THE BOYS OF BULLAROO

Tales of War, Aussie Mateship and more

GARRICK JONES

This is an IndieMosh book

brought to you by MoshPit Publishing
an imprint of Mosher's Business Support Pty Ltd

PO Box 147
Hazelbrook NSW 2779

indiemosh.com.au

Copyright © Garrick Jones 2018

The moral right of the author has been asserted in accordance with the Copyright Amendment (Moral Rights) Act 2000.

All rights reserved. Except as permitted under the Australian Copyright Act 1968 (for example, fair dealing for the purposes of study, research, criticism or review) no part of this publication may be reproduced, stored in a retrieval system, or transmitted in any form or by any means, electronic, mechanical, photocopying, recording or otherwise, without the written permission of the publisher.

Cataloguing-in-Publication entry is available from the National Library of Australia: http://catalogue.nla.gov.au/

Title:	The Boys of Bullaroo
Subtitle:	Tales of War, Aussie Mateship and more
Author:	Jones, Garrick (1948–)
ISBNs:	978-1-925814-81-1 (paperback)
	978-1-925814-82-8 (ebook – epub)
	978-1-925814-83-5 (ebook – mobi)
Subjects:	Fiction LGBT; Fiction Romance; Fiction War and Military

This book is entirely a work of fiction. Names, characters, businesses, organisations, places and events are either the product of the author's imagination or are used fictitiously. Any resemblance to actual persons, living or dead, events or locales is entirely coincidental. The author, their agents and publishers cannot be held responsible for any claim otherwise and take no responsibility for any such coincidence.

Cover design by Anna Tiferet Sikorska at www.TiferetDesign.com

Cover images under license from Shutterstock and Depositphotos

To the men in my family and those around me
who served in the conflicts
of the twentieth century.

Contents

Sergeant Jack 1

Cross My Palm with Silver... 55

The Boy Who 101

The Stock Route to Starlight... 141

The Connaught 161

Charlie and Me.. 191

Sergeant Jack

I awoke in a panic.

There'd been a sudden lurch, a squeal of brakes, the sound of voices, and loud clanging noises outside the train carriage. It wasn't the noise, or the sudden waking from a deep sleep, that had me panicked; it was the unwanted memory of a huge explosion, the scream of escaping steam from a ruptured locomotive boiler, and the lurch of the carriage in which we'd been sitting, violently torn to pieces around us as we were flung through the air.

Instinctively, I ran my hand through my hair, trying to remove invisible shards of glass.

But there were none—even though that sudden flash of memory had been my unwelcome, yet frequent, visitor for two years now, I still reached for my head and tried to brush away debris that wasn't there.

I'd reserved a compartment to myself—I'd been surprised to learn when I'd come home that a first-class sleeper compartment did not necessarily guarantee sole occupation—unlike most European trains. It depended on when the cabin would be turned down for the night. Oft-times passengers travelling shorter distances, during daylight hours, could be accommodated together. I preferred to travel alone.

I was still nervous of train journeys, and this was my third since returning to Australia earlier that year, and on all of those I'd taken an entire compartment so that I could travel alone. People were still too solicitous of those of us who were of an age to have returned and who were maimed in some way. "At home soldiers" we called the countless men and women who believed they had fought the fight from ten thousand miles away. Politeness was such a fragile thing—I believed it better not to find myself trapped in situations from which there was no escape. Trains were one such hazard to my tightly held, but limited, self-control.

I raised the shutter of the compartment window to see why the train had stopped.

Strathfield? How could that possibly be? I must have nodded off. I checked my pocket watch—it was only fifteen minutes since we'd steamed out of Central station. The lurch of the train had merely been the engine coming to a halt; the loud clattering and sound of voices the normal sounds of a busy railway station at twelve minutes past ten on a weekday morning.

Strathfield was the first major hub in suburban Sydney, and it was from this station that the northern, southern, and western lines peeled off to service all parts of the State of New South Wales. I'd quite forgotten that fact, until reminded by the carriage attendant, when he'd informed me there would be a change of staff at Strathfield. He was due to move to a train heading to the Northern Tablelands, whence I'd arrived myself barely two days ago.

I leaned my head against the carriage window, watching the hustle and bustle not two feet from where I was sitting; all of those people oblivious to the one-armed man whose heart, quite often, seemed overwhelmed with either bitterness or anger—or sometimes, at my most vulnerable, sorrow and loss.

"I'm about to go now, sir," the carriage attendant said, after knocking gently at the compartment door. He was standing in the corridor; I felt that he had been observing me for a few seconds before speaking, waiting for a moment for my face to settle. "Is there anything I can do for you before I leave?"

"No, thank you very much," I replied. "You've been most helpful."

"Very well, sir, then I'll wish you a pleasant journey. The new attendant will be along shortly to say good morning."

"There's no need. I'd rather you pull the blinds to the compartment and tell him I'd like to be left alone. I'll call if I need anything."

"Very good, sir. Good day," the man said.

As I heard the compartment door click shut, I realised I hadn't even looked at him during our brief conversation. I'd been staring at the wheels of a porter's luggage trolley, my eyes roving over the tiny flecks of reflected light from the grains of mica that were embedded over the surface of each wheel to give it traction. Focusing my attention on the minutiae of a physical object was one of the things I did when something shocked me in a public situation—usually flashes of memory brought on by a noise, or a sudden movement, or even a stranger's face. Usually faces that reminded me of lost mates.

A doctor had taught me this method, a way of distracting my attention away from feelings that threatened to overwhelm me. In the early days, I'd drowned in those feelings—constant companions for months during my blackest times in Combermere Barracks. My friends had names: Bitterness, Anger, Sorrow, and Loss.

I snorted softly. All that time in England, in a military hospital at Windsor, and I hadn't even seen the castle—the home of the king.

I closed my eyes and willed the pain to pass.

After the ritual that seemed common to every country in which I'd caught a train—the shout of "all aboard!", followed by the blast of the station master's whistle, and a "toot-toot" from the locomotive—I felt a soft lurch as the Western Plains Express glided from Strathfield station in a cloud of steam, on its twelve-hour journey to parts west, to the great outback of my sunburned, orange land.

The compartment was luxurious, by any standard. The wall of mahogany opposite my seat concealed a wash station and a fold-down bed. The attendant who'd showed me to my seat had taken my overcoat and hung it in the wardrobe section, closest to the compartment door. Between it and the washing area was the bed, which he explained could be turned down in an instant should I wish to sleep, even though my journey would take no longer than five hours.

Sometimes I still found the simplest of tasks the most frustrating fiddle. I managed to open the wash station, one door at a time, and turned on the tap to splash water on my face. The washbasin itself was a fold-down affair, shell-shaped, with a mirror above it, and underneath that a small shelf with a pair of hand towels, neatly folded, and embroidered with N.S.W.G.R.—New South Wales Government Railways. But for the life of me, I could find no hand soap. The silver-plate soap dish was empty.

I turned from the wash station and pressed the buzzer to summon the attendant, and then stared at my face in the mirror while I waited for him to arrive. It took only a few moments—but, in those thirty or so seconds, there was enough time to see how much I'd changed in the six years it had been since I'd set off to Egypt, my heart bursting with excitement, and my voice shrieking "Rule Britannia" along with the rest of my friends in the Light Horse, as we sailed for the Middle East in the October of 1914.

Physically, my face still looked the same as then, albeit older. I looked youthful enough—I would be twenty-five in a few months' time. It was the hardness in my eyes and the firm set in my jaw that was the most striking difference; my mother had noticed it immediately and had burst into tears. "Where's my sunny, laughing boy?" she'd wept into her handkerchief, not ten minutes after our reunion.

"How can I help you, sir?" the attendant asked. He'd knocked and I'd heard him open the compartment door, but he was hidden from view by the open half-door of my wash closet.

"There seems to be no hand soap," I said. "Would you be so kind …?"

"Of course, sir, I'll be right back," the man said. I heard the compartment door click shut and returned to the perusal of my face, turning my head from side to side to check I was still in one piece. I'd often daydream that I'd been left disfigured, as so many men had been that I'd met at the end of the war; their faces a ruin—eyes, jaws, noses missing.

"Here you go, sir," the attendant said, after returning less than a minute later. "There's cedar wood, or Ivory soap, if you'd prefer something unscented … are you quite all right, sir?"

I'd turned from the mirror to inspect the small tray of soaps he held before him, waiting for me to choose, then, as I glanced up into his face, I froze.

The shock was physical, as if I'd been punched in the stomach.

"Jack?" I said, my voice a barely audible thread. "Jacky?"

But then my voice caught in my throat and I gasped for air. As I stared into the man's pale grey-green eyes, I realised it was not Jack—it never could have been, I'd held Jack in my arm as he'd died—but the attendant was so similar at first glance that I'd been shocked to the bottom of my soul. I tried to apologise; words would still not come. Something terrible had risen from within me and grabbed my heart, squeezing it so tightly that I sobbed loudly.

"Sir!" I heard the man shout, and then I felt his arms around me as I fell into darkness.

*****

Ammonia—it jolted me awake.

"You're all right, Captain Taylor," a stranger said, his face not ten inches away from my own. "You fainted, that's all."

I slowly remembered where I was and tried to stand up. I was propped up in a half-sitting position, legs out on the long bench seat of my compartment, pillows behind my head.

"Stay still for a moment, if you please. My name is Ian Fletcher, and I'm a doctor. I just want to have a quick look at you," the man said, replacing the stopper on his silver-gilt bottle of smelling salts.

"It's mister," I said.

"I beg your pardon?"

"It's Mister Taylor, not captain. The war's over," I said, trying to smile. "Unless this is another of my bad dreams."

"You're very lucky this young man caught you as you fell," the doctor said. "You could have done yourself a lot of mischief had he not been here."

I smiled at the carriage attendant, who was standing behind the doctor, looking at me with a slight smile, one that masked a look of concern.

"Thank you," I said to him.

"I'd be grateful if you'd lie still, if you please," the doctor said, and then turned to the young man who bore such an uncanny resemblance to Jack that it still made my blood run cold. "Would you mind?"

"Surely, doctor," he replied. "What would you like me to do?"

The doctor asked him to hold the end of the stethoscope at the base of the "v" between the middle and ring fingers of his hand and hold it flat against my chest. He talked as he examined me, tugging at both of my earlobes at the same time, and then pulled down my lower eyelids with his thumbs as he mumbled to himself, all the time listening to my heartbeat.

"Bush medicine," he explained, as he knocked one knuckle against my forehead.

"Here, listen," he said to the attendant.

"Who, me?"

The doctor nodded and then removed the stethoscope from around his neck and positioned its tubes in the young man's ears. "Keep your hand on his chest."

"What am I listening to?"

"Pat out the rhythm of his heartbeat on your leg."

The doctor checked his pocket watch, observing the rhythm of the man's pats on his thigh.

I was intensely aware of the young man's other hand, pressed against my chest, holding the stethoscope in place. Someone had opened my shirt down to the waistband of my trousers and had spread it open. When I glanced down and saw the thick hair of my chest protruding between the fingers of the attendant's hand, I swallowed, and then forced myself to close my eyes. How long had it been since anyone had touched me, other than a doctor or a nurse? I knew precisely, yet the knowledge of it grabbed painfully at my heart.

"That's enough," the doctor said, after a minute or two, and then held out his hand for the return of his instrument. He sat on the bench next to me.

"He reminds you of your brother, or someone close that you lost in the war?" I couldn't answer, so I nodded. "I guessed as much. It was the shock that made you faint—your pulse quickened substantially while you were looking at him and when he was listening to your heart. It's not uncommon; I fear it will be many years yet since men like you fully recover."

"Men like me?"

"Men who are half of what they were when they left."

"So, we will recover?" I asked, my voice scarcely hiding the pain.

"Too soon to know yet, the war's barely finished. And this last business was far worse than the Boer War—no trenches and year-long bombardments there," the doctor replied, patting me on the knee. "Only time will tell. However, I need to get back to second-class, young man. I've a wife and young son with a bad cold in the other carriage and I can't leave them alone for too long. I suggest you sit down and talk to—"

"Falmer, sir," the attendant said, "Emerson Falmer."

"Falmer, then. Talk to Emerson for a while; tell him about some of your experiences in the war so your mind can untie the connection you've made. Otherwise you'll get off the train still carrying that ghost with you and wondering how it came to be that you mistook an employee of the railways for whomever it was who was so dear to you."

"But, I'm sure he has other duties—" I began to say.

"Only you and an older lady with her maid in First today, sir."

"And before I go," the doctor said, as Falmer helped him into his jacket. "What are you taking for your amputation?"

"They're in my jacket pocket," I said.

"These?" the attendant asked, after opening the wardrobe and retrieving the pills from my coat.

"Hmm, opiates. I hope you keep to the prescribed dosage?"

"Of course," I said

He stared at me for a while before he spoke. "Take my advice, Mister Taylor, no matter how bad the pain is and how hard it is to put up with, I'd advise only one dose a day, just before you go to sleep to help you through the night." He held up the bottle and rattled it. "Sometimes the cure can be worse than the complaint. I bid you good day, sir."

The moment of embarrassed silence that followed after he left was only broken when I glanced at Falmer and caught him watching me. He'd been inspecting the pronounced, but narrow, ridged scar that cut across my chest. We both smiled at the same time.

"I call it the Great Dividing Range," I said, and then chuckled.

"Well, it certainly cuts a swathe through that jungle on your chest," he replied. "I'll help you dress when you're ready."

"No need," I said. "I can manage most things, except for the neck stud."

"Well, I'm the man to help you. I did it for years. I was what they're calling a 'batman' these days—finished my war as a sapper after serving as orderly to my lieutenant-colonel at Ypres and Bullecourt—fifth division, sir."

"You came back and he didn't?" There was something in his voice that prompted my question.

"I was out boiling water for his tea when a shell went straight through the door of his bivvy. We all lost someone close to us, Captain Taylor."

I could see the supreme effort it took the man to remain calm. I guessed he was doing it for my benefit; every man's story was hard in the telling.

"My name is Arthur," I said. "If we're going to have a little tête-à-tête about the war, then we'd best be on first-name terms, don't you think?"

"Very well, Arthur, then you must call me Emerson in that case."

I held out my hand to him and he took it, shaking it firmly.

"I think tea might be in order. I'll get the dining car steward to bring some along while I get you up on your feet and get you dressed."

"Make sure he brings two cups," I said, and then, when he raised an eyebrow, added, "I insist."

"Very good, sir."

*****

"Lift your chin if you please … there, that's got it!"

I had to admit that Emerson Falmer had a nimble way about him. I hadn't expected it, to be perfectly honest. He was a big-framed man, although quite slender in the waist. It was the major difference I saw, now that we'd spent some time talking over tea, and I'd been able to compare him to Jack in my mind.

"It's that collar stud that's the hardest," I said, as he stepped back to check me over, smoothing the lie of my waistcoat with the palms of his hands.

"How will you manage?" he asked, as he began the intricacies of the double Windsor knot, one that I found so evasive with one arm. I'd been taught by one of the nurses who'd looked after me how to loosen my tie and then slip it over my head, so that it was easy to put back on again. However, whoever had taken off my tie had undone it completely. The look he gave me as he wound the lengths of the tie over and under each other told me without words that it was these little, daily things that might prove the most difficult.

I'd told Emerson that I'd been interested in applying for some property under the Returned Soldiers Settlement land grant, but the only land available when I'd applied was in the area I'd grown up in, and that was the last place I wanted to settle. I wanted to start over—I think I'd said, "make a clean break from my past", when what I'd actually meant was to get as far away from my family as was possible.

I was on my way to take possession of five thousand acres of grazing and agricultural land that I'd bought with the proceeds of my inheritance from my father, who'd passed away while I was serving overseas. The father of a chum from the army worked as a broker for Elder Smith, and he'd been my first port of call when I'd decided to make a go of it on my own. The land was still being worked by the five sons of the deceased estate; they all wanted to go their separate ways. It came with a large squatter's house, not far from a permanently running creek.

"I'll stay in a hotel in town until after I've had a chance to have a good look around the property," I explained. "And then I suppose, once I've seen the lie of the land, I'll advertise. Station manager, cook, handyman, a few farmworkers, jackaroos, and one or two roustabouts to start off with—maybe a dozen in all will do for a start."

"Mixed farming?"

"Cattle and sheep," I replied. "I'll put a few acres under barley, a few paddocks for feed, and maybe I'll breed some fine horses."

"Really? Now that's my area."

"Horse breeding?"

"I wasn't always a 'ladies' maid', Arthur. My family's from the High Country; I grew up with horses."

I must have looked puzzled; it was hard to reconcile an officer's orderly with a man brought up in the saddle. I felt a little foolish—making a judgement on a man's abilities with no real knowledge to back up my assumptions. But I saw that he was weighing up something in his mind. "You'll advertise in *The Land*?" he asked.

I nodded. "Of course, that is unless there's some other new weekly I don't know about."

"No, *The Land's* the place. I keep my eye on the positions vacant every time it comes out," he said.

"Oh? Why?"

"I didn't get to choose what I did in the army, Arthur—I applied to the Light Horse, just like you."

"What happened?"

"I don't know if you know how it works, but I was picked out—I think it was my very fine moustache," he added, with a wink, and a smile.

I couldn't begin to imagine the disappointment he must have felt; everyone wanted to fight Johnny Turk or Kaiser Bill with their bare hands if need be.

"I was working at the Australia Hotel when I went to enlist. I should have kept my mouth shut when they asked me."

"But, I thought you said you came from The Snowy?"

"I left home. It's a long story and I won't bore you with it."

I hoped one day I might get to hear that story, but I couldn't help thinking if he did reply to my advertisement, I wasn't sure if I'd be able to cope with a constant reminder of Jack around me, day in and day out.

"May I ask you a personal question, Arthur?"

"It depends," I replied, a little warily.

"It's nothing like that." His soft curve of his lip, almost, but not quite a smile, put me instantly at ease.

"Go ahead."

"You said you had an inheritance from your father. Why didn't you simply buy something nice in the city, perhaps overlooking the sea? Put your feet up and take time to recover from your time 'over there'?"

Sergeant Jack

"Oh, I couldn't think of anything more boring, Emerson. Despite the physical challenges, I need to do something—anything to keep me busy and stop me feeling maudlin. But a selection was something Jack and I talked about all the time. Our daydream—two mates running a station together …" I was aware that my voice had caught in my throat and begun to fade.

Right at that moment, the train slowed.

"Valley Heights," he explained. "They're putting on an assist for the climb through the Blue Mountains."

"An assist?"

"It's another engine. They do the same in Murrurundi on the down journey when you go home to New England from the city."

I checked my watch. I couldn't believe only an hour had passed since I'd blacked out, and here I was, chatting with a comparative stranger about the most intimate things. That's what soldiers did who'd been in the war.

"Not thinking of marrying your lady?" he asked.

"Which lady?"

"I'm sorry. I couldn't help noticing the photograph in your watch case."

"That's my youngest sister, Edith."

"She's lovely."

"She certainly is," I agreed. "No marriage for me, I'm afraid. The war's robbed me of any chance of settling down with anyone—and one thing I realised while I was away is that I'm simply not a man for the ladies."

Our eyes met for an instant, holding an uncertain gaze. I couldn't help noticing that he'd begun to blush.

"How did you meet?" he asked casually, patting my tie into place. "You and your friend, Jack, I mean."

"Induction day," I replied. "We'd been sworn in, signed for the pay for our horses, and were lined up, ready to be split into four-man sections, and then paired up as training partners."

"Pay for your horses?"

"The horses didn't get paid," I said, laughing. "If they thought the horses we'd brought with us were up to scratch, the army bought them from us. If not, they were sent home, and we'd be given a Waler."

"Really?" His voice carried a hint of disapproval. Everyone knew that the breed, which had originally been known as "New South Walers", were competent enough and bred specifically to be for the cavalry. On the other hand, every horseman who'd ever lived would rather be riding a friend, who he'd most likely trained himself, than take on an unknown nag—one that probably brought along with it God knew how many problems, learned from another man's hand.

"Yes, but in hindsight, I'd rather have thrown the thirty quid in their faces, taken whatever nag they gave me instead, and sent my 'Kingsman' back to spend the rest of his days at home on the station with Edith …"

I felt the tears start in my eyes. It was too painful to cry over Jack, yet oddly enough, whenever I thought of my boy—my proud, handsome, valiant, and trusting horse …

"You were telling me how you met your friend?"

"Well, it was Jack who chose me."

"I sense there's part of that story you're leaving out," he said, with a glint in his eye.

"Do you really want to know?"

He nodded.

"He bagsed me," I explained.

"How?"

"He said, to the sergeant, at the top of his voice and in front of the twenty of us who were waiting to be divided up, 'I'll have the tall, skinny one with the Dapple Grey and the gamahouche lips, if you please, sir.'"

To my delight, Emerson roared with laughter.

Wiping the tears from his eyes, he asked, "And how did that go down?"

"Four days in the lock-up and the admiration of the entire regiment. Even the sergeant pissed himself laughing."

*****

Jack, my darling, darling Jack.

He'd had the heart of a lion and the feet of a gazelle. Brave and fast and the truest friend a bloke could ever wish to have. He could shoot and ride like no man I'd ever known, and his laugh would light up the room, and with it my heart, no matter how crowded or how far from each other we were at the time.

At the start, I couldn't understand why someone so full of life could be interested in someone like me: a shy, quiet man, who'd been brought up in a cold, Christian house—one that saw any sign of affection as a weakness. In those days, I was so innocent I didn't even know the mechanism by which I, my three brothers, and my sister had been conceived, or brought into the world. Of course, on a farm it was impossible not to know how animals were made and dropped; but in my naiveté, I simply couldn't equate either of those activities with my parents.

When Jack had announced to the world that he'd chosen me because of my fulsome, rosy lips, I'd laughed along with everyone else, although without the slightest idea of why it was so funny. It took me a month before I finally plucked up enough courage to ask him what gamahouche meant. I'd hesitatingly asked one night while we were eating supper at an otherwise empty table in a corner of the mess tent. We'd arrived late, as usual, when there were only thick slices of bread and fillings left on the service benches. He'd laughed so hard that I found my uniform splattered with yellow and white flecks—bits of the egg sandwich he'd been eating at the time.

Once he'd stopped laughing, he leaned across the table and whispered that I should mimic what he did. He slowly poked his tongue in and out of his pursed lips, making slurping noises as he did so. I copied him. "Keep going," he said, under his breath, laughter in his eyes. "Now imagine you're wrapping your tongue and smacking your chops around my old fella—"

I whacked him with my enamel tea mug.

Sometime later, while out together having a stroll late at night, and after another painful admission of ignorance, Jack explained to me what most men did with their hand when they wanted to relieve tension. I'd shyly admitted that I had no idea what the other boys in the regiment had meant when they'd talked about "batting".

"Fetching mettle … wanking … pulling … having a tug …?"

He slapped me across the back of the head when I shook my head at each of the phrases. I still didn't know.

"Oh, God, Taylor! Didn't your brothers teach you?"

"Teach me what?"

"You know, about … 'self-abuse'?"

"Self-abuse? Um … I'm not sure I know exactly what that entails, Jack. I've heard the expression of course, the vicar was always rattling on about it to us boys, but he never told us what it actually was."

He howled with laughter, much to my deep embarrassment.

"'Self-abuse' is masturbation, Arthur—playing with your knob until you spend on your belly."

"Oh, good God!" I said, as the penny dropped. "So, *that's* what self-abuse is." I'd thought the vicar had been referring to over-eating, or smoking cigarettes.

"It's like growing a moustache, ploughing a field, or whacking your bollocks against the pommel of your saddle on the gallop—it's a rite of passage for every man, Taylor!"

He explained to me that it was generally known as "The Brothers' Duty"—meant to be taught by older boys to their younger male siblings, something I found hard to imagine when I thought of my three brothers: George the bully, Cyril the coward, and Howard the nothing.

"Please don't laugh at me, Jack," I said, shyly. "You won't believe me when I tell you I've never …"

His look of amazement started to turn into a laugh, but then, when he saw what an effort it had taken for me to confess, shook his head sadly, and ruffled my hair.

"You haven't? Not ever?"

"No, Jack. Don't make fun of me. If you knew my parents …" I was truly mortified.

He shushed me, gently, and then rubbed the back of my neck. When I eventually raised my eyes to meet his, I saw something strange there.

"Truly? Never?" he asked, very quietly, after what seemed an age.

I shook my head. "No."

"Jesus, Taylor," he'd whispered, in disbelief. He lit a smoke for both of us, handed me one, and then cursed softly. After staring at his foot and making circles in the sand with the toe of his boot for a few moments, it seemed as if he'd come to some decision. He looked around, and then spoke. "Everyone's in bed, Artie; I suppose I'd better step up to the mark and pretend to be your brother—not only for your own sake, but for the reputation of the regiment—can't have a soldier in the Light Horse not knowing how to wallop his codger. Over here, behind the mess tent."

He beckoned me with a toss of the head. I followed him meekly.

"Sit on that barrel and watch. I'll show you how it's done; then it's up to you."

He stood in the darkness, just enough light from the quarter moon and the stars for me to see what he was doing, and then after glancing around to see we were truly alone, dropped his strides and pulled his undies down below his knees, and demonstrated exactly what "self-abuse" was.

"Your turn," he said, after a few minutes, wiping his hand on his handkerchief.

"Don't look," I said, timidly.

"You did—your eyes were the size of dinner plates," he said.

And he was right; I hadn't been able to take my eyes off what he'd been doing, and I was so hard and excited that I barely put my hand on myself and the job was done.

"It's all over your boots," he said to me, as I leaned, panting, against the barrel I'd been sitting on while watching him do the deed.

I hadn't noticed; I'd been staring into his eyes for the entire five seconds that it had taken me to spill.

We shared mutual relief on many, many nights after that, either one watching the other, in turns, or sometimes both going at it at the same time. We concocted races to see who could get there first; we laughed and joked while we went at it, daring each other to bring ourselves off in public places where there was the risk of being caught. We did it in wadis, on horseback, even once during target practice when no one else was around.

Of course, we never touched each other. However, in time, all things change, one way or another.

It had been precipitated by a night when we'd sneaked down to the bayonet field at two in the morning, unable to sleep, and worried over a forthcoming stoush with a savage band of rebel Arabs with a reputation for disembowelling their captives. We'd stood, face-to-face, the bayonet-dummy between us, both pressed up hard against it, our pants down around our ankles. I could feel the movement of Jack's hand through the hessian. "Co-ordinate, Taylor," he'd said. Although I couldn't see it, I could hear the smile in his voice. "Otherwise we'll be banging knuckles through the straw." In the split second before our carefully timed ejaculations, as we leaned against it, the dummy slipped sideways on its suspending noose, and we found ourselves stumbling into each other. It was too late to stop; and, to be honest, I simply didn't want to—I discharged all over Jack's hairy belly.

"What the—" he started to say, but he was caught in the throes of his own release, so I put one hand on his shoulder to steady myself, leaned back, and allowed him to spend all over me. "Come on, Jacky," I'd whispered, in encouragement. I'd done it to him, after all—I thought it only fair to cop his mess on my tummy.

"Well, that was ... interesting," I managed to say, after a few minutes, delightfully aware that our hips were still touching.

"You did that on purpose, Taylor." His face was wreathed in smiles.

We both knew it was an accident. But, even in the dim moonlight, I saw in his eyes that something had changed. It was the look of a man who'd but a moment ago been told that he'd won the lottery—disbelief mingled with surprise and wonder.

As I stepped back and bent down to take my handkerchief, I glanced up. Jack was staring into the sky, languidly rubbing the result of our mingled release through the hair around his navel. He was still hard. "Stand behind me and hold me, Artie, please," he whispered. "I'm not done yet."

So, I stood behind him, one arm around his chest, the other across his belly, painfully aware that I too was achingly erect and hard up against his buttocks as he clenched and released for a second time.

"What about you?" he murmured, after he was done.

"Put your arm around my shoulder," I said, scarcely believing that it was me who was speaking. I took care of myself, pressed up against his hip, and when my time came, he swivelled to receive my offering across his thighs.

We didn't talk about it, nor did we repeat the experience, until one night after one spot too many in a whorehouse.

It wasn't really a brothel as such. In Alexandria, they were called "Can-Can Halls". Jack and I had been minding our own business that night, rolling durries outside our tent—we'd both been promoted to lance-corporal, so shared a two-man tent, rather than the eight-man "bell tent" that we'd spent so much time in when we'd arrived in the desert, all of us sleeping feet-to-feet, arrayed like human spokes in a wheel.

Harry "Howitzer" Duncan and two of his rowdy mates, already well into their cups, egged us on to join them for a drink at Madame La Zola's. Harry's nickname came from the supposed size of his member, which was reputed to be the same length and thickness as a shell used in the field artillery piece after which he'd been nicknamed.

"It's probably really the size of a .303 rifle cartridge," I'd quipped, when this bit of information was shared with me. Two years in the army had made me as laconic as the rest of my mates.

However, that night in Madame La Zola's my jest was proved untrue as I watched Harry drop his trousers, retrieve a truly enormous bull's-pizzle from his underpants, and thrust it into a blowsy-looking girl with dyed blonde hair and too much makeup who was standing on the bar, taking on all comers. Harry's performance was as the result of goading and cheering by the lads and the girl was obviously supplied as part of the "entertainment" at the establishment. She was bent over at the waist and held out a china cup, rattling it for donations from the crowd of men who were waiting for their turn.

I was revolted.

We staggered back to camp shortly after, Jack whispering, "Come on, Artie, let's get out of this hell hole," and then taking me by the arm. We grabbed a bottle of grog on our way out, throwing a few piasters on the bar, and then headed home, arms around each other and passing the bottle.

It was incredibly clear that night, the moon full in the sky, and very little sound in the camp when we got back to Maadi.

Our tent was nicknamed "The Lupanar of Pompeii" by the boys. Unless it was an inspection day, the interior looked like some house of ill repute in Alexandria. We'd stowed our camp stretchers to one side, a large Turkish carpet covered the sand on the floor, and a brass pierced-work lantern hung from the ceiling bracing-rod of the tent. We called it the "donger", as that was the sound it made when men came into our tent unawares and whacked their noggins. We usually slept on the carpet, sleeping bags under us. If it was hot, we'd either lie naked under a sheet or in our undershorts.

While Jack was getting undressed, I went to see to our horses, and then tied up the inner skirt of the tent on the windward side to let the heat out and to allow a breeze to come through during the night. The flysheet practically came down to the ground on both sides, so we still had privacy, should anyone bother wandering past our tent in the middle of the night.

By the time I'd finished, Jack was naked, lying on his back with one hand behind his neck. "I can't help feeling a tiny bit envious of Harry," he said, glancing down at his penis, which he was holding at the base and slapping against his navel with a soft thwack.

"Why on earth would you feel envious, Jack? I think yours is perfectly fine."

"Yeah?" he said, with a half-drunken grin. "If you like it so much, why don't you give it a kiss?"

"Fuck off," I said, laughing while I began to undress. I'd never heard swearing until I joined the army; now I could turn the air blue with the best of the boys.

I lit a smoke, threw open the tent front-fly, and stood in the doorway in my undershorts while I caught some breeze.

"Where's mine?"

"Get off your lazy arse and roll one of your own."

"I've got both hands full," he pretend-protested.

"You've only one hand busy from what I can see," I said.

"You've got one free," he quipped.

"Wish in one hand and piss in the other …" I replied.

"If I wasn't half blotto, I'd suggest a quick trip to the bayonet range.

I heard there's a dummy there with our names on it." He began to run his hand through the hair on his belly. "It'd be fun, Arthur. I know you think about it as much as I do."

For a moment I hesitated. His member lay against his hip, tumescent, and twitching in time with his pulse—I recognised those mesmerising contractions as his extreme arousal, and felt myself tenting my shorts.

"You're drunk, Jack Hastings; you'd fall flat on your face before we got halfway there."

He wanted to play "grown-up games". I could see the heat in his eyes—he'd seen me inspecting his erection, and was now staring at the unmistakable protuberance in my underwear.

"Take 'em off slow, Taylor," he whispered, with a wink. I let out a loud pretend-sigh of "do I have to?", and then slowly slid the waistband of my shorts down with the thumb of one hand, my cigarette dangling from the corner of my mouth as I performed a clumsy nautch-dance, while humming "Bara, the Bare-Bellied Vixen from the Sphinx". It was a ridiculous song, composed by one of the boys in the N.C.O.'s mess one night while in his cups, to a vaguely oriental melody. I stopped my belly dance when my penis, uncomfortably stretched downwards in my shorts, sprang out and slapped against my navel.

"Oh! Egad! It's a man!" Jack said, in a surprised falsetto, feigning coyness.

We both howled with laughter, only to be stopped by a shouted "Shut up and go to bed, you noisy fuckers!" from our W.O., whose tent was pitched thirty yards away in the same dry wadi as ours.

"The bayonet field will still be there tomorrow, Jack," I said, sniggering while I relit my smoke, which had gone out.

"You're a wet blanket, Arthur, you know that?"

I snorted. "Who needs a straw dummy anyway?"

"You're a dirty boy, Taylor."

"That's the pot calling the kettle black!"

"All right then, but before I go to sleep, how about you and me look after things? I've got a bag full of change that needs spending." He cupped his scrotum and bounced it in the palm of his hand a few times.

"And you know how much I like watching you spilling your sixpenny bits over your gut."

His grin was truly enormous; he knew my answer without me having to reply.

I was more than keen, so closed the flap of the tent, pulled my shorts all the way down to my ankles, and then kicked them onto his face. He pressed them to his nose. "Ah, Madame La Zola!" he said, in a mock-French accent. "Do I smell a big Aussie prick in your knickers?"

I laughed, and then kneeled next to him.

"Cigarette," he ordered, reaching out for my smoke.

"Open wide," I replied, batting his hand away. He watched me while I took an exaggerated, deep drag on my fag. He waggled his eyebrows and then pursed his lips, parting them as I blew a stream of smoke into his mouth. Maybe it was the effect of the grog, I'm not sure, but I'd been looking at his mouth, the point of his tongue only just visible, resting softly between his lips, when he muttered my name with the same softness he used when trying to wake me first thing in the morning.

As I glanced up into his eyes, he slipped his hand behind my neck, and began to rub it gently.

"What is it, Jack?" I asked. There seemed to be a lump in my throat the size of an apple.

"May I, Arthur?"

I nodded, and then he pulled his face up to mine and kissed me. It was such a gentle kiss, our lips barely touching—I thought my heart would stop with the wonder of it. As I drew back, I felt our mouths peel apart, detaching hesitantly, as if reluctant to abandon their connection.

"What's the matter, Taylor? Never been kissed before?"

For a moment I said nothing, and then slowly shook my head.

"Damn!" he said. "Do I have to teach you everything?"

I nodded.

"Come here, then. If that was your first, we'll pretend it didn't happen and start all over again—this time I'll make it a good one."

He pulled me down on top of him and opened his lips as I kissed him. I could feel the warmth and soft wetness of his mouth. It was … luscious.

"Strewth," I whispered.

"Give me your tongue, Artie," he said, softly, rubbing my chin with his thumb.

"What?"

"Just do it."

I think the groan I let out during the first deep kiss of my life broke something inside me, something that could never be put back together again. I knew at that moment I would never be the same person I was before Jack Hastings kissed me—but I didn't care. I realised that what had broken was the wall I'd put up around my heart to protect me from the truth—I didn't just care for him as a buddy, I loved him with every ounce of my being, and I had done for a very long time.

"Oh, God, Arthur," he said, when we eventually broke apart, saliva running down my chin, and my lips swollen from the gentle, but greedy, invasion of my mouth.

I rolled onto one elbow, to catch my breath. Was it all right for a bloke to tell his mate that he loved him? In the way I felt about Jack, I mean? I had no idea. I was far too shy to speak the words that hovered on my lips.

"What were you going to say?" he asked, as he saw me open my mouth to speak, and then change my mind.

"My tongue's sore," I said, instead.

His eyes were bright, even in the soft light that flooded in under our tent's raised skirt.

"Yours is sore? Well, you could always suck on mine for a while," he replied, cheekily. "I thought we took turns with everything?"

I placed my hand on the flat of his belly and gently rubbed it through the hair around his navel. "I'm not sure that I'm up to taking turns tonight, Jack," I said, my voice grainy and breaking slightly on the vowels—it was the heat in my ears and the lump in my throat that made it hard to speak.

"What on earth do you mean?"

"Why wait for the next buggy when you could share the same carriage?"

He gasped when I reached down and took him in my hand.

That night was the first time we'd touched each other. I had no idea why we'd waited, but it was sweeter for the waiting. Later, as he lay on top of me, both of us wet with sweat, our emissions slippery between us, he muttered gently into my neck that he loved me. I pulled his mouth to my own and, unable to cope with the immensity of my feelings, did what any Aussie bloke would do under the circumstances—I pushed them down inside me and talked about the fire that still raged in my loins.

"I think I've got another one in me," I whispered. "You game?"

"Gimme a sec, Taylor," he said, and then laughed softly as he slid his hand languorously through the mess between our tightly pressed bodies. "I need to catch my breath first."

"Take your time," I said.

Now the ice had been broken, I wanted more. I felt happy with myself—happy that I'd been able to give him pleasure directly, with my hand.

"May I?" I asked.

"What are you doing?"

"Exploring," I replied, as I began to fondle him again.

"Already?"

"Shut up and take it like a man, Hastings," I said. "Why don't you just lie there and let me do the work."

Despite my admonition, he obeyed me for only a few seconds before he groaned loudly, and then gathered some of our previous mess up in his hand and used it to return the favour. I thought I'd pass out with the sheer astonishment of the sensation—my left leg began to shudder.

"That's my boy, Arthur," he whispered into my ear, aware of my excitement, and then arched his neck and moaned with pleasure as I twisted my wrist. "Come on; show me what you can do—"

"Don't stop what you're doing down there," I ordered. "But, shut up and kiss me right now—I'm almost ready to give you another pint of my best, Jack."

At the moment we climaxed, the image that flashed through my mind was of that popular country fair attraction where they arrange for two locomotives to collide head-on in an explosion of steam, the contents of their boilers spewing out between them. It seemed to me—perhaps fancifully—that it could not have equalled the force of our simultaneous, combined eruptions.

"You've got stuff in your hair," he whispered, several minutes later.

We'd fallen apart and were lying side by side. He was kneading the back of my head and running his fingers through my long, black locks.

"That's what happens when you rub my head and don't wipe your hands first," I replied, with a laugh.

"And where's the fun in that?"

I ran my forefinger through the mess on my stomach and drew a line down his face from his forehead to his chin. "And now you've got it all over your face."

He kissed me.

"Thank you, Lance-Corporal Arthur," he said, snuggling against my shoulder.

"Thank you, Sergeant Jack," I replied.

"I got promoted?"

"For bravery in the field."

"Bravery for what?"

"Standing up to an intense cannon bombardment," I replied. I took his hand and rested it on my penis. "I know it's not a Howitzer or anything …"

We both turned and buried our faces into the cushions behind our heads and laughed ourselves silly.

"Permission granted to discharge your weapon over me anytime," he said, once we'd settled for a bit.

"Dirty boy …" I replied.

"Anything for you, mate," he said, with a wink.

"Anything?"

He rolled on top of me and kissed me again, this time playfully.

"Now where were we before you grabbed my old fella and forced me to do your bidding?" he asked, chuckling into my neck.

"Where would you like us to be, Jack?"

He was very quiet for a moment before speaking. "Somewhere south of nowhere, Arthur. What we did was just too ... too bonzer for words. Let's stay lost for a while, eh?"

Lost? I could do lost—especially in the arms of the man I now realised I'd fallen in love with.

My mate, the best man I'd ever known—my cobber and the love of my life, my Sergeant Jack.

*****

At quarter to one, I made my way to the dining car.

The train had been standing at Mount Victoria station for fifteen minutes and was due to depart shortly. Emerson had explained that it was to take on water and to wait for a local connecting service for passengers who'd spent time at the Hydro Majestic Hotel and at the resorts at Leura and Katoomba.

I'd been hesitant about eating in the dining car, tossing up whether to order something in my compartment or to brave the excruciating ordeal of eating in public. However, Emerson had assured me that the chef had received instructions from the concierge of my hotel regarding the preparation of my food. I'd confessed to the hotel chef, in a moment of extreme frustration, that I was sick of eating food that was cut up into cubes, or stews—things that could easily be managed by a man with one arm.

And so, it came as an extraordinary surprise when, after the soup course, and then fish—both of which were easily managed with the correct utensils—the dining car *chef de cuisine* arrived with a service trolley, the carriage steward at his side, and then ceremoniously began to carve the most delicious-looking steak that I'd seen since leaving the shores of my homeland, six years beforehand. Everything was *à la française*—from the chef's tall *toque blanche*, to the steward's white-cotton-gloved silver service, the name of which, in French, had always amused me—*service à l'anglaise*.

However, the wonder of the table setting was a round, silver platter, which sat precisely within the well of the china plate upon which it had been placed. Welded all around the edge of the platter was a short-sided strip of silver, standing up nearly half an inch or so—it looked rather like if someone had cut off the bottom section of a large, round tinned-meat can. The short, vertical edge of the platter provided something against which I could push my fork and load it, without the embarrassing "stabbing" motion I'd become used to.

"Where can I get such a wonder?" I asked.

"It's yours, sir. Consider it a gift of the staff on the train. It's a small thing when you've given so much to your country."

I was puzzled, yet embarrassed, and at the same time grateful. It was not until almost the end of the journey that what he'd said resonated and made complete sense.

After the table had been cleared and reset, and as I waited for dessert to arrive, I couldn't help recalling the last humiliating meal I'd had after arriving home.

Home.

Such an evocative word. I'd been told that although there were equivalent words in other languages, the English word "home" was so laden with layers of meaning that it was considered unique among other tongues. During the war, men spoke of nothing but dreams of going home. Jack had become so used to my despair of returning to a life of misery, austerity, and meanness, that he'd avoided it. I'd poured out my heart to him, explaining my previous life of loneliness, and the uncaring spirit of everyone on the family property—and it was from my expressions of misery that was born our great plan. It was his grand idea that when we returned to Australia, we'd build a life together on a farm of our own, away from our families, to get on with our lives, forget the war, and to share our hearts for the rest of our lives.

So, two months ago, on the day I'd stepped off the train at Quirindi station, I was not surprised to see only two people waiting for me—my youngest sister Edith, and one of the station roustabouts. She was the only one of my family who'd come to greet me and to accompany me back to the homestead.

I was grateful my brother was not there.

George, the eldest of us siblings, had been sickly when he'd been very young. Mother had doted on him, much to the detriment of those of us who'd followed on after—it was if someone had turned off her maternal feelings after he'd been born. He was the only child she ever touched, unless she had to, or really spoke to with any degree of familiarity. He was her pet, the child who could do no wrong. It was as if my two other brothers, Edith, and I had been afterthoughts—unwanted clutter in her life that she could not pack away into the luggage room at the back of the house. As it was, she'd rarely spoken directly to any of us, either using George or Father as her go-between.

As for George, well, he grew up mean-spirited—a spiteful child with a volatile temper, who played on his early ill health. Although overweight and decidedly un-athletic, George blamed the world and those around him for everything he could not do, or when he did not get his own way. He was naturally lazy and excessively dull-witted, and had learned to manipulate situations through cruelty and deflection, blaming one of us—me usually—for anything that he broke, or for any chore he'd been assigned that was left unfinished, or that he'd performed badly. "Arthur did it!" Was the phrase that seemed to hover on the tip of his tongue when we were young.

He went out of his way to make my life miserable—telling lies, beating me when I was a toddler, and once, when we were sitting on the top stile of the mustering ring, packed with unbroken horses, he pushed me into the milling herd. Edith had screamed as I disappeared under a mass of thudding hooves and shrieking mares; had she not, I may have been seriously injured. But, her screams had alerted one of our aboriginal jackaroos, who'd torn across the stockyard and rescued me. Of course, George blamed me, telling Father it had been me who'd tried to push him, and that I'd lost my balance and fallen.

Over the years, my relationship with George had turned from fear to hate. It was only Father's presence that had kept us from each other's throats, and it was timely when war broke out and I left home.

On the drive from the railway station, back to the homestead with my sister, I heard of how much life had changed since Father had died. "George the bully" had appointed himself head of the household and had occupied Father's study, from which he ruled like a tyrant over a petty kingdom. Everyone had acquiesced to his blustering, cavalier, and selfish management of their lives. It was no real surprise to me—they were all faceless drones as I remembered them, apart from Edith.

Father had made them like it with his stern, cold, Christian dictates and his distant and dismissive manner with every member of his family—except for me, that is. For it was I who had saved him from drowning one day, when he'd fallen into the drench trough and had become trapped underneath a terrified and heavy ram. I'd jumped into the race and pulled the sheep off him, and then thrown my father over my shoulder. I'd clambered over the stiles and thrown him onto the ground, breathed into his mouth, and pumped his chest. There had been frequent times after that, and only when no one else was around, that he'd say, "Just tell me what you want, Arthur; I owe you my life. Anything! Just tell me what you want."

When the motor—one of George's purchases immediately after Father's death—pulled up in the driveway outside the homestead, the entire family was lined up waiting, as if posed by an old-fashioned photographer who'd told them to stay still and not to smile. One by one they kissed my cheek, each glancing at the empty sleeve of my jacket, which was pinned into the inner seam under the armpit. My bright smile gradually faded as I realised they didn't want the maimed serviceman who'd come home; they wanted the bright, cheery, and pliable boy who'd left six years ago.

"George says you're to go to see him in his study when you arrive," Mother had said, wiping her eyes and sniffling. It wasn't a request from him, it was an order—I could tell from the tone of her voice. She turned her back on me and walked back inside, followed by the rest of the family, leaving me open-mouthed and astonished, my baggage at my side and Edith grasping my elbow.

"Tell George to blasted-well get off his fat arse and come to greet his brother. I've travelled ten thousand miles to get here, and now you leave me standing at the front gate like a shag on a rock?" I yelled at their retreating backs.

It was then that my mother turned, mournfully, in the doorway and said, "What happened to you, Arthur? Where's my sunny, laughing boy?"

"He died 'Over There', Mother; so that you can continue to afford to wear the fine dresses you so love." Despite myself, it was hard to hold back the tears. "Aren't you at least glad to see me home?"

"Not like this," she'd replied, staring at my empty sleeve.

Twice, I'd made an attempt to swallow my pride and had walked to Father's study door, but then had changed my mind. I could hear my brother clanking and clicking away—he loved to buy old clocks and to disassemble them. He'd no talent for putting them back together again, and Edith had told me there were boxes and boxes of clock bits and pieces stored away in the loft above the stable. He wasn't too busy to see me—he was merely "putting me in my place" by making me wait.

I decided to take a ride around the property, and did not get back in time for lunch, taking a sandwich in the kitchen instead. It was lovely to chat with Alice, who'd been our cook when I'd left, and although still young, had become timid and touchy. When I'd gone to hug her, she'd flinched. I thought it odd, but then I'd noticed dark marks on her wrists, showing below the cuffs of her long-sleeved blouse.

"I hope Mister George is not making too many demands on you, Alice?" I'd asked, carefully, when she'd told me how demanding the new cooking schedule had become—fresh cakes and pastries on a daily basis, instead of twice a week.

"No," she'd replied, hiding her face, refusing to meet my eyes, and involuntarily rubbing one arm.

It told me everything I needed to know. George's demands had not been only culinary ones. It made me very angry, and determined to talk to him about it. I strode off to his room. His door was locked and he didn't answer me when I banged on it and called out to him.

"Gone to town for more clocks, probably," my brother Cyril said, poking his head out of his own room to see what the ruckus was all about.

It gave me a chance to try to calm down. It was my first day home, and perhaps I'd misunderstood. So, instead, I retrieved my book from my valise, promising myself I'd perhaps ride out with George on another day and try to pour oil on troubled waters. I'd already decided I couldn't live back home, and there were financial and property dealings that needed to be sorted out between us. Somewhere away from the house might be more conducive to avoiding a confrontation. I wanted to settle my affairs, and then move on, to make a new life for myself elsewhere.

I spent most of the hot afternoon in my old bedroom, lying on the counterpane with my book on my lap, and staring out through the French doors, which I'd flung open to allow the breeze to come through into the room. Even the occasional sound of magpies from outside and the soft buzz of blowflies didn't evoke the sense of "home" that I'd expected.

I changed for dinner, asking Edith to help me with my collar stud, and then joined the family at the table. We waited, and waited, and waited.

"Can we start without George?" I asked, after fifteen minutes of silence and nervous glances between members of my family.

My mother glared at me.

Eventually he arrived, looked around the room, and then sat at the head of the table and said grace. He would not meet my eyes.

No one spoke, sitting quietly while Alice began to lay out dishes of food on the table, to be passed around so each of us could help himself.

Lamb chops—I stared at them for the briefest moment before turning in amazement to glare at my brother.

George had started eating and had his head down, looking at me from under his eyebrows, an amused smirk at the corner of his mouth. He'd planned this. For a moment, I considered picking a chop up and gnawing on it—manners be damned—but realised that was precisely what he intended me to do. So, I helped myself to the food laid out on the table, and then rose from my chair and excused myself to my mother.

"I'll eat in the kitchen," I said, and then left the room, taking my plate with me.

He followed me, as I expected, a few minutes later and leaned in the doorway, watching me as I chewed the meat from the bone, holding the chop with my fork.

"What do you want, George?" I asked, wiping my chin with a kitchen tea towel.

"Want?"

"Of course you want something, George. I know you only too well. You haven't changed over the years, except you're fatter, and the size of your arse is now three-foot wider. Comes from parking it in Father's chair the moment he died, I suppose."

"I don't have to stand here and be spoken to by someone like you—"

"Yes, you do, George," I snapped, my voice rising in volume and dark with anger. It was the first time he'd heard me speak with violence in my voice, and it contented me to see his complexion lighten by several shades. "That is, if you wish me to consider your offer."

"What offer?" he blustered. "I've no idea what you're talking about."

"I'm a killer, George," I said, interrupting him. "I'm not the pliant boy that walked out the door six years ago that you can bully into doing your will. I've spent the past six years fighting through excrement to save my life. I know what shit is these days—I can smell it a mile off. You reek of it, and I know you want my parcel of land. Do you take me for a complete fool?" I added, slamming my hand so hard on the table that the plate I'd been eating from flew onto the floor and smashed into countless pieces.

"Savage," he said, shaking the shards from his shoes, and then spat on the kitchen floor at my feet.

Alice gasped behind me.

"You're safe where you are, Alice," I said. "I might need you to be at hand to sound the alarm if I decide to flatten this miserable excuse for a man. I won't let him touch you."

"Try your worst, Arthur!" There was fear in his eyes, despite his attempt at bravado. His eyes had widened considerably when I'd mentioned Alice's fear of his violence.

"Ah," I said, softly, my voice now more full of threat than before. "You'd like that, wouldn't you? A chance to punch your disabled brother—tell me, George, how many white feathers did you receive 'anonymously' in the mail while I was away?"

"Shut your stupid mouth," he growled.

"Oh, that many?" I said, smiling at him. I could see the red rising into his face. I knew I'd touched a nerve. No one in the area had particularly liked my brother before I'd gone away to war. I couldn't imagine that situation had changed over the time I'd been away. From what I'd read and heard, no one in the whole of Australia had been backward about coming forward to present symbols of cowardice to those who'd been seen to shirk their duty.

"I came out here in the spirit of putting things to rest between us," he said.

We both knew it was a lie.

"*Putting things to rest between us?*" I said, quoting him, and then, with a small laugh, couldn't help adding, "Really? What sort of simpleton do you take me for? Here I am, come back, despite your probable earnest wish that I remained in Flanders fields in an unmarked grave—"

"I wished for no such thing!" he protested.

"Don't tell me it hadn't crossed your mind. How much easier this would have been for you if you could have simply taken what you wanted after I was dead. Go on—tell me! How much, George?"

I knew precisely why this whole scenario had been written by my brother, and then played out the way it had, and why he was now in the kitchen. He knew I'd be too proud to sit with the family and eat food with my hands, and planned the meal so I'd be forced to leave them, humiliated, so he could speak with me alone while I was feeling vulnerable. However, I was made of sterner stuff—the war had taught me that much. I fronted up to him, our toes touching, and shouted into his face. "How much?"

"I'll give you nineteen-and-eleven, Arthur. And I think you should consider it. It's a fair offer."

Father had left me twenty thousand acres of land in his will. He'd divided up the property into lots, each to be distributed to us after his death. He'd asked what I wanted, countless times, and finally, just before I'd left for Armidale to join up, I'd told him. On the day I'd left for war and after I'd said goodbye to my family, he and I had travelled to town together and had gone to see his solicitor. I'd watched as he amended his will, and then he accompanied me to the station and waved me off at the train. My father always maintained a stern, emotionless expression. Nothing could have prepared me for the tear that slid down his face as he wished me safe travel.

In his new will, Father had specified my allotment, according to my wishes. Apart from the parcel that contained the homestead and which would go to Mother, the rest of his children would fight it out between themselves for their plots. I'd asked him for the acreage nearest the main road. It was rolling and open, and had its own ready access to the Namoi River, so I wouldn't be beholden to the rest of the family property for water. My selection was not only the closest to the road and to the railway, but it was also the most fertile; George knew it. If he ever decided to branch out, away from sheep or cattle and into agriculture, none of the rest of the land was as fecund as my parcel. I'd chosen it because of those very reasons. My thinking was that if I returned from war and decided to bring up a family of my own, I wanted to grow things, not to raise them.

"Nineteen shillings and eleven pence an acre, George? To get me out of your lives? I suppose you don't want me here—I'm an embarrassment, is that it?"

"What use are you, Arthur? You've come back but half a man—you're a cripple—what can you do around the property to help?"

"Why don't I do what you do, George? Sit in Father's chair and play with myself all day with the door closed?"

"You disgusting—"

"How about I simply give up the land? I suppose that's what you really think you deserve—to be handed everything on a plate, as if it was God's gift?" I didn't let him finish; he'd steer the conversation away from where I intended to lead it. My ire was up and I could feel it boiling in my belly.

"Why are you playing stupid games, Arthur? I could take you to court and swear you coerced Father into changing his will."

"So you could, George, if I didn't have letter after letter from him, giving me instructions as to what I should do with 'my land' if he died while I was away, and how eternally grateful he was that I'd saved his life, and that the land was but a small thing as repayment. Anyway, the land's no longer mine to sell."

He'd gasped when I'd mentioned Father's letters. Edith and my father were the only two members of my family who'd written to me in the entire time I'd served abroad. "What do you mean—it's not yours to sell?"

"Do you remember Eric Miller?" I asked.

"What about him?"

"I know how much you hate him. Remember that time he beat you senseless at school, calling you a sissy and a bully ..."

"Shut up, Arthur! I'm warning you—"

"Warning me what, George? Going to slap my face and run crying to Mother that I teased you?"

Although his fists clenched and released over and over, I could tell he was scared.

"Eric Miller. What about him?"

"Oh, yes, Eric," I said, staring into his eyes, daring him to make the slightest move. "If you want to buy the land, you'll have to negotiate it with him, not me. I shook hands with him on the sale three days ago. We met at the Australia Hotel in Sydney and had dinner. He filled me in on the changes here, and how much everyone around here hated you these days."

"You what?"

"I sold the land to him. Ten guineas an acre, George. I spit on your nineteen-and-eleven pence!"

The fury in his eyes made me smile; to taunt him I moved even closer, our noses inches apart.

"You disgusting traitor," he shouted. "You've sold your family out for money." He spat the words out, incandescent with rage. "If you weren't a fucking cripple, I'd—"

"You'd what, George?" I picked up the chair in which I'd been sitting and threw it across the room. Alice let out a tiny shriek of terror. "Go on," I added, furious by now. "Hit me! Hit me like you hit Alice. I know what else you do to her you disgusting degenerate. Go on—hit me! I'll give you one free shot."

He growled and then took two steps and attempted to whack my jaw. It was an ineffectual slap, rather than a punch, but it was all I was waiting for.

Something inside me snapped.

Maybe it was a lifetime of built-up anger and resentment, or the fact that I'd given five years fighting for my country while George had hidden away like some spoiled brat in the broom cupboard, afraid of the dark. But I felt it go, like a "twang" in my mind—such was the violence of my fury. I reached behind his head and grasped a handful of his hair and then thrust his head down violently, bashing his face onto the table. The crack resonated around the room and Alice screamed loudly from the corner of the kitchen, where she'd taken refuge.

"Traitor?" I heard myself shriek. "I'm a traitor? You disgusting tub of lard!"

I grabbed him by the neck and threw him onto the floor, next to the splintered chair, and jumped onto his chest, pinning his arms down with both knees while I pummelled his face with my fist, cursing him for his miserable meanness and cowardice—he'd stayed at home all tucked up safe and warm while I'd gone away, lost not only my arm, but the only person in the world I'd ever loved, and when I'd come home he'd tried to cheat me out of the true value of my inheritance.

I only came to my senses when I became aware that my sister Edith was kneeling behind George's head on the kitchen floor, holding my wrist with both of her hands, and shaking with the effort to stop me striking. "Arthur! Arthur! Stop!" she was screaming.

It was only when I realised that she was sobbing in fear that I stayed my hand.

"Get out of my house!" my mother said from the kitchen doorway in the silence that followed. The rest of the family gathered behind her, open-mouthed and aghast at my violence.

"Mother—" I started to say.

"Get out! You ... you animal! I never want to see you again. Get out!"

I ran from the room, out through the kitchen door as fast as I could, threading my way between the trees in the orchard behind the house. I leaped over the vegetable garden wall, and then tore down through the home paddock to the river, a mile from the house.

Exhausted and retching, I fell on my knees, breathless, my hand braced against one of the tall gums along the riverbank, and then leaned forward, vomiting through the sobs that tore through my body.

Home? The word burned in my chest. This wasn't "home" this was hell. At least on the battlefield and in the trenches I knew who the enemy was—I never expected it to be those who were supposed to love me and to welcome me back.

"Jack … Jacky, why did you leave me?" I heard myself cry out to the quiet bushland around me, and then I howled like a wounded animal, and threw myself into the river.

I floated in the dark for what seemed like a long time, but which was more likely not more than a few minutes, my head resting in the mud at the edge of the water, until I heard the loud rustling of starched petticoats heading my way through the night.

"Arthur! Artie?"

Edith had come looking for me, as I knew she would.

"Oh, damn," she said, when she finally saw where I was lying.

Despite my despair, I laughed. It was hard to realise that my little sister was no longer fourteen, but a beautiful, willowy, graceful, and intelligent young woman of twenty. "Damn, Edie? Really? Bad language?" I asked as she threw herself, fully clothed, into the water at my side.

"I hate them! I hate them! I hate them!" she howled, and then began to sob, shaking as violently as I had done only a short while before.

"I hate them even more," I said, trying to put some sweetness into my voice, pulling her into my arms as I sat up in the reeds. It was how we'd spoken to each other when she was a tot—*I love you. I love you more. No, I love you more. I love you even more*, and so on.

She laughed at my teasing, her sobs turning into hiccoughs.

"Your dress is ruined," I said, rubbing my chin over the top of her head.

"So's your beautiful suit," she replied, as she tightened her arms around my waist.

"You're so grown-up," I said, kissing her forehead.

"And you've come home such a man. I've become unused to what one should be, Arthur. And now, here you are, a hero, and so handsome, and so brave."

"And I find my tiny sister has turned from a gosling into a swan. You are truly beautiful, Edith. Why aren't you married?"

"George would never let a man near me."

"And no 'special' gentleman friends?" I asked, trying to change the subject away from me, while trying to get her to smile.

She shook her head. "What about you, Artie? Did you find someone to love?"

It felt like an hour before I was able to speak, and then I sighed loudly before I answered. "Yes, I did, Edie … someone really special. So special that I believe I'll never, ever love again."

"Killed in the war?"

I nodded, grateful it was too dark for her to see the look in my eyes and the tears that had started to run down my face again.

"Was she wonderful?"

This time my pause was not quite so long—I was tired of grieving alone. "He had eyes of milky-green, Edith," I said, my voice so broken that I could barely whisper. "And he had the softest, most beautiful hair—it was the colour of the sand on the beach—" And then, I had to stop. I simply could not say another word.

There was no great reaction of shock, or dismay, or disgust. My extraordinary sister simply nodded against my chest, as if I hadn't just revealed the greatest secret of my life. "He was a very lucky man, Arthur … for you to have loved him so much," she eventually mumbled. "What was his name?"

I don't know if it was the surprise of her acceptance of my revelation, or the fact that I could not speak it, but his name stuck in my throat, as if reluctant to be spoken, and I collapsed against her, howling my misery, and sobbing into her neck. She held me and shushed me, rocking me against her breast and murmuring, over and over, "It's all right, Arthur; it's all right. I love you … I love you."

Perhaps an hour later, I found myself lying on my back with my head in her lap, her back against a peppercorn tree, while she ran her fingers through my hair.

"I can't stay here, Edie," I said. "I'm sure you understand that now?"

"Yes, I know. What will you do?"

"Come back to the house and help me pack. I'll saddle one of the horses and ride into town and stay at the hotel near the station overnight. Then I'll catch the first train to Tamworth in the morning."

"Why Tamworth? Wouldn't it be better to go to Sydney? Surely you've friends in the city?"

"Well, yes, I do have friends there. You know George; he's bound to go to the police and have me charged with assault. I'm not going to give him the chance to accuse me of running away. You can tell them where to find me—I'll stay at the Post Office Hotel."

"Take me with you, please. Don't leave me here. I can't bear it."

"I'll send for you, Edie. I promise I will."

"He won't let me go—take me with you now."

"Let me get myself settled and then I'll send for you. I promise. I've any number of mates from the army who'd be only too happy to come to escort someone as lovely as you away from this place—and not one of them would be as considerate with George as I was not long ago, if he tried to stop you leaving."

"Where will you go?"

"Jack and I had planned to buy a farm together somewhere out west. I suppose I'll do that. Hey, my little pumpkin, how'd you like to be the 'missus' of the homestead?"

"Oh, Artie!" she cried, and then threw her arms around my neck.

As we walked back to the house in the dark through the paddock, her hand in mine, she begged me to tell her all about Jack. I told her how he'd laughed, the light in his eyes when he'd looked into mine, his bravery, the way he'd kissed me …

"He sounds just perfect," she said, as we slipped into my bedroom to pack up my things.

"He was. Truly he was. You would have loved him, and he would have loved you too."

She held me in her arms and we rocked together, eventually breaking apart when the floorboards began to squeak under our feet.

The house was quiet; they'd all gone to bed mortified most likely. I didn't write a note, but hitched up the sulky to one of the quieter mares, having realised I couldn't take my luggage with me on horseback. I'd pay one of the men at the hotel to drive it back in the morning.

"Artie?" she whispered, as she helped sort out the reins. "Is it true what they said in the papers? About the horses, I mean? Were they all put out to pasture and looked after?"

My hand froze on the buggy shaft as I was tightening its cinch. I couldn't tell her the truth—that the directive came that no horses were to come home. Clipped of their manes and tails, given one last feed, and then led to a veterinarian to be shot and skinned for the leather. So many men had walked off into the desert with their best friends, and then returned without their horses and a bullet short, explaining that "he stepped in a hole and broke his leg …"

"Yes," I mumbled, the tears falling onto my hand.

"Promise me you'll tell me the truth one day," she said, hearing the lie in my voice.

I shook my head. "I can't," I said, before my throat closed over.

My poor, beautiful, and loving "Kingsman", his belly ripped open as we'd jumped over the Turks' trenches at Al-Khalasa, bayonets and swords thrust up by the enemy as we'd soared over their heads. As Kingman had fallen under me, I could hear his terrified screams, and Jack's voice shrieking my name.

I'd heard talk of "berserker" moments in the heat of battle. In retrospect, I suppose that's what had happened to me. Nonetheless, at the time, it had felt like someone else had stepped into my boots and taken over, someone who knew that Jack was nearby and could not get to me. I'd had fleeting glimpses of the man I loved fighting in a mass of men, calling out to me as he'd tried to make his way to my side. But, at the same time, I was also aware that the Turks had an automatic weapon mounted on a small rise not twenty yards from where I'd been standing, and that the gun was shredding our mates. I'd been more afraid for Jack than for myself—all I could think of was that I had to save him. I had pulled out my sidearm and started to fire into the press of crescent-helmeted men around me. I'd known I had to get to the gun emplacement before we were all but stripped of our flesh by the "rat-tat-tat" of rapidly fired machine gun bullets.

The next thing I remembered was laying on Kingsman's flank, covered in blood with Jack behind me, holding me in his arms, a sea of dead Turks around us.

It's how I came to my promotion to captain, my transfer to the No. 8 squadron of the Australian Flying Corps on the Western Front, and my nickname—Captain Arthur, the Beast of Al-Khalasa. I'd single-handedly bayonetted and shot my way through the enemy trench and taken control of their antiquated Gatling gun, and then mowed down their entire emplacement before Jack managed to struggle to my side. I was responsible for the death of thirty-six men. It was a burden I knew I'd carry for the rest of my life.

My dagger was found in the eye-socket of the commander of the area, one of the most ferocious and fearless fighters of the Turkish forces from nearby Beersheba. For that, after the war, I was awarded the Turkish War Medal for bravery.

Our side gave nothing to the enemy after the conflict—neither high esteem nor medals—only our scorn and our dead. In the end, I couldn't help thinking that both the Germans and the Turks had more honour than we did, and they valued the honour and bravery of all men, on both sides, more than the glory of victory.

*****

I lingered in the dining car after dessert and coffee and watched the world go by. The scenery in the Blue Mountains was very beautiful, even though not as spectacular on the descent into Lithgow as it had been on the way up from Valley Heights to Warrimoo.

When I eventually got back to my compartment, Emerson was attending to my portmanteau.

"It's the dish from the staff, Arthur," he explained. "As it's not too heavy, I thought I'd put it in your luggage rather than giving you something else to carry."

"You know … don't you," I said, gently.

He looked embarrassed and began to blush. "Yes, Arthur, we all do. We know who you are, but we've had orders that you're a very shy person and like to be left alone. I didn't think it my business, as friendly and open as you've been with me, to intrude into your privacy."

I sighed. There'd been such a hoo-ha when I'd come back on the *Osterley*, trying to arrive "incognito". Alas, I'd become a celebrated war hero to the Australian public and there was no escaping the attention.

"I appreciate it, Emerson, truly I do. You've treated me with great courtesy, respect, and openness, and I do hope we can continue to keep in touch—although I'm not sure how."

"May I suggest something?"

"Of course."

"Perhaps if I give you an address, you might write to me here, care of the railway, once you've moved into your property, and before you advertise for help. I'd be happy to apply for some time off and show you what I can do with horses."

There was such hope and enthusiasm in his eyes that I made an instant decision.

"How much notice do you have to give to the railways?"

"Six weeks. Why?"

"Whether it's as station manager, horse-breaker, stud-master, or general 'layabout', I think you're exactly the sort of man I'd like to have around me, Emerson. If you're willing to take a chance, that is?" I held out my hand, and he shook it enthusiastically.

"I promise you won't regret it, Arthur. I'm very moved. Blimey! Stone the crows …"

I asked him to sit, as I could see the start of tears in his eyes. Perhaps this is what he truly wanted to do, to move back onto the land? Once we started to discuss how he'd go about setting up a strong breeding program, I could see I hadn't made a mistake in being so hasty—like me, he knew his horses. I'd get over his similarity to Jack. Already I could see how different they were—the warmth in his eyes was that of nascent friendship, not of love.

Shortly before the train arrived in Bathurst, he knocked on the compartment door to warn me that there were explosives on the track ahead—small percussion charges, used to alert men who were working on the line ahead that a train was approaching.

"Thank you, Emerson. I'm glad of the warning. I'm still extremely nervous of rail travel." He looked puzzled, but I could tell he was too polite to ask, so I explained, "It's how I lost this," I said, glancing at my empty sleeve.

"You fell under a train?"

"No," I replied. "I was in a train accident in France in 1917."

"Not that disaster at Modane?"

"No, ours was a week earlier, and just outside Paris."

"Please don't tell me it was that dreadful affair at Pontoise—the civilian train that was bombed when some Americans started shooting at the Jerries?"

"How terribly sad that you should hear of it," I said. "I had no idea it had reached the papers here."

"It didn't, Arthur. You forgot, or perhaps I didn't tell you, that I was at Poissy when it happened. Such a dreadful thing."

"Yes, it was—and it was only because of our own foolishness that we were on that blasted train."

He blanched. "That's not where …"

"No," I said. "Jack died in hospital in England four weeks after that, at the beginning of January in 1918."

"I'm so sorry, Arthur."

"Sit. I don't mind talking about it, oddly enough. As the doctor said earlier, it's probably good for me to talk of the war, to help lay my ghosts to rest."

"Shall I order tea?"

"I've just had coffee an hour ago, but, why not?"

"Righto, I'll be back in a flash."

I watched him close the compartment door. I knew he'd return quickly—he'd explained that there was an electric telephone connection between his attendant's cubicle and the dining car. In ten or fifteen minutes, the charming steward who'd served me at lunch would arrive in the corridor outside my compartment with a tea trolley laden with an excess of silverware and china, and, despite having eaten my fill not an hour since, a plethora of cakes, biscuits, and sandwiches.

Of course, if I were to recount my accident to Emerson, there would be a few personal things I'd have to leave out. Earlier in the day, and quite unexpectedly, Jack and I had been issued with a three-day furlough, so on the spur of the moment, decided to go to Paris to see the sights. We'd only missed the evening troop train because we'd been waylaid by the lads as we were leaving the airfield, coerced into joining an improvised cricket match. We were forced to spend the night in a double-bed in a *pension* near the station—it was the last time we made love and slept together in each other's arms.

Those few innings with the boys that made us miss our train led to a dreadful turn of events, one precipitated by the combined stupidity and misplaced enthusiasm of a hundred trigger-happy American youngsters, fresh off the boat from the U.S.A.

When Jack and I returned to the station in the morning, the civilian train to Paris was already packed. The Germans were mostly aware of passenger services and they tended to leave civilian trains alone. Troop trains nearly always travelled at night—they were harder to hit in the dark. When I saw two American infantry platoons lined up at the far end of the platform, I merely assumed they were waiting for another train to follow on after ours. I had no idea that two empty carriages were being shunted onto the rear of our train for them, to drop them off at Cormeilles-en-Parisis, ten miles and thirty minutes away.

The train was barely a mile from the bridge over the river at Pontoise when Jack pulled at my sleeve. "Look, Artie," he said. Five *Großkampfflugzeuge* were flying parallel with our train, about two hundred yards away and forty or fifty feet from the ground, checking we were indeed a civilian service.

"It's all right," I said to the fellow passengers in our compartment. "They're German bombers, but they won't attack a civilian train. Trust us, we know—*nous sommes, tous les deux, les aviateurs Australiens.*" My French wasn't wonderful, however they understood, seemingly relieved and laughing.

It was then that I heard rifle fire coming from the back of the train.

"No! Stop! You idiots!" Jack screamed, leaning out of the carriage window, facing the back of the train, and waving his arms. But, it was too late. Over his shoulder, I could see the German bombers peel off into formation, and then I heard the roar of their engines as they gained altitude, ready to start a bombing run.

"Get down! *À terre! À terre!*" I shouted. I'd barely got the words out and thrown myself around Jack, pulling him onto the compartment floor, when there was the most God-Almighty bang from the railway line ahead of us. Our carriage rose in the air, and twisted sideways, landing with an enormous "crump", accompanied by the screams and shouts of our fellow travellers, and the distinctive, piercing shriek of escaping steam from the engine's ruptured boiler. For a moment, I thought we'd escaped uninjured, but then I heard the whistle from above of a descending bomb.

My world, and the carriage in which we'd been thrown about, disintegrated into splinters of wood, flying metal, and shattered glass. I had a few, fleeting images of bodies flung past me as I was hurled through the air before I hit the ground with a violent thud and the world went black.

When I came to, I was sitting up, a terrific pain in my chest, and my ears ringing. I raised my right hand and ran it through my hair, surprised to find it full of small pieces of glass. I put out my left hand to steady myself; it touched nothing and I fell onto my shoulder—I didn't understand what was going on. And then, in front of me, I saw an arm underneath my left leg. I was puzzled for a moment, and then numbly realised that I seemed to be impaled by a long brass rod, which had traversed through the flesh across my chest, like the spike of some diabolical and bloodied *rotisserie*.

It took only a few seconds for me to register that the length of brass was actually one of the front restraining bars of the overhead baggage racks in the compartment in which we'd been sitting, and that the arm under my leg was in fact my own.

"Jack!" I screamed; terrified when I realised what had happened. He'd been in my arms when the bomb had hit us. "Jack! Jack!"

And then, I remembered nothing; just indistinct shadows and disembodied voices for another four weeks.

*****

"It must have come as a terrible shock when you woke up and found yourself in a hospital in England," Emerson said.

"It wasn't so much of a sudden, eye-opening, out of the blue 'Where am I?' sort of affair. I'd been aware of coming and going in and out of consciousness for some time—vague impressions of doctors and nurses and the smell of antiseptic in the air. I remember being very cold and asking after Jack, over and over, before everything went dark again. And this time I knew I'd been unconscious for a long time."

"Why?"

"Because when I 'woke up', I knew I'd actually been conscious for an extended period—days, maybe weeks, but not minutes—I'd merely been asleep in my mind. I was sitting up in bed with a bandage over my eye and a book on my lap, which I'd apparently been reading, or someone had been reading to me. 'Excuse me, Miss,' I remember saying to a nurse who was passing by the end of the bed. She nearly dropped her tray in surprise, and then called out for a doctor before rushing to my side. I recall that I was puzzled that she should have been so startled that I'd spoken to her, and it took all of the doctor's efforts to calm me when he arrived a few minutes later—I couldn't stop asking after Jack. I was so agitated that I had to promise the doctor I'd quieten down first and allow him examine me before they'd tell me about my mate. So, I took a few deep breaths and let the doctor and the nurse do what they had to. I learned that everyone in the hospital had thought that I'd had a brain injury and that I'd never come back to who I was before the accident—the doctor remarked that my sudden return seemed like a miracle.

"While he was examining me, and to help fill in some gaps in my memory, the doctor told me that Jack and I were very lucky to be treated so quickly, because we'd been sent to a military hospital nearby, and not left with the hundreds of injured civilians at the small infirmary near the crash site. As we were the only officers in Commonwealth uniforms pulled out of the carnage after the accident, it wasn't hard to discover who were were—there weren't many Australian pilots in that part of the world—and so, once my identity had been revealed as Captain Arthur, the Beast of Al-Khalasa ..."

"The man who killed a hundred Turks with his bare hands, cut off his own arm from under his horse to free himself, and then killed a hundred more?" Emerson said, sombrely, but with a slight grin.

Exaggerations existed by the score—it was a story similar to those I'd heard a dozen times both in England and back home, and which I'd actually seen reported in print more than once or twice. I felt no joy in it; in fact it was disheartening, especially as the true story was a nightmare of disappointment in myself that I'd taken the lives of so many and yet had survived myself.

"To cut a long story short, they shipped us to the cavalry hospital at Combermere Barracks in Windsor, not all that far from London—in Australian terms, that is."

"And Jack?"

"He was only two rooms away and had been asking after me constantly during the three weeks that had passed since we'd arrived. In the early days, before they'd operated on him, the doctor told me that the nurses had wheeled him to my bedside, where he'd spent hour after hour holding my hand and talking softly to me. One night, he'd even dragged himself from his room and had hauled himself somehow onto my bed, and had then stretched out next to me and fallen asleep, his arms around me. Although they'd discovered him not long after, they'd left him there until morning, everyone so moved by what they described as 'the bond of friendship forged by war'."

"But …?"

"Yes, there's always a 'but', Emerson, and, as you already know, he died in my arms."

"You don't have to tell me anything more, Arthur. I understand completely how dreadful it must have been for you."

"There's only a little more, if you have the stomach for it?"

"Go on."

"Well, after the doctor eventually finished fooling around with me, he told me that although Jack's operations had been technically successful, an infection had set in."

Emerson's face dropped, but I continued.

"He was asleep when I was led into the room—swathed in bandages, just his face and one side of his head uncovered. He'd been stripped of the skin over the right side of his body in the explosion, most of the pelvis on that side torn way, and several ribs above it. It was a miracle that he'd survived. If he'd pulled through he would never have been able to walk again, and would have had difficulty breathing for the rest of his life. However, it was the way the doctor had said 'if' that made me realise Jack was fighting a losing battle."

"And he died of his infection?"

"Yes," I said, quietly. "He died in his sleep."

"And you were there with him?"

"Yes, I was. That was a blessing."

It was only on special occasions, moments when I knew I would be alone and to be able to let my grief flow freely, that I allowed myself back into that memory of our last hours together.

Emerson seemed contented enough with the small amount I'd related, even though, as a soldier, he probably suspected that what had come to pass had been far worse than my quick, glossed-over description.

It was all anyone ever needed to know—Jack died in his sleep and in my arms.

*****

As it played out, what had actually happened was an uncanny mirroring of what he'd done while I was unconscious.

When I'd been led to his room, I couldn't bear the pain of the moment in front of strangers, so asked for a few minutes alone. I sat quietly on the edge of his bed, and then, after a few minutes, took his hand in mine, and lifted it to my lips. He stirred and opened one eye. "Artie, is it you at last?" he mumbled. It was then that I realised he was blind. They'd spared me that knowledge.

The desperation in his voice was unbearable, yet I forced myself to stay strong. "Yes, it's me, Jack. I'm sorry it's taken me so long to get here."

"I knew you'd come; either on this side, or on the other, Arthur," he mumbled. "I've been hanging on for as long as I could, until you could get here."

"What do you mean hanging on? You're not going anywhere, Jack Hastings; you're going to be just fine, I promise you." Even I could hear the fear in my voice.

"You always were a terrible liar, Arthur Taylor. Don't make promises you can't keep."

I leaned down slowly over the bed, carefully trying not to hurt him in the doing of it, but he whispered, "Lean on me, Arthur. I don't care how much it hurts, but I can't die without the feel of your body against mine once more."

I allowed myself to settle against him as I stroked his hair and then kissed his ear. He turned his head and whispered, "On the lips, Arthur. Don't worry if there are people watching, where's my courageous cobber?"

"Oh, Jacky," I said, my heart breaking. And, as I kissed him, I began to cry. It wasn't a sob, or even a shudder—it was a stream of tears that fell from my eyes and ran down my face, its saltiness flowing into our kiss.

"Captain?" I heard, over my shoulder. "I'm sorry—you really have to let him rest. I'll bring you back in an hour."

The doctor who'd brought me to his bedside must have seen dozens of friendships played out like this in hospital beds over the years. He explained that they needed to change Jack's dressings and that my friend would never want me to see how terribly he'd been wounded, but to remember him as he was—a perfect, strong, and healthy young man.

"Is there anything I can do?" I heard myself asking, even though I knew it was more to settle myself than admitting I knew there was nothing that could be done.

"You can rest up, and get yourself better, Captain; that's about all anyone can do right now. You'll need all of your strength to look after him once he's recovered." I looked up at him, to see the truth in his words, but he wouldn't meet my eyes.

When I woke up, it was dark. I checked my pocket watch, which was on the nightstand next to my hospital crib, and was astounded to see that it was after two in the morning. I quietly eased myself out of bed and padded, barefooted, down the corridor to Jack's room, and then stretched out beside him on his bed, spooning up beside him as best as I could manage.

"Artie?" he said, quietly.

"Yes, Jack. It's me; sorry if I woke you."

"Let's talk about our station—I haven't been able to stop thinking about it. It's what's kept me going while I was waiting for you to come back to me—our life together working the land. Just you and me, the red dirt, some bonzer nags, and the bright blue sky ... what are we going to call our piece of Australia?"

"How about we call it 'Mulwidgee Station', Jack?"

"Mulwidgee, eh? You old softy."

Mulwidgee meant "the place of the two strong hearts" in the language of the local aboriginal tribe where I came from. It was a story I'd heard in my childhood, and which I'd often told him when we'd been out in the desert, even though I didn't really believe it was a true story of The Dreamtime, but a white fella's mishmash, based on something the early settlers in the district had misheard, but didn't really understand. Victorian-era, romantic stories of the noble savage held a fierce fascination for our ancestors in the outback.

"Tell me the story, Arthur," he whispered.

"You sure you want to hear it again?"

"A man could never get tired of hearing that story—and with your voice telling it." He pulled my arm close around him, snuggling up to my form, as if he was a kid waiting for his father to tell him a fairy-tale, to help him go to sleep.

Despite the tears in my eyes and the croak in my voice, I took a few deep breaths, and then began the tale of Mulwidgee.

"Once upon a time, there were two brave warriors, who were promised by their separate tribes to the only daughter of the chief of another people's clan. The girl came into the world with a brolga's foot in her hand, exactly like the two warriors, even though none of them lived within cooee of the others. At the moment of their birth, a fiery star flew through the sky overhead, and the spirits of the land claimed them all as their own.

The girl grew up to be a wisewoman of her tribe, married to the land. However, her father was proud and pig-headed; he'd made a bargain with the elders of each of the tribes the two men belonged to and was determined to see it through. So, when the two young warriors came of age, her father sent for them, to see which of them would be the worthiest to marry his daughter, or whether she would take them both as husbands. When the men arrived, they found that their spirits were carved from the same tree as hers, and refused to marry her, but offered to live out their lives as her friends and her guardians. The father of the girl was furious, and slipped into their shelter at night and killed them both while they slept. The girl lost part of her spirit world with the death of the two men, so she cut out their hearts and buried them both at the base of a Coolabah tree, so the men would always be together. At the place of Mulwidgee, it was she who remained as their guardian, watching over their joined spirits until the day she died."

"Promise me you'll do that," Jack said softly after I'd finished.

"What, Jacky?"

"Bury me under a Coolabah tree; take me home and plant me under Australian skies on the land that you settle, so that I know from time to time you'll visit me and tell me what you've been up to?"

"Oh, Jack," I said, pulling him closer to me, almost unable to breathe with the pain in my heart.

"Ouch, you clumsy bastard. Not so hard!" He started to laugh, but then sighed. "Let's talk more in the morning. Now, kiss me goodnight and let's get some sleep."

He was fast asleep a long time before I was, but eventually, I felt my eyes closing and I too fell into slumber.

I awoke with a soft voice in my ear.

"Captain Taylor! Wake up, sir. Can you hear me?"

A nurse was shaking me anxiously, a night light in one hand, her other gripping my shoulder. For a moment I had no idea where I was. "Jack?" I whispered.

"I'm sorry, captain," the girl said.

I knew he'd gone, sometime while we slept. His body was cold and unresponsive in my arm. I howled my grief, calling out for him and telling him not to leave me. "Too soon! Too soon!" I shouted, until I felt strong arms around me and I was hauled out of the room. I may have started to wreck it; I don't know. But, the next thing I remember was waking up, my eyes still closed, wishing I'd remained unconscious, wherever it was that I'd been. For this time, I could not bear to bring myself back into the world around me—a world without my Sergeant Jack.

*****

"I'll see you in a few weeks then," Emerson said as he took my overcoat from the compartment wardrobe, getting everything ready so that I could exit the train. "The conductor will come aboard once we've pulled into the station; take your time, Arthur."

I peeked through the shutters, horrified to see crowds of people on the platform, which was festooned with bunting.

"Oh, no!" I whispered to myself.

"You're a hero," he said, smiling at my exasperation.

"I don't want this, Emerson," I said, and I truly didn't.

"Arthur, may I tell you something?"

I nodded, so he sat next to me and smoothed the lapel of my jacket, so that I was forced to look at him while he spoke.

"Perhaps the reality of what you did was not a brave thing as such. Perhaps it was an act of desperation; or perhaps it was plain old blind luck. However, having said that, it's too late to change all of that now. These people waiting for you have already made up their minds on who you are and what you did. For them you're a symbol of the only good thing that came back from the war. In you, they'll see something of every man who went away and who didn't come back, and they'll hope that their lost ones were as brave in their final moments as they believe you to have been."

His words stung me to the core; I'd never thought of it like that.

"You may not like it, Arthur; but it is what it is. I suggest you imagine your Jack at your side when you step off the train, and think how proud of you he would have been to see an entire town turn out to welcome you into their fold."

Instinctively, I put my hand out to touch my portmanteau. Indeed, Jack was at my side in a way, or at least part of him was. While his body was buried in a military cemetery in the rolling green hills of an English countryside, I'd had his heart embalmed and I carried it in a beautiful green enamel sealed container wrapped up tightly in the leather satchel at my side.

If the land I'd bought, and had not yet seen, did not have a Coolabah tree, then I'd plant a dozen in a wide circle and bury his heart at the centre, as I'd promised him I would—on the land I'd settled, and under the bright blue Australian skies.

I blinked back tears as I stepped from the train carriage onto the station platform.

"Goodbye, Emerson, and thank you," I said to him as he opened the door for me.

"I'll see you in a few weeks, Arthur. Now, remember your Jack and be brave," he said soberly, but with care in his eyes, as I disembarked.

"Captain Taylor?" A florid-faced man asked, holding out his hand.

"That's me," I replied, shaking it.

"My name is William Pottle, and I'm the mayor."

I looked around at the smiling faces of the people on the platform. Despite the flags in their hands and their gentle, warming, and welcoming applause, they were just like any people in my wide, brown land ... perhaps, in time, I could truly start to build a new life here.

The mayor had not stopped pumping my hand, and a few voices began to sing a different song than the one I'd left home to. Instead of "Rule Britannia", it was a tentative rendition of "Advance Australia Fair", a song most of us were familiar with, but which, until recent times with our newly found, and enthusiastic, post-war Australian patriotism, had not often been heard.

"Forgive everyone," Mayor Pottle said. "We're all a bit emotional. It's not often we get to have a national hero come to live with us."

I smiled my brightest smile and thanked him.

"Welcome, Captain Taylor, welcome!" he said. "Welcome to Bullaroo."

Cross My Palm with Silver

The sun had not long gone down and it had been a spectacular sunset, mainly due to the smoke from hundreds of square miles of bushland burning out of control on the eastern slopes of the Blue Mountains. Now, the waters of the harbour were inky-black, streaked with reflections of blue, red, and green from houses on the other side of the bay and from a few brightly lit ferries that were scurrying across the still-busy port, carrying commuters home to Mosman and to Manly.

"Beautiful, isn't it?"

Whalan didn't even turn his head to reply. He heard the voice and knew instantly who it was, and why the man had followed him out onto the balcony.

"Yes, you're right," he replied, staring out into the dark, over the roofs of houses below the Potts Point mansion. "It's a cracking view."

"Harvey," the man said, holding out his hand.

"Morris," Whalan replied, smiling at the lie both of them had put forward, and at the same time, at the man's firm handshake.

"Are you a business acquaintance of Howard's?"

Whalan shook his head. "Yes, 'Harvey', I am. But not in the way I think you mean it."

"Really? Now I am surprised. You don't look the type."

"Type? What type do you mean?" Whalan smiled, and then finally turned to look at Detective Stanley Archer—the man's real name. Only last week the detective had spent five hours in the witness box giving him the glad eye, while Whalan had sat next to his instructing solicitor in Darlinghurst Court, passing papers to the barrister for the defence, and it seemed he still hadn't recognised the young man with the shy, come-hither smile.

Whalan remembered the particular way in which the policeman stretched his neck before speaking—not before every utterance, that would have been annoying, but often enough to know that he'd injured it at some point in his life and it still gave him grief. Stanley Archer looked perhaps a few years older than him, with an old-fashioned "craggy" look that Whalan found immensely attractive—a grown-up version of Ramón Novarro, the movie star. When he spoke, it was as if he was trying to hide his teeth, which, when he did smile, were even and white. He sported an uncoloured mole on his left cheek underneath his eye, equidistant from his nostril and his earlobe. Whalan had noticed it immediately—it gave him a masculine, rugged appearance that stirred something "down below".

"We've been staring at each other all evening, 'Harvey'. I'd like to sort something out before we start discussing whether I'm 'the type' or not," Whalan said.

"If you want to … but there's no need."

"Come with me," Whalan said, and then tugged on the breast pocket of the man's dinner jacket.

"Where are we going?" Stanley asked, smiling, allowing himself to be led into a corner of the balcony. It was where the balustrade met the wall, in shadows, and where no one who was inside could see them.

"Here."

"And what's here?"

Whalan ran one arm around the man's waist and drew him closer, before starting to close his eyes. "The thing I wanted to sort out, before you got the wrong idea," he whispered. "This isn't business, this is personal."

"I don't …"

The kiss was wet and lingering. Whalan smiled to himself as he broke from it, noting the policeman's reluctance to detach from his mouth. "I think you do …" he mumbled, and then allowed himself to be pulled back into the man's embrace by a gentle tug on his bow tie. "It'll come undone if you pull any harder," he murmured into the kiss.

"What?"

"My bow tie."

"And if your bow tie comes undone, will your pants fall down?"

Whalan laughed.

"Jesus, you're a big, strong bastard, aren't you, Morris," Stanley Archer said, his arms still around Whalan's waist. "And you're pretty forward—kissing a stranger like that. I could be anybody."

"Could say the same for you ... 'Harvey'. However, you didn't seem to mind, and it's not as if we didn't spend the best part of half an hour inside smiling at each other before we came out here."

"Struth—that kiss was a bit of all right, though. I could happily go another round of those."

Whalan chortled, carefully putting one hand into his pocket to adjust himself in his pants, aware that the man had noticed and was grinning as he did the same to himself.

"Look, as much as I liked that," Stan said, "it's a bit risky for me. What if anyone came out here and saw us?"

"They won't," Whalan said with a glint in his eye.

"How can you be so sure?"

"One of my mates is standing guard."

"Ah, so you planned this then?"

"Maybe?"

"I see," Stanley said. "Then, if you did, how about another smooch? If no one's going to surprise us, as you say."

"Maybe ..."

"All right. I get it. How about a smoke then?" The policeman knew the other man was up for it, but he enjoyed playing this game too—the game of "maybe yes". Flirting was fun when there was something nice at stake, and Stanley Archer really liked what he saw.

"Sure. Smoke would be nice, thanks."

"Your name's not Morris, is it?" Stanley asked, as he tapped the end of his cigarette on the back of his hand to knock in the loose tobacco.

"No, and unless you've stolen someone else's cigarette case, yours isn't Harvey either."

The policeman smiled. His initials were plainly engraved on its tooled silver surface. "Were you worried that I wasn't who I seemed to be? Is that why you kissed me?"

"It was one of the reasons."

"What was the other?"

"As I said just a minute ago—this is personal, not professional."

Stanley stretched his neck. Whalan heard the crack. "Ouch!" he said.

"It doesn't hurt."

"Shame—I was going to offer to kiss it and make it better."

Stanley laughed. "What do you mean when you say 'personal, not professional'? I'm starting to feel like an idiot—either that, or someone who's really put their foot in it in a very bad way. Do I know you from somewhere else? It can't have been the army, you look a bit too young, yet you're so familiar … there's something about your smile."

"Well, 'Harvey', you couldn't take your eyes off my mouth for half the day last week," Whalan said. "Maybe that's why my smile's so familiar?"

"Last week? I'm sorry; I don't remember. I'm not in the habit of ogling good sorts in public, and I think I'd remember someone like you if I'd met you somewhere private."

"And yet, you seem happy enough to give me more than a quick brush of the lips when we've only just met."

"Never say no to a free wet one from a looker; that's my motto."

"I suppose you get plenty of French kisses?"

"If I got plenty, do you think I'd be so keen for more?"

"Maybe kissing me is a diversion, while you struggle to remember whether you and I've hit the sack before, and maybe you can't recall where it was, or what my real name is? I'm sure you've got a little book full of the telephone numbers of the dozens of guys you've jazzed in the back of your car."

Stanley couldn't help laughing. "Morris", or whoever he was, pressed all the right buttons. He was sure that if he told him the truth, the younger man wouldn't believe him. It was years since he'd been this interested in anyone, and as for kissing—he'd quite forgotten the lusciousness of another man's mouth under his own, or the tingle it gave him when he opened his own lips for another man's generous tongue. And the jazzing bit? Hell, it'd been what felt like a century since he last dipped the wick.

"Oh, there are too many names in that little book to remember who's who," he said, with a wink, as he lit Whalan's cigarette. "I have this sneaking feeling that you're not letting on about something—either I've done something with you that I shouldn't have, or we've met somewhere embarrassing, or you work somewhere that's going to make this awkward, or—"

"Now, that's flattering." Whalan laughed, and then leaned forward for another kiss. "Forgetting me already, and after barely a few days too," he added, just before their lips touched. This time when their mouths came together, it was lingering, and deeper.

"Jesus ..." Stanley said.

"No. As flattered as I am, Jesus died nineteen hundred years ago. Let me give you a clue. I said it was last week ..."

"What was I doing last week? I was in ... oh ..."

"Yes, Detective Archer, you were in court. My real name is Whalan—Whalan Richards. I was the articled clerk in the Botherwell Case prosecution in the Crown Court at Darlinghurst last Wednesday, and you spent most of your time in the box looking at me as if you wanted to lick my Adam's apple—from the inside."

Stanley took the cigarette from his mouth and slapped his forehead. "What a fool I must seem! I'm so sorry—you must think I'm the most terrible degenerate, coming on so strong to a stranger like that."

"I think nothing of the sort, and it was me who kissed you first, remember? My own mother wouldn't recognise me in my wig and robes."

"I'm so sorry—Whalan. Of course I recognise you now you've jogged my memory. I don't flirt with everyone. This is a first for me—I'm usually so shy when it comes to this sort of thing. You have to believe me; I've never given anyone the glad eye in a work situation before ... I'm so ashamed of myself."

"No need to be ashamed. I don't kiss everyone either."

"You don't?"

Whalan shook his head. It was true. The demarcation between what he did for money and his personal life was quite clearly drawn in his mind. Kissing definitely belonged in the latter. He'd never kissed a client, nor would he.

"Then why the mouth-to-mouth with me?"

"Because I had a fat for you all the way through the case last week, and when you walked in here tonight out of the blue, I went out of my way to make sure you followed me onto the balcony. In my line of work you get to figure out who wants what with a glance, and I wanted to kiss you just as badly as you did me."

"You did, huh?" Stanley said, with a soft snort, pleased, yet a little embarrassed. "Anyway, what makes you so sure I was going to trail after you?"

"Because, Mr. Detective, I dress to the right, and for the twenty minutes after you arrived, and before I left the room, you seemed to be alternating between counting the veins on my knob and watching my lips as I spoke. In the business, we'd recognise that as wanting to go downstairs for a feed after chewing on my face for a week of wet Sundays."

Stanley Archer opened his mouth to deny it, but then looked into Whalan's broad smile. He knew the jig was up.

"Guilty as charged, your honour."

They laughed and then leaned together, shoulders touching, forearms on the balcony rail.

"I'm working tonight, sad to say," Stanley said.

"So am I."

"Pity."

"If I thought you were a punter, then we'd already be down to business, and you a fiver lighter."

"Five quid? You're worth ten times that."

Whalan smiled and then ran his hand under the detective's cummerbund, over the small of the man's back. "Did you go to charm school while you were training to be a policeman, Stanley?"

"Honestly. Five quid? How much of that do you get?"

"Two."

"For what? Or do I have to cross your palm with silver before you tell me?"

Stanley was teasing, and they both knew it. Whalan knew the detective was not a customer; he had too much of a sense of his own desirability to ever fork out money for sex. No, the man was flirting in a way that meant something else. Something not restricted by prices and negotiations about what went on in the bedroom. He'd seen it in his eyes last week, the way that he'd caught Whalan's eye over the top of the bible as he swore his oath, and then had flicked his gaze back and forth at him right throughout his testimony and cross-examination.

Of course, Whalan had hung around as long as he could after the end of the session, hoping the tall, beautifully dressed policeman would leave the courtroom through the public entrance. But, after twenty minutes, he'd realised that Detective Stanley Archer probably had other police business to do and had left through the passageway behind the cells, underneath the courthouse.

He'd rather hoped he'd run into the man again, and in the meantime, had done a bit of surreptitious digging—he had his contacts. Thirty years old, two years in the army at the end of the war, commendation for bravery, Darlinghurst cop shop, and then, earlier this year, moved from the detective branch of the N.S.W. Police Force to the Criminal Investigation Branch, as it was now known. Never married, worked out regularly at a gym in the Haymarket, lived alone in a flat overlooking Coogee beach. Bit of a loner.

It didn't seem to add up to the forthright man who'd but a few minutes ago had all but stripped Whalan of his clothes and had his way with him on Howard Fifield's balcony.

The silence had become a little uncomfortable, Whalan thought. It was one of those lengths of time when each person wanted to say something, but then thought better of it, in case they played their hands too soon.

"Beautiful, isn't it?" Stanley said, also aware of the momentary awkwardness, and repeating the phrase he'd used when Whalan had first come out onto the balcony.

"Yes, you are," Whalan replied, with a soft chuckle. "But I think you meant the house, detective."

"Wahine" was a striking, two-storied building, constructed in the late-Victorian colonial style, surrounded by deep, shaded balconies on all sides, and situated in two acres of garden. A private paradise, a few miles from the centre of the city with its own jetty and small, private beach—its owner had returned from the war a decorated hero and a military surgeon of renown.

"How did you get into this business, Whalan?" the policeman asked.

"Don't you mean why?"

"Isn't it the same thing?"

"No. How I got into it was through an introduction. Why I got into it was a necessity, if I wanted to continue studying and to pay my rent."

"Okay, I won't pry," Stanley said, and then took one of Whalan's hands in his own and massaged the knuckles. "I'm pretty quiet, believe it or not. I understand privacy—I keep myself to myself most of the time."

"Quiet? I'd love to see you when your engine's running, if this is quiet," Whalan said, before slipping his fingers between the detective's.

Quiet? A loner? Whalan said, to himself. The man who'd just been invading his mouth and who had sucked Whalan's lips into his own with a groan? He didn't know whether to be doubtful or to be flattered. They'd both been immensely aroused while they were kissing—Whalan had felt Stanley's erection pressing into his belly, and had become so excited that he'd felt the sweat pooling behind his collar.

"I promise you, I'm not like this with everyone; in case you were wondering," Stanley said. "There's something… something special about you."

"I bet you say that to all the blokes, Archer."

"Only the ones with the key to my ignition."

"Oh, really? Shall I get in line then for a ride?"

"You can hop in my back seat any day, Whalan."

That was the last thing Whalan had expected to hear. It was his turn to think, "you don't look the type". But then, he'd been sleeping with men for money for three years now and nothing really surprised him. Sometimes the most "blokey" guys were the ones who liked to lie on their faces and bite the pillow while he did the deed—they were usually the married ones, with the excuse that "it was the only thing their wives couldn't give them".

"Really?"

"As long as you return the favour," the man added, with a very cheeky grin and a wink.

That was better, Whalan thought. An ambidextrous man with a sense of humour—much like himself, he realised. He idly wondered if this flirtation would come to anything, despite the kissing. Sometimes things became too complicated long term—a copper and a soon-to-be solicitor seemed like a disaster in the making.

"I'd be delighted; however, it's going to have to be another night, Stanley. I'm afraid I'm going to have to shove off and get to work, otherwise I won't be able to pay my rent, and my landlady will toss me out on my ear."

"Is that really why you do it?"

"Why else do you think I'd be here, if it wasn't for the money?"

Stanley shrugged. "I guessed you were one of Howard's boys."

"I'm not a boy, in case you didn't notice."

"I noticed. How do you get muscles like that?"

"Hold cheeky coppers over my head and do squats."

Stanley laughed. "No, really, how do you do it? Your biceps and thighs are as thick as telephone poles."

"I haul barrels after work at Toohey's Brewery, down at Broadway. Sometimes, if they have any work going, I do Saturdays and even Sundays on the sly."

"I like strong men, Mr. Richards."

"So do I, Detective Archer," Whalan replied, with a wink, copping a quick feel of the policeman's tented trouser front.

"Naughty big bastard, aren't you? Keep that up and I'll have to kidnap you and have my way with you."

"Any other night, I'd be up for that, and like a shot too. But tonight …"

"Yes, tonight; sorry. How did you get to be here tonight if you're not one of Howard's boys?"

"You know Manny Leibowitz?"

"Sure. He's one of Tilly Devine's push."

"It was Manny who put 'The Rowers' together as a team—gathered us from all over Sydney."

"The Rowers?"

"That's what we call ourselves—there's eight of us normally. We're all pals now; young professionals who can't make ends meet. We come here maybe three, sometimes four, times a year on occasions like this one—all dressed up to the nines. Manny organises it, and lets us know when it's on; we get a ticket to George's in Castlereagh Street for a fancy, rented tuxedo, and we get picked up in a charabanc in Martin Place and delivered here. We wander around with the guests and we're nice to everyone and go about our business. Manny takes us home in the early hours of the morning with enough money in our pockets to pay for food and lodgings for a few months."

"Two quid will pay for all that?"

"What are you talking about—two quid?"

"That's what you said your cut was."

"Oh, no." Whalan laughed. "I usually take home at least six, sometimes eight."

"Eight quid? That's four times in a night? I've got maybe one good one in me, and at best two dribbles after that if I'm lucky," Stanley said, open-mouthed.

"I don't shoot."

"I'm sorry, I'm confused."

"I don't boil over with my clients, Stanley. The only thing that sees my spunk on nights like this is the rag in the table beside my bed when I get home and knock one out before I go to sleep."

"I still don't understand …"

"Each one of us blokes has things he will do and things he won't. The punters don't all want the same thing. If they want someone who'll squirt for them, they know I'm not the one to ask to go to a room. But, see that guy through there? The tall one with the curly hair parted in the middle?"

Stanley leaned against Whalan and followed his gaze. "That's 'Henry'. He's one of The Rowers, too. He earns £2/19/6d a week as a cashier and he's got three small kids and a wife to support. 'Henry' can pump out four loads a night, no problem. No one touches him; he doesn't touch them. He simply stands there with his daks around his ankles, talks dirty to the customers, and delivers while they watch. Some guys have more juice in their knackers than others. As for me? Well, donating my spunk to a stranger for money is further than I want to go—as I said, we all have our limits as to what we're prepared to do with our clients."

"How do the marks know what you're up for?"

"Promise me this isn't some convoluted sting operation, Stanley. You could be pumping me for information. Sorry, but ever since the consorting law, everyone's a bit nervous. I know that sounds insulting, however, as you're a copper and I'm in the legal business …"

"You think I'm leading you on?"

"No, I don't. Sorry, I shouldn't have said that. I opened my mouth when I should have thought first."

"You're right. I'm a copper here at a private party, and I suppose it's pretty obvious I'm not here to buy. Give me your hand."

"Why?"

"Just do it, Whalan." Stanley quickly unbuttoned his flies and pulled out his erection. "Cop a handful of this and then tell me if you think I'm fooling around."

"Damnation, Stanley … that's enough for a family of four."

Stan was amused—they both knew it wasn't quite true, but he had to admire the quick thinking and the flattery. "It does the job," he said, aware that Whalan was enjoying what he was doing to him with his hand.

"Well, I do believe you, Detective Archer, and I apologise; that wasn't worthy of me. Maybe we perhaps make another time to meet up? I'd really like to spend a bit longer getting to know you … and this."

"You'd better let me put it away then—if I'm not careful you might end up getting very well acquainted right now."

"Something to look forward to, then; somewhere down the line," Whalan said, firmly massaging Stanley's rod—he gave it one last squeeze with both hands, and then ran them behind the man's back and grabbed his buttocks, pulling the policeman towards him so they were pressed up tight against each other.

"Now, that's really not fair, mister," Stanley said, with an enormous toothy grin, as Whalan ground the hardness in his own pants against the detective's erection. "If you don't want a mess on your fine trousers, then I think it's time to put junior to bed."

"Allow me to do it for you then, Stanley, please? A real gentleman wouldn't allow you to go back inside in a state of 'undress'."

"Knock yourself out," he said, with a wink.

"Left or right?"

Stanley sighed and then smiled before replying. "Straight up is about the best you'll manage right now."

Whalan pulled him back into the corner they'd been in earlier, and then angled the detective's body so the broad stretch of the veranda was behind them. He squatted down and took Stanley into his mouth for a few seconds, slurping and moaning as he did so, before tucking the man's penis back into his trousers and buttoning his flies for him.

"Fuck me!" Stanley growled, his voice thick with arousal. He reached down and pulled Whalan to his feet and then kissed him.

"I do believe that you've already offered me your arse once tonight, Detective Archer."

"Holy Mother of God ... your mouth, Whalan."

"I could say the same about your cock, Stanley."

Whalan watched the confusion in the man's eyes, and then the slight refocus as he decided to speak. "I don't think I've been this turned on since ... well, I can't remember, Whalan, and that's God's truth. It's been quite some time since I—"

Stanley didn't get a chance to finish his sentence. Whalan pressed his mouth to his own, and then took Stanley's hand and guided it down to his erection, which he'd released with one hand while buttoning up the detective's trousers with the other.

"Holy Christ, do you choke many blokes with this? How thick is your fucking prick?" Stan said, after reluctantly withdrawing from the kiss.

Whalan laughed, and then kissed him again. "I think you like to talk dirty, detective."

"I think you may be right, mister …"

"I know I'm right. You forget why I'm here tonight. Lots of these buggers like it when you tell them what they want to hear … and the dirtier the better."

"Spare me the details of what other blokes want, Whalan. But feel free to talk as dirty as you like with me; I'll give as good as I get."

"Only with dirty language?"

"If you're as good as you say you are, then there's no need for me to answer that."

Whalan took his cigarette case from his pocket and opened it for the policeman. "Thank you," Stanley said, unable to avoid noticing that the case was a cheap wooden one—the bloke was not flush, that was for sure.

"No need to thank me," Whalan said, lighting both of their smokes. "It's only a cigarette."

"I was thanking you for the quick gobbie," the detective whispered against the side of Whalan's neck, blowing cool, blue smoke over the man's shoulder as he spoke.

"You're welcome. To be perfectly honest, and this is no bull, I'd have liked to spend as long as you could last down there, saying hello to 'Junior'. I've got a bit of a thing for bringing a nice bloke off in my mouth—it's been so long now, I'd almost forgotten."

Stanley couldn't help raising an eyebrow. "What about the blokes who pay for it?"

"I don't do that with clients."

"Really?"

Whalan shook his head. "No. No kissing, no sucking, and no taking it up the arse. Those are private pleasures."

"How do I get my name on that private list?"

"That list's been empty for years, Stanley, and there's only one name there right now—yours."

*****

Stanley Archer stood at the front gate of Wahine, a cigarette dangling from the corner of his mouth, his hands in his pants pockets, looking up into the clear, starry sky.

"Remember the stars over France, guv?"

Stanley turned to his offsider. "Piss weak when you could see them, compared to this extravagance above us, eh, Edward?"

He and Constable Eddie Taunton had served together in France, and then had both joined the police force when they came home, just over ten years ago. Eddie had no real desire to climb the ranks, but they'd been buddies and so had wangled things so they could work together. Eddie was Stanley's runner, as he had been in the trenches—only these days he was more of a "nark" and a friend than a carrier of messages.

They knew everything about each other—everything.

"How's it going inside then, Stan?"

"Quiet, so far. Max 'Pretty Boy' Hilliard's up there in a corner, miffed, and holding court."

"Miffed?"

"The lad he wanted's already been bagsed for the night."

"Uh huh?"

"I don't like the sound of that 'uh huh', Eddie."

"Bit of vengeance served up cold?"

"Who, me?"

"Yes, you, Stanley. It's me you're talking to, remember?"

"I hate that—"

"Ouch! Don't say it. You know how much I hate that word."

"Sorry. But I hate the bastard even more than you do the word."

"Let it go, Stan. It's bad for your indigestion."

Stanley Archer kicked one of the stone gate pylons, which stood guard to the entrance to the house. He'd only come tonight as a favour to Howard—to keep the dogs away from each other's throats. Howard had expected a few members of the two rival razor gangs to turn up and he didn't want any problems. Stan was police guard for the night; not expected to do anything, merely show his face so everyone knew they had to be civil.

He'd done it for a few reasons. The first being that he'd served with Howard and considered him a friend. The second was that it did him no harm to do innocuous favours for Tilly Devine, mainly because she wasn't averse to tipping him off about what her rival, Kate Leigh, was planning. He liked neither of them really; they were hard-nosed, vicious bitches. On the other hand, Tilly's push had a code-of-honour of sorts—one that looked after orphans, took care of single pregnant girls, and provided some help to the poor in her area. Kate, however, was cold and calculated—her gang too happy to wield their razors and to carve up bystanders if they got in the way.

Stan's and Max's mutual loathing? Well, it had started off with a bit of tit for tat with Tilly Devine. She'd tipped him off about a planned bank raid in Rozelle by an out-of-town mob, and in return he told her he'd heard that Max was planning to trash her sly grog shop in Rushcutters Bay. So, she'd stashed half a dozen of her best at the back of the shop, and there'd been a hell of a fight. Stan and Eddie had turned up as part of the investigating squad—the aftermath of the razor-gang stoush was something that still turned his stomach.

Max had somehow known it was Stanley who'd tipped Tilly off, even though he had no proof, and had started to snipe at him in public and spread rumours that he was "on the take". It had come to the point that Stan had called in to see Kate Leigh, and had asked her to tell Max to mind his manners—when she'd seemed reluctant, Stan had shown her a list of the addresses of her stash houses, and told her to curb her mutt. He hadn't threatened anything; just let her know that he knew where she kept her girls—and her goods.

Stan had heard on the grapevine that Max had been beside himself when Kate had ordered him to leave Stanley alone. But, as the sniping had stopped and he'd rarely seen Max out and about, he'd put it completely out of his mind until one day, when he'd come home to find Harriet, his German shepherd, disembowelled on his kitchen floor, sliced cleanly by a razor from chin to tail, and with the word "Pig" written in her blood over the wall. He'd never been able to get anyone to confirm it had been Max, but there'd been a distinct coolness between them ever since, one that had turned to mutual hate.

He'd only spoken of Harriet's death once, when Max had calmly passed on condolences for his loss in the middle of a crowd of cinema goers outside the State Theatre. "I hope I get to pass on the same sad news to your mother one day, Max, even though I might need a spade," Stanley had replied, angrily, fully knowing that Max's mother had died years before and was buried in Waverley cemetery.

"What's up, Stanley?" Eddie asked, staring back up into the bright sky above them.

"Why do you think anything's up?"

Eddie laughed softly.

"What?"

"You've had your hands in your pockets playing with yourself ever since you came outside to check on me, Stan. That's how I know something's up."

Stanley pulled his hands from his pants pockets with a sigh, and then lit a cigarette. "Want one?" he said, holding his case out to Eddie.

"Wash your hands first, and I'll think about it."

Stanley laughed.

"So, Detective Stanley Archer—someone take your fancy up there? You going to finally dive in and empty your bollocks into someone who isn't worthy of cleaning your boots, like you used to do?"

"Fuck you, Eddie. He's not like that."

"Gotcha, you sly bugger!"

"Baited and reeled in."

"In one, yes!"

"This one's different—he's a nice bloke, Eddie."

"One of Howard's mates?"

Stan shook his head. "Working man with holes in the soles of his shoes."

"Had them next to your ears already, have we then?"

"You've got a dirty mind on you, constable, you know that?"

"You're talking to the man who used to stand guard outside the storage tent while you gave it to that Frenchie. Remember?"

"He's dead. Remember? Now, can we move on?"

"Sorry. That was unkind of me. What's the name of this bloke upstairs, then? Have you got that far yet? Have you even asked? Or has it been a matter of being too polite to speak with your mouth full?"

Stan couldn't help himself; he chuckled, and punched Eddie's biceps with his knuckle. "Name's Whalan Richards."

"Whalan ... Whalan Richards," Eddie mumbled, and then pulled out his notebook and began leafing through it. "Hang on. I knew that name was familiar. You silly bastard ... Whalan Richards is the articled clerk for McGuire and Tanner, the—"

"Instructing solicitors on the Botherwell Case. Yes, I know."

"Well, Mister Smart Arse, I can tell you something about him you don't know."

"Save it, Eddie. I'd like to make up my own mind."

"It's not a bad thing, Stan ..."

"Then you'd better tell me."

"Harry McGuire slipped me a quid or two to check him out when he applied to them for his articles."

"And ..."

"Good boy done wrong."

"What do you mean? He's a good boy who's done wrong, or he's a good boy who's been done wrong?"

"I'll tell you in a few words."

"And they are?"

"Circuit Judge Smithy Gibson."

Stanley cursed under his breath. There was no need for explanation. Gibson was a country judge who, during his circuit tours, would ingratiate himself with the locals, and then leave after a dinner invitation with something of value in his pocket that he'd filched after asking to be excused to use the lavatory.

"You were away when the case went to trial," Eddie said.

"Yes, that's right. What's this got to do with Whalan?"

"Everything, Stan."

Eddie explained that not only had Gibson been convicted for theft, but also, at the same trial, for sexual assault against a young man, from whose parents he'd stolen items of value. The judge had been inclined to putting the hard work on young blokes as he moved from town to town and court to court. Those who'd refused his advances had their reputations ruined by Judge Gibson's false and malicious rumours about them. He'd made the mistake of tying one of the men up in a room above a pub, as a "demonstration" of how a case he'd judged had played out, and then had tried to suck the young man's penis. Unfortunately for the judge, the lad had kicked him in the groin and yelled his head off, alerting the landlord and the local cops who were having a beer after work downstairs at the bar. They burst into the room to find the young man still tied up and screaming his head off with the judge's dentures around his cock, while his honour lay writhing on the floor clutching his privates. That was the case that had come to court.

Whalan had been one of Gibson's victims. He'd been repulsed by the judge's unsubtle groping and offers of money, and as a result, after he'd already left town, Gibson had written his parents a letter, saying that Whalan had forced his way into the judge's hotel room and had tried to seduce him, offering to sell him his body for ten shillings. Whalan had been a kind-hearted country boy with a good future ahead of him, sent to Coventry by gullible parents who'd prefer to believe a turd like Gibson rather than their own son.

"Despite that old bastard and everything he went through with his unloving parents, look what he made of himself, Stan. A solicitor's articled clerk! Who knows where he'll end up?"

Stanley gripped Eddie's shoulder and shook it gently. He was pleased that his mate had shared what he knew. It helped him understand Whalan's situation a little more clearly, now that he knew he'd been booted out of home.

"Say, Eddie? What do you know about the 3/9d racket?"

"What? That soldier nonsense down at Sharland's Hotel?"

"Yeah, the way the soldiers on the game let the punters know what they're up for."

"If you hadn't been away at that arsehole place out west visiting your pal from the Snowy, you'd have been able to find out yourself, and maybe catch a nice bit of infantry tail while you were about it."

"Bullaroo," Stanley said.

"Yeah, Bullaroo, as I said—arsehole place out west."

"It isn't all that bad, Eddie … you should come up with me one weekend. That shack I bought on the river is the bee's knees for a spot of quiet fishing and some quiet country life."

"Whatever you say, Stanley. You know me and 'quiet country life'—I'd rather chew my arm off up to the elbow. Now, the 3/9d racket worked like this: soldiers who were available sat at the bar and laid out silver coins in front of them. That's why it's called the 3/9d racket."

"The four silver coins, from a threepence to a florin, add up to three shillings and nine pence?"

"Exactly. Now it all depends on which coins are laid out and whether they're placed face-up or face-down on the bar."

"Heads means something different than tails?"

"Yes, Stanley. Each coin, whether heads-up or tails-up, would let the punters know what they were up for. Heads meant they'd play the man's role, tails, they was there for the taking …"

"Were."

"No, it's still going on …"

"Jesus, Eddie, no! They *were* there for the taking—it's the grammar … never mind. Go on!"

"Not all of us went to a private school, detective."

"Sorry, Eddie, my turn to be unkind. Back to the system. So, starting from the smallest amount, threepence was for …?"

"Pashing. No threepence, no kissing. Threepence on the counter, heads-up, meant kissing but with teeth together, tails-up, open slather. Same for the other three silver coins—sixpence for a tug, shilling for a gummy, and two bob for the job."

"So, if the man laid out three bob—a shilling and a florin—all heads-up, the shilling would mean the soldier was happy to offer his dick to the punter for a gob job but not do it to the other man, and that for the florin, the soldier was prepared to stoke the fire, but not bend over himself …"

"That's right, it's clever. If the punter saw there was only a shilling and a florin, then he'd know that because of the missing threepence and sixpence, the soldier wasn't interested in kissing, or in tossing the bloke off, or even letting him touch him."

"You're right, it's very clever …" Stanley said.

"Why did you ask?"

"I remember reading the charge sheet on that politician who made a fool of himself at Sharland's; although, as it was already before the courts, I didn't really take in the details of how the game was worked. I only ask now, because I think that's how they're working it tonight with both the men and the girls upstairs."

"How do you know that?"

"Well, Whalan told me there were seven other young fellas—they call themselves The Rowers. I noticed that one of them seemed to be standing in a corner, holding a coin album and showing it to the men I assume must be the punters. I think he must be the one who sorts out the wheat from the chaff—their 'bookkeeper'—the one who keeps tabs on who's prepared to do what and with whom. The other clever thing about it is that it's a way of negotiating so that you could never be stung for opportuning. No talk of what goes on in the sack—the punter just needs to point at different coins to let on what he wants to do—or have done to him."

"And the marks most probably don't pay the working boys and girls directly either. You know, Manny Leibowitz came in earlier …"

"Yeah, I saw him up there chatting with Howard, and Whalan said he was the organiser, the one who looked after The Rowers," Stanley explained. "So, you think the punters pay him, and then he pays the workers at the end of the evening?"

"Sounds very clever to me, Stanley."

"No passing of money directly from client to the lad or the girl, all the negotiating done before they get down to business …"

A car drove into the gateway, so they moved aside to let it through. Two young men, dressed in tails, alighted, and then waved to Stan and Eddie, who tipped their hats in reply.

"Theatre?" Stan called. He recognised them both as friends of Howard.

"Review at the Theatre Royal. All tits, no dicks," one of them called back.

"Wonder what the cabbie thought of that?" Eddie asked as they moved back onto the lawn to allow the taxi to leave.

"Sure he's heard it all before, my friend."

They lit another cigarette and Stan went back to examining the stars for a moment or two.

"So, guard duty over up there is it?" Eddie asked, still curious about the gleam in his friend's eye.

Stan nodded. "Howard's happy that all's well. I rang Cyril and Freddy Bailey to come keep an eye on things while I get to know Mr. Whalan Richards, and so that you can go home."

"The Bailey twins are coming over to keep an eye on things while you 'get to know' Whalan Richards? I suppose you mean that in the biblical sense, Stan?"

"Shut up, Eddie. You know what I mean—one has to test the waters before one takes the plunge. Here, give the boys this fiver from me when they get here, and tell them to keep their flies done up until Max Hilliard and his hoods have left, alright? And let them know the girls are not on the house—if they want to hokey-pokey, they'll have to pay the going rate."

Stan sighed. He didn't earn a lot, but so far this evening, his wallet was twenty-five quid lighter.

"Leave you enough dosh, Gov?" Eddie said, with a wink, taking the five-pound note and inspecting it before putting it into the breast pocket of his coat.

Stanley put his hand in his pocket and pulled out a handful of change. "Hm," he said, "five shillings and nine pence ha'penny. That should be enough for the old 3/9d game."

"What, Stan, you planning on fucking yourself to death or something?"

Detective Stanley Archer laughed loudly and then turned on his heel. "Maybe, but only with one fella, Eddie. Keep up the good work," he said, over his shoulder, as he threw his cigarette butt into the garden, and then walked up the front steps to the entrance of the brightly lit hallway of Wahine, whistling "If I Had a Talking Picture of You".

He stopped and gave Eddie a wink as he polished the toes of his shoes on the backs of his trousers.

*****

Detective Stanley Archer twirled the threepenny bit between his fingers, watching how it caught the light.

They'd been lying side by side on top of a beautifully embroidered white Marcella quilt in the "Blue Room", talking for an hour or two. Their coats were draped over an armchair in the corner of the room, both of them still fully clothed.

"Hm," Stan murmured, momentarily distracted by a gentle, teasing kiss.

"There was only three and six on the sofa table, detective," Whalan said, twanging one of Stanley's elasticated braces. "I don't remember any threepence?"

Stanley rolled onto his side and thrust his hand into his pocket, drew out a handful of his silver and copper coins, and then placed them one by one on Whalan's chest, starting at his neckline and lining them up, down and over the waistband of the man's trousers and along the fly flap, which he patted while growling, low in his throat.

"You left all the two bobs for my dick, Stan."

"You noticed? My, oh my—and they're all tails-up too!"

Whalan pulled the policeman's head to his own and kissed him again, this time roughly, only stopping when the saliva began to run from the corner of his mouth and onto his shirt collar.

"So is that what you want me to do to you?" he murmured against the policeman's cheek.

"A ride there for a ride back is what I really want ... but yeah, it's been an age, but I'd really love you to give me a long, hard one, Whalan."

"I think I can accommodate that," Whalan muttered.

"Well, you're going to have to wait until four a.m., 'Muscles'. As much as I like you, I'm paying for your time to keep you off the floor and to get to know you, not to play doctors and nurses—not yet, anyway. If you want to come across when you've clocked off, then I'm happy to give you whatever I've got."

"I think I can wait, Stanley. The kissing's on the house ... as it wasn't negotiated for, then you're not paying for it."

"Damn me, but you are one fine specimen of a man."

"You're not half bad yourself, Mister Policeman."

"Oh no," Stanley said, nipping the point of Whalan's chin between his teeth. "You're totally wrong there … I'm not half bad, I'm the full quid mate, and I'm very, very bad."

"Oh yeah? I can't wait for you to show me …"

His last words were stopped as Stanley moved away from his chin and began to attack his mouth again. "Oh damn …" Whalan kept saying in his mind over and over, until the words disintegrated into a moan.

★★★★★

He'd been astounded when Robbie, the "bookkeeper" for the evening had come to him and told him that he'd been booked out for the entire evening, by the one man, who'd forked out twenty quid for the pleasure of Whalan's company for the rest of the night. On nights like this, when they were all working the same function, The Rowers drew straws between themselves on the way to the party to see who'd take care of the punters and direct them to the right boys. Whoever was chosen became the "bookkeeper". The other men all put in something at the end of the night, so that the man who drew the short straw wouldn't be out of pocket, and would go home, like his mates, with money in his pocket.

After his initial surprise, Whalan plucked Robbie's sleeve and drew him to a corner of the room, asking him to keep an eye out for the handsome detective with the distinctive mole on his face, and asked him to tell the man that, although he'd be busy all night, he'd pop out for a breather and a smoke every so often. He didn't want the policeman to leave without getting the chance to make a time to meet up, perhaps for a drink at a pub, later in the week.

"Fancy him do you?" Robbie had asked, with a cheeky smile.

"Damn it, Robbie, never met anyone like him. I don't know what's up with me."

"Lucky stiff, Whalan. Some of us never meet anyone who makes the heart beat faster."

"You seem to meet a lot of blokes who make the blood beat faster in your cock, though, Rob."

The two men laughed, and then Whalan stopped suddenly. He'd seen Max "Pretty Boy" Hilliard sitting in the corner with two of his thugs at his side. He threw Whalan an odd, lopsided smile that wasn't at all friendly.

"Please tell me it's not Max who's filled up my dance card …"

"Nah, I wouldn't do that to anyone, Whalan. He knows he only gets one at a time at Howard's shindigs. Besides, the man who's booked you is a new bloke—someone you'll like."

"I don't like my marks. They're just pound notes to my eyes. I only pretend to like them."

"Famous last words."

"What do you mean by that?"

Before Robbie could explain, Howard Fifield arrived and interrupted the conversation.

"Your client's an old friend of mine, Whalan. I know you're a kind and decent man; I hope you'll show him the same courtesy and respect that he'll offer you."

"Well, of course, Howard," Whalan said, somewhat puzzled. Perhaps it was an old war buddy of Howard's who'd been disfigured, or lost a limb?

"There's a bottle of champagne and some nibbles set out. Enjoy yourself; you're in the Blue Room—last door on your right at the end of the corridor."

Whalan had gone to the room and prepared himself for whoever might knock on the door. There was an expected protocol to it. He laid out his sixpence, shilling, and florin on the sofa table, all of them heads-up—the king staring him in the face—it was a double-check to make sure the punter knew exactly what he'd be getting and nothing more. *No kissing, you can suck my dick, I'll pull you off, and I'll slip you a length*—that's what the three coins meant when placed face-up. It was a numismatic language—a metaphorical crossing of the palm with silver.

Then he waited. He'd found it odd at first—that it was the mark who should be the one to undress him, and not the other way around. But it was another precaution—if someone else made the first move, then Whalan couldn't be charged with prostitution or procurement for an illicit act.

When the soft knock at the door came, he'd steeled himself and stood, waiting at the end of the bed with an enormous faux smile on his face, before calling out, "Come!"

"Is that an invitation to enter, or to splatter on your face?" Stanley had said, with a wink, after poking his head around the door.

*****

At four o'clock in the morning, his envelope containing eight pounds in his jacket pocket, Whalan alighted from the charabanc, along with the other seven members of The Rowers.

"Want to share a taxi, Whalan?" Robbie asked, cheerfully.

"No thanks—I've a lift waiting."

He pointed down Martin Place to the corner of George Street, where a solitary car stood, its engine still running, and where a tall, handsome man with a skin-coloured mole on his face waited, his hand raised in greeting.

"You lucky fuck!" Robbie said, with an enormous grin.

"Your day will come, Rob. You just have to wait long enough."

He patted his friend on the shoulder, gave him a quid from his envelope as his share of the "bookkeeper's" pot, and then trotted off down the slight incline to the man who'd promised he'd be there waiting to take him home.

*****

Whalan never made it back home that day.

In fact, he'd been back to his boarding house only three times—to collect an initial change of clothes and to pick up his razor and toothbrush, and then to pack his belongings, and finally to hand over his last week's rent.

Four months later and they were now considered an "item" by those in the know. Stanley's flat was compact, but big enough for both of them without getting in each other's way. It was on the top of the hilly part of Beach Street, and at the top of a block of relatively new flats, with a dark winding staircase to the front door, and an open, wrought-iron balcony at the back door, which led down an iron fire escape to the communal backyard and the washing lines, shared by the other flat dwellers.

Three minutes' walk to the tram loop to the city, the same to the beach and the shops. Whalan loved it—his morning runs with Stan on the beach, his tram ride to work through the cuttings at the back of Coogee and Randwick and then through the outskirts of Centennial Park. Twenty minutes from work, and a hundred miles from care—that was his motto.

Their relationship was still very physical, gentle enough for such hefty men, but then, at other times, rough and demanding.

Although Stan had arranged for Whalan to be officially registered as one of his phizz-gigs—under the pseudonym of "Muscles"—with a recorded informant's weekly payment of five pounds, Whalan understood he was not required to pass on information he heard while working at the solicitors' office. The registration and its pay was Stan's way of helping him to earn extra money to go towards his studies, even though Whalan continued to pick up the odd shift at the brewery and continued to see two of his regular clients—brothers, who liked Whalan.

Stanley was ambivalent about it, but said nothing, keen to let their friendship develop naturally. He demanded nothing from Whalan, except that he be honest. He understood that sex for money was not the same as the passion he shared with him, and genuinely felt no jealousy. However, it didn't stop him from dropping Whalan off at the grand house overlooking Randwick Racecourse twice a month, and then waiting in the car for him to drive him home. The brothers paid for and shared Whalan's services—sometimes he'd be their sole guest. At other times, when the brothers were feeling adventurous, Whalan would arrange for one or two of his friends from The Rowers to attend, to make up a foursome, or more.

On those nights, the nights when several men were guests of the brothers, Stanley was jealous. Not of Whalan, or of the brothers, but of the idea of five, six, or even seven naked men, grinding together, doing whatever in the dark. It made him so hot in the pants that he had to control himself from having his way with Whalan on the way home, confessing his extreme arousal over what he'd imagined had gone on.

So, on his birthday, in January, Stanley had been surprised to be invited to meet Whalan at the Coogee Bay Hotel for dinner, and not in the dining room, in a suite on the top floor, where, instead of supper, he was presented with a smorgasbord of three naked blokes. Whalan, Rob, and Henry had helped him out of his clothes, slapped him on the arse, and told him to dive on in, with the added bonus of telling him that nothing was not on the menu.

Later, the following morning, back at home and lying in bed in each other's arms, Stan had thanked "Muscles"—admitting that it had been a fantasy come true, that he'd loved every second of it—but had decided that once had been enough. While he and Whalan were shacked up together, his pal was all he needed.

"But you can still remind me of it while you and I are doing it, mate," he'd added. "I can't stop thinking of that moment when Henry sprayed across our faces while Rob was up to his balls inside you, and you were pumping me so hard that I thought we were going to go through the bedhead, the wall, and then fall out into the beer garden outside."

"Was I that rough on you?"

"Yeah," he replied, licking his lips. "More please, and any time you wish."

*****

On the following Saturday, they arrived back at Wahine, to celebrate Howard's birthday.

He and Stanley had been born only a few days apart, and in the same hospital at Waverley. They'd been the best of buddies during the war, and, since returning, Howard had become a man of reputation and substance, society's darling, and the first port of call for anyone who didn't mind paying up four guineas a pop for attentive treatment from a handsome man. As he'd come home with a reputation for stitching up all sorts of battlefield wounds, Howard also became extremely popular, and therefore extremely wealthy, as a result of the nature of injuries that turned up on his doorstep late at night. The crime world bosses of

Sydney loved a man who could fix nearly anything and could keep his mouth shut.

The cops left him be. So many of them had served "over there" and still judged a man by his reputation, rather than what he now did. Stanley was one of them.

Their history, apart from having served together, had been lustful and vigorous not long after settling back at home. However, Howard had an insatiable yearning for young ex-soldiers and other twenty-somethings with good manners and flexible sexual leanings—back in those days, Stan had not been as open-minded as he was now, so although they'd managed one or two encounters a year, their relationship had developed into a deep friendship, with only the occasional foray between the sheets.

It was no small surprise to Whalan to see Eddie, Stan's offsider and war buddy, already at Wahine when they arrived, drinking champagne, in a very nicely tailored, American-style tuxedo.

"Spiffing!" Stan had said to his mate.

Whalan was only surprised because he knew that Eddie was married—not happily, that was true, many men weren't—and didn't imagine for one moment that he played around on the side. He simply wasn't the type. No doubt, he'd find out in the course of the evening why he was there.

"Taken Whalan up to Bullaroo yet?" Howard asked, as they waited for dessert to be served.

"Yes, but we didn't do much fishing," Whalan said, with a wink.

"I wouldn't have minded being the fly on the wall on that weekend," Howard said.

"Anytime you like, Howard. You're our pal; happy to put on a show for you—privately, that is."

"Dessert be fucked!" Howard said, roaring his head off with laughter. "Let me clear the dining table—you'll be right at eye-level!"

"Dirty buggers!" Eddie said, and then laughed with the others. He was used to the games these men played with each other. Good-natured flirting and dirty talk with no real expectation of anything actually coming to fruition.

"While we're waiting, I may as well tell you that there's another reason there's only the four of us here. I hope you got the invitation for the official birthday bash next week?"

"We did and we're looking forward to it, aren't we, Muscles?"

Whalan raised his glass as a toast. "Although, I have to say it's going to be odd being at one of your parties as a guest and not for work…"

"You'll cope, I'm sure," Howard replied. "However, that leads me on to what I was just saying—the other reason. You two missed my Christmas party—visiting family at Toukley I believe?"

"Yes, we visited my elderly aunt, who lives in a rundown house right on the beach up there," Stan explained.

"Well, I found it odd at the time, but it's got even stranger since then. Pretty Boy Hilliard turned up with two new louts."

"Maybe 'Arthur and Martha' went to their families over Christmas?"

Howard shook his head. "No. There are rumours, Stan."

"You heard anything, Eddie?" Stan asked.

"The new blokes who were here with him … Eye-tie looking fellas?"

"They're actually Turkish, Edward; however, the rumour is that Max slashed Arthur and Martha, cut their throats, shot them through their mouths, and then threw the bodies off The Gap at Watson's Bay."

"You sure?" Stanley was gobsmacked. Shooting through the mouth, usually with a shotgun, was the razor gang's traditional way of dealing with a snitch—someone who blabbed; a person who couldn't keep their mouth shut.

"One way to check," Whalan said. "Their girlfriends are two of the women who work at your parties, Howard. You could get in touch with them to see whether their men are still about. Sally and Mary—give Manny a call; he'll get hold of them. At least you'll know one way or another if the rumour could be true…"

"You're pretty quiet, Eddie," Stan said, aware that his offsider hadn't replied when he'd asked him if he'd heard anything, and who now had his head down, playing with his silverware.

"Word's out that Max has a secret and someone didn't keep their mouth shut."

"Why didn't you tell me?"

Eddie merely looked at Howard and then at Whalan. "Ask them. I don't know what it is, but I think it's something humiliating. Taking a razor to those two losers—members of his own push—and then cutting their throats before shooting them through the mouth?"

"Have you said anything?" Howard asked Whalan.

"No!"

"Hang on a second! Said what?" Stan was getting a little annoyed. Everyone knew something except for him.

"Whalan's being discreet, and it's one of his better qualities, after his massive thighs, that is."

Stan laughed for a moment, and then leaned on his forearms on the table, suddenly deadly serious. "If Whalan's being discreet, and I agree, it's one of the things I love about him, then I suppose *you're* going to tell me, Howard?"

Love? Whalan's ears had latched onto that word. It was one Stanley never used about people, only ice cream, and the things Whalan did to him with his tongue.

"No, I'll tell you, Stan," Whalan said. "It should come from me. After all, I'm one of only three that truly knows about Max's 'secret' … he likes to dress up."

"What do you mean, dress up? I don't understand—"

"In women's underwear," Howard added. "Is what Whalan's trying to be so careful about."

"Oh …" Stanley's "oh" was one of total surprise. He couldn't have been more astounded if he'd been told that Max liked to be taken by a donkey in the middle of the Pitt Street rush hour to roars of applause from the prime minister. However, he could see it on Whalan's face—there was more.

"I'm sorry, Stan," Whalan said. "But in the business, what goes on behind closed doors is expected to stay there. How would you like it if I blabbed about what we get up to between the sheets?"

Stan ran his hand over Whalan's before replying. Whalan couldn't believe it—it was the first time that his copper had ever demonstrated any affection in public.

"Depends on who you were telling it to, and whether they were up for a bit of rough and tumble with you and me."

Despite his joke, Stanley was getting nervous. If Max was truly paying out on people who he thought were spreading rumours about his private activities, and Whalan had said he was one of only three who knew about Max's fetish for wearing ladies' undergarments …

"And that's not all he likes, is it, Whalan?" Howard said. "You'd better tell him."

"Are you sure, Howard?"

"If you don't, then I will."

"Very well," Whalan said with a sigh. "Max likes to take it up the bum while he's wearing lacy brassières and panties, strings of pearls around his neck, long, black, silk stockings, and too much cheap perfume."

"Lots of guys get their kicks, though—in all sorts of ways," Stanley said. "That can't be all of it."

"We have to write things on his body in lipstick."

"Write things? Like what?"

"Words like 'slut' and 'whore' on his chest …"

"Oh …"

"And he calls us 'daddy' while we're at it—some of his phrases are really over the top too. For example, he has a pet name for his arsehole that doesn't bear repeating—I'm sure you can work it out. We're all big grown-up boys—words don't offend us—it's how they're used that makes the difference. The whole experience is pretty stomach turning, to be honest," Whalan added, biting his lower lip, and playing with his spoon.

"Surely that sort of thing goes on a lot … it's not nice, but it's hardly world-shattering."

Stanley saw the quick glance between Whalan and Howard, and waited.

"His own father fucks him," Howard said, quietly.

Stanley's face dropped. "What?"

"His old man ties him up every Sunday morning when he comes home from church and fucks him on the dining room table while his mother's cooking the roast."

Whalan nodded. "He loves to tell us that his daddy gave it to him harder last Sunday than we are, while we're sticking it to him."

"That's sick," Eddie said, eventually.

"Do you think it was 'Arthur and Martha' who were spouting off? Is that why they've disappeared?"

Howard shook his head. "That's why the four of us are here tonight."

"You said there were only three of you who really knew. Who are the other two?" Stanley said, alarmed.

"Henry and Robert," Whalan replied.

"We need to get someone looking after them, Eddie," Stanley said.

Eddie pulled out his notebook. "Addresses?"

Whalan sighed. "Do you really have to? Henry's married, and Rob still lives at home. What about their families?"

"What about you reading in the paper that they've been found with the backs of their heads taken off by a shotgun, Whalan?" Stanley said. There was kindness in his eyes, despite the steel in his voice.

Whalan gave Eddie both of his friends' addresses and telephone numbers, with the assurance that the surveillance would be discreet.

"Do you mind, Howard? I'd just like to have a quiet word with my mate out on the balcony."

"Knock yourself out, Stan. Dessert will be another few minutes."

Stanley lit them both a cigarette while they leaned on the balcony outside, in exactly the same place they'd been when they first met.

"You're going to have to keep your eyes open, my friend," he said to Whalan.

"I'm a big, strong boy, Stan. I can look after myself."

"Against a shotgun?"

Whalan didn't answer, but leaned his head on his man's shoulder. "You held my hand."

Stan nodded. "Yes, I did. And I'm sorry I haven't done it sooner."

Whalan turned him in his arms and kissed him.

"There's something I don't understand though," Stanley said, breaking from the kiss.

"Go on."

"You and Robbie giving it to Max I understand—but Henry? He's a shooter, not a player."

"Henry unloads over his lacy knickers and stockings, and then while Max is sucking it out of the silk, Henry fucks him with a length of chair leg—"

"That's all I want to hear, thank you, Whalan! I wish I hadn't asked now," Stanley said.

Whalan chuckled, and then said, "Let's just hope that dessert doesn't come with custard."

"Eww ... filthy bugger."

"And aren't you glad of it too."

"Never been gladder, handsome. Now let's get back inside and work out how we're going to keep you safe."

"Maybe I could just stay in bed and you could send your copper mates in one after the other. Then I'd always be 'under' police protection."

Stanley pinched his mate's arse. "That dreadful pun was unworthy of you, Whalan," he said, as he opened the French doors and led him back inside, where he could see that dessert was just being served.

*****

Two days after Howard's official birthday celebration, Stan was at work, still feeling a little hungover.

It had been the best party he'd been to in ages, Max "Pretty Boy" Hilliard conspicuously absent, even though Howard had assured Stan that he'd posted an invitation. Towards the end of the evening, Stan had drawn Whalan to one side and said, "Remember your birthday present to me? Wouldn't it be nice to do something the same for Howard? After all, he's been so good to us ..."

The following morning, he'd awoken in a tumble of naked men and twisted sheets, Whalan in his arms, Howard stretched out over his legs, and Robbie using the doctor's fulsome buttocks as a pillow. Henry had long gone, it seemed, although he felt the dried trail of the young man's donation across his chest. He'd had a ball—several actually.

Paperwork! Bloody forms! He'd thought the C.I.B. was bad, however, since he'd been seconded to the consorting squad, while still working out of Darlinghurst, he had a stack of reports as high as his teacup waiting to be filled out and sent on up the chain.

He'd just struck a match to light his smoke when the young officer in charge of the switchboard ran into the room, calling out his name urgently across the other desks in the office. He was in such a hurry that he still had his telephone headset around his neck and was clutching the plug and lead in his hand.

"Sir!" he called out. "There's been something go down bad at Kingsford. Harry Smith's been on the phone and he was howling into the receiver; said something about he just went to get some fish and chips."

Stanley froze, his lit match in his hand, his cigarette trembling in the corner of his mouth. Harry Smith was the copper who was supposed to be looking out for Henry and his family. The whole room turned to look at him.

"Get Whalan on the phone right now, then ring Kingsford police station to find out what they know." The young telephonist ran from the room. "Eddie! Eddie! Anyone seen Eddie?" he screamed down the corridor towards the tearoom.

Eddie appeared, white-faced, in the corridor, a cup of tea in one hand, and a cigarette in the other. "Stan? What's wrong?"

"I think Max has got to Henry. I'm trying to get hold of Whalan now. Get your arse over to Robbie's house and take a few blokes with you."

"Go home, Stan. Pick up some stuff and put Whalan on the train to Bullaroo—he'll be safe there. Call me at Robbie's when you get home and please tell me Whalan's all right. We'll take it from there."

"Sir!" the telephonist called out from the end of the corridor. "No one's answering at your place."

"Fuck me!" Stanley swore. "Ring the station at Randwick and send them down there to check. Tell them I'm on my way." He couldn't believe the panic in his voice. Mr. Calm-in-any-situation was starting to come apart at the seams.

"He'll be all right, Stan. He'll be all right. He's a big strong lad," Eddie said, clasping Stan's forearm.

"Thanks, Eddie. I'm sure you're right. Now, hop it! I'm off too. I'll speak with you in about twenty minutes."

"Right you are, Stan—and, mate?"

"Yes?"

"Drive carefully and give Whalan a hug from me, please?"

Stan nodded, alarmed to see the fear on Eddie's face. He'd never looked afraid before, not even in France when Fritz was upon them, bayonets out and jumping over the sides of the trenches, swarming like cockroaches from under a dark and damp cellar door.

The first thing he saw as he drove along the footpath outside his house was Whalan, leaning against the front wall of their block of flats, surrounded by black police cars and a dozen cops. He looked calm enough, but gestured when he saw Stan's car ploughing through the garbage bins on the footpath. "Here he is!" he seemed to be saying. Stan pulled on the handbrake as he pushed his foot to the floor on the brakes—his car fishtailed to a halt in a cloud of blue, burning-rubber smoke.

"You okay, mate?" he whispered into Whalan's ear as he clenched him in a bear hug.

"Yeah, I'm okay," Whalan replied, shakily. "Dunno about the other bloke though."

"That's the spirit," he said, patting his back.

"No, Stan. I'm being serious. I think I killed him."

"Who?"

"Benny the White."

Benny the White was one of Max's closest henchmen.

"Was Max here?"

Whalan nodded. Stan stepped back; he'd never seen him so still inside.

"Where's Benny then?"

"He's around the back, sir," one of the local coppers said from behind him. "Your mate here killed him with your 'fridge."

*****

Whalan had been studying and had decided to make a cup of tea. He'd just put the kettle on and was about to go to their new Frigidaire to get the milk, when he happened to glance through the kitchen window and saw something odd. It was the top of a tube, gradually appearing from below. But then, as more of it came into view, he saw it was two tubes;

two metal tubes welded together, side by side. Jesus, it was a shotgun! Someone was coming up the back staircase and was holding a shotgun vertically—that meant they weren't alone. If they were by themselves, they'd be holding it horizontally. It had to be in that position because the person carrying it was trying to avoid poking someone in front of them or behind as they came up the stairs. His heart pounding in his chest, he'd flattened himself against the wall and watched through the partially closed wooden venetian blinds. Pretty Boy Hilliard and three of his hoods appeared on the narrow wrought-iron balcony outside the back door. He watched Max raise his finger to his lips for silence, and then count silently—five, four, three, two …

Whalan was good at thinking on his feet—he glanced around the room to see what he could use as a weapon, or a shield. He remembered what an arse of a job it had been to get the new 'fridge into the kitchen—it just fitted down the narrow passageway from the back door to the kitchen door. So, when he heard the crash of the door being smashed open, and even though it was as tall as he was, and probably weighed the same, he heaved the appliance up off the ground and into his arms, and then ran out of the kitchen into the passageway, yelling his head off. He closed his eyes, expecting a shotgun blast, and ran down the corridor as fast as he could, pushing the screaming and shouting men ahead of him out of the door and onto the balcony.

He heard their yells as they scrambled down the back stairs, and thought they'd all got away, until he looked over the railing and saw Benny the White, who'd obviously fallen over the edge of the balcony and was lying on his back, three storeys below him, screaming with pain, and one arm across his face.

"Come back, Max, you fucking snivelling coward," he'd called out, and then had ducked as a shotgun blast came from below.

He leaned over to see Max trying to reload, screamed with rage, picked up the refrigerator again, and then heaved it over the edge of the balustrade. It missed Max, but landed on top of Benny, who'd been clutching at Max's trouser-leg, yelling for help.

*****

Cross My Palm with Silver

"I was stronger than I thought I was, Stan. I suppose carrying all those beer barrels for the past three years ..." Whalan said to Stanley later that evening, as they sat curled up together on the rocks at the base of the cliffs near Giles' Baths, at the north end of the beach.

Whalan had been inconsolable when Stan had told him that not only had Henry been executed, gangland style, along with his wife and three babies, but that when he'd eventually got to his house, Eddie had found Robbie shot through the mouth too. Rob's parents were also dead, single bullet wounds to their heads, tied to their kitchen chairs. It was the way the razor gang operated—they'd been made to watch their son's execution.

"We've got to get you away, Whalan. Please see sense," Stanley said, kissing him behind the ear. They were soaked to the skin from the spray of the breakers crashing on the rocks around them.

"I'm not going anywhere. Sorry. You'll have to lock me up to stop me, but this is personal. Max came after me; not the others. It was me he was after."

"To get at me. Try to understand that."

"I don't fucking care."

"Well, I fucking love you, Whalan, and I don't want to see you hurt. There! I've said it. I've been biting my tongue for too long now. If anything ever happened to you ..."

Whalan pulled Stanley into his arms and nearly crushed him with the force of his hug.

"Never say that again, Stan, please?"

"What? That I don't want to see you hurt?"

"No ... that you love me. Because if I hear it again, then I'll believe it, and I don't know what the fuck I will do—"

"Jesus, mate," Stan said softly, taking Whalan's chin in his hand, and then kissing the tears away that began to roll down his face.

"What will we do now?"

"Now that I've confessed?"

"No. About Max."

Stan thought for a second before speaking. "Any good with a sledgehammer, Richards?"

"Sure. Why?"

"Quick trip to see Kate Leigh and then we might start off by breaking a few kneecaps."

"What? Just you and me?"

"Nah, Whalan. This is serious now. The crew that killed Robbie slashed the copper who was looking after him, and then cut his head off. Left it on the kitchen table between Robbie's parents with an apple in his mouth."

*****

Detective Stanley Archer slowly opened one eye. Howard Fifield was standing by his side, checking his pulse. It took him a moment to latch on to his surroundings and to remind himself of where he was.

"Where's Whalan?"

"Just calm down, Stanley," Howard said. "He'll be back in a moment."

"Where'd he go?"

"Against my advice, he and Eddie have gone down to Rushcutters Bay to buy you some lunch—something about a chip sandwich, as disgusting as that sounds."

Stanley chortled and then stopped as a spasm of pain ran through his shoulder.

"Steady on, Stan. You're one hell of a lucky bastard. There's one bullet fragment in there that'll have to either work its own way out, or stay there until the day you die."

"I remember the shots, Howard. But, I don't really remember much afterwards, apart from Whalan throwing me in the back of the car and driving me here. It's been a bit of a blur to be honest until this morning."

"Well, shock's a nasty thing—it's bound to play havoc with your memory for a few days after a gunshot wound. Having said that, you're lucky to be under the care of the best ex-combat surgeon in the city, even if I say so myself. And, had Whalan not been sitting in the gutter with his head in his hands, he might be in a bed next to you—or worse."

"When did you do this?" Stan asked, glancing at the sling that supported his heavily bandaged arm and shoulder.

Cross My Palm with Silver

"Five days ago, my friend. This morning, when I came in to examine you, was the first time you've really been clear-headed and more like yourself. Four bullets, Stan ..."

"We had no idea it was coming, Howard—all I saw was the barrel and the round magazine of the tommy gun poking out of the car window. I was so damn angry that Kate had lied to us. Max wasn't at the Redfern house. They'd tried to put up a fight, but it turned into a bloodbath the moment we walked in the door—it was all I could do to pull Whalan away. You know what it's like—we all saw men in the war lose their marbles with anger."

"Nine dead, I read in the paper."

"Yes, and six of those were turned into bloody smears by our mild-mannered mate with a sledgehammer."

"He's never been mild-mannered. Well-mannered, yes. But there's always been a lot of anger inside him."

"Can I tell you something, Howard?"

"Of course you can. Let me adjust this sling while you do it."

"I love him ... I don't know any other words to use, but I do. All the time I had my foot to the floor trying to get home to him last week, I promised myself over and over again that I'd say it to his face if I got there and found he was unharmed."

"And did you?"

"What?"

"Tell him."

Stanley smiled. "Yes, later that night on the rocks near Giles' Baths. He'd been crying his heart out over Henry and Robbie."

"He wasn't the only one."

"They were such great blokes, Howard. But, I don't have to tell you that."

"Anyway, I hope he told you that he loved you too ... I've seen it for yonks—in both of you."

"Yeah, he did," Stanley said softly, his eyes full of wonder at the thought.

"Then I wish you both well; I'm going to miss you both very, very much."

"Miss us?"

Howard threw the morning paper on the bed; the headline was in 72pt bold:

Mass Suicide in York Street

"What?"

"Yes, seems like Max and eight of his cohorts jumped from the top of the AWA building in York Street last night."

"Suicide? What the hell?"

"Yes, it's almost unbelievable that on the way down they happened to slit each other's throats and that Max died from a shotgun blast that destroyed his rectum. Terrible accident."

"Wait! Max was shot up the arse? No, you're joking aren't you?"

Howard shook his head and snorted. "As I said, Stanley, well-mannered, but not mild-mannered …"

"Whalan did this?"

"You were touch and go for a bit. He was wild with fury."

"But, he couldn't have done this alone."

"No. As far as I understand it, he went with Eddie to see Kate and told her that unless she gave up Max, he'd ruin her."

"I'm confused …"

"He'll tell you some sort of cock-and-bull story so you don't get too angry. However, do you know who her law firm is? The people who look after her legal stuff?"

"Not—"

"Yes. McGuire and Tanner, the solicitors who employ our friend. Seems like Whalan forged a power of attorney, went to the Commonwealth Bank and opened new accounts in his and your name, and transferred all of Kate's stash into them."

Stanley laughed, despite the pain in his shoulder.

"What a little ripper!"

"So, he and Eddie and a few of your boys from the cop shop turned up at Max's hideout in Erskineville and then threw him and his vermin into police cars and marched them to the top of the AWA building. He made Max watch while one of your coppers held each of the men's arms behind their backs. Whalan cut their throats, lifted them over his head, and then hurled them down onto the street below, one by one, as the others watched. One each for Henry, his wife, and their three kids, Robbie and his parents."

"Jesus, Howard." Stanley closed his eyes for a moment and rested his head back against the pillow. It was hard for him to reconcile the kind and thoughtful man he'd fallen for with someone so driven by violence that he had to … He stopped. He'd seen worse in the war. He'd just forgotten what men, even some of the quiet, timid ones, could do when they lost people they cared about and when overtaken by grief, or hate.

"And then, when there was only Hilliard left, they pulled down his pants and Whalan carved your 'favourite' four-letter word across his buttocks with a razor and then gave him both barrels up the arsehole with Max's own shotgun. Prosaic, really, in some way."

Stanley was speechless, and rather glad he hadn't been there to see it firsthand. Violence went with his job as a copper, and it had been part of his life since he'd first arrived in France during the war. He'd been able to stomach the worst things imaginable while they were happening—it was only when he'd played them over in his mind afterwards that the true horror of what he'd sometimes seen made him sick.

"Don't think badly of him. We saw worse violence 'over there', Stan. And, he did it for his friends and for you. We all thought you wouldn't pull through, you know? I think he would have torn the world apart with his bare hands if I hadn't been able to save you. You've no idea how very carefully and lovingly he laid you onto my examination table. After I told him to stand back, he threw himself down in the corner of the room and sobbed. He was so inconsolable that I tried to give him a shot to calm him down. But he pushed me aside and ran outside—you've never heard such keening. I thought he would bring his soul up with his sobbing. I could hear him howling at the sky for ages while I operated on you."

Stanley wiped at his eyes with his forearm. He'd never expected to find someone who cared that deeply about him. "I suppose I should be flattered," he said in a whisper.

"I just wish I'd met someone who loved me as much as he does you; and that's the truth of it." He smoothed back Stanley's hair from his forehead and gave him an affectionate smile. "Anyway, that sounds like him and Eddie coming back now. You'll have plenty of time for him to fill you in on your trip."

"Trip?"

"Yes, I booked the tickets myself."

"Where are we going?"

"Canada," Howard said.

"Canada?"

"Well, Kate Leigh thinks you're sailing to California on Saturday. Whalan's arranged to meet her on board before the ship leaves to sign the papers that will transfer the last fifty thousand pounds of her money back into her account."

"Wily bastard, that's clever insurance."

"It surely is. Only you two will have steamed out the day before on your way to Vancouver."

"But why Canada?"

"He can finish off his training to become a solicitor in Canada without too much worry—same legal system basically—and he thinks the Royal Canadian Police Force will welcome a detective with as much experience as you into their arms."

"Holy cow!"

"And Mrs. Leigh can use every skill at her command to try to stop you leaving on Saturday. However, you'll already be halfway between here and Auckland with fifty thousand pounds of her money in your Canadian bank account, waiting for you when your ship steams into Vancouver harbour."

*****

"Beautiful, isn't it?"

"What's more beautiful is the smile of the man standing next to me."

"What man? I'll punch him in the face."

"Why don't you shoot him up the arse with your shotgun, Whalan?"

"There's only one thing I want to shoot up his arse, Stan, and I think you know exactly what that is."

"My arm's still sore, but I'll give it a go."

"A go? What sort of a promise is that? It's been nearly two weeks …"

"There's that head steward who looks after the captain's table …?"

"Nah. Those days are over. It's you and me now, and a new life, just us. No razors, no guns, no—"

Stanley stopped his words with a kiss. They were alone on the first-class promenade deck and it was late at night. Even Whalan's 'Beautiful, isn't it?' was an echo of their first meeting on the veranda at Wahine. Now they stood in each other's arms, not quite half-a-world away, but as good as, again watching blue, red, and green lights rippling across the dark waters of a busy city harbour.

"I could always sit on it?"

"Hooked up with a fucking romantic. Just my luck."

"A romantic sex-fiend."

"Is that you?"

Stanley laughed, and then pulled Whalan back into his arms and kissed him again.

"Ready for some romance and some copper cock?"

Whalan laughed softly, and then pinched his bum. "Wait until we tie up at the wharf. I want to see the whole of Auckland harbour as we sail in … what are you doing back there?"

"Why don't you watch the ship sail into the harbour, while I help with a little tug?"

Whalan groaned. "And you talk about my puns …"

Stanley's good hand slipped around Whalan's waist and he deftly unbuttoned his flies.

"Remember the quick gobbie you gave me on Howard's balcony on the night we met?"

"Hm, hm …"

"Well, as you accuse me of not being romantic …"

"What? Sucking my dick in the dark is romantic?"

"It will be if I mouth 'I love you' while I'm doing it."

"Wait! Did you just put money in my hand?"

"Yes, Whalan. It's a shilling, now shut up, and let me get to work."

Whalan slipped the coin into his jacket pocket and closed his eyes. Of course he wanted this as much as Stan; it was their game. They'd played it a lot since they first met—the metaphorical game of crossing one's palm with silver.

He started to rummage through his trouser pockets, feeling for florins, although he was doubtful he'd last long enough to line up a few on the handrail of the promenade deck.

How the hell would he know if he'd got them all tails-up in the dark anyway?

The Boy Who ...

"What, you again?"

"Yes, sergeant."

"Are you still nineteen?"

"Yes, sir, but—"

"And have you miraculously grown three inches in the past few days, Henderson?"

"No, sir, but—"

"Then what the fuck are you doing here?"

"I have a letter for Doctor Sylvester, sergeant."

He glared at me. I could sort of understand it; I'd been turning up regularly at the Bathurst recruiting centre since we'd gone to war, in the vain hope that someone could swing it and allow me to sign up like all my other mates. However, I did know the minimum enlistment age was twenty, and that the minimum height requirement was five-foot-six.

"Sit down in the corner and wait. He's busy. Give me your letter and I'll send it in," Sergeant Mitchum snapped, seemingly annoyed that I'd turned up once again. I could tell it wasn't real anger; more concern than anything. I'd had it all my life—those looks of "take a look at yourself, mate—you'll snap in half if the wind blows the wrong way".

My mother had died of tuberculosis when I was nine. My father struggled hard to make ends meet to keep my sister and me in clothes and well fed, but he was struck by a car not a year later and died in our local hospital from his injuries. Gwyneth brought me up, even though she was sixteen at the time, leaving school early and taking a job at the big property just outside town. Mrs. Falmer, the station manager's wife, looked out for us, without making us feel like it was charity. Meals, clothes, textbooks for me, money for outings. But, we'd promised Mother we'd do our best to make our own way. So I'd found work after school, two afternoons a week, mixing and grinding ingredients and making pills for the older Mr. Pettis, the chemist, and the other afternoons and weekends helping Dr. Fletcher at the local hospital.

An hour went past before the medical examination door opened and Peter Sylvester came out, his hand extended. "Hello, you must be Donald? Is that right?"

"That's me, sir," I replied, shaking his hand.

He was quite different than I'd expected—younger, better groomed. Despite a beaky nose, rather like my own, he, too, sported round gold-rimmed glasses that he wore, also as I did, low down, on the tip of my nose. I smiled when I saw my own constant gesture mirrored back at me—he pushed his glasses back onto the bridge of his nose with the forefinger of one hand. It made me take to him instantly.

"Please, come in," he said, showing me into his surgery. "Take a seat, Donald. I've an hour for a quick sandwich and a cup of tea before the next intake. Can I make you a cup?"

"No, thank you, sir. Sergeant Mitchum relented and gave me one a short while ago."

The doctor smiled at me, and then sat at his desk, studying Dr. Fletcher's letter. "Ian speaks very highly of you, young man, although he's fairly cranky that you seem to want to throw away a promising future to join the army?"

"I feel it's my duty, sir."

"You didn't matriculate?"

"No, sir. It was the Latin that was the problem. Highest marks in all the other exams, but my school doesn't offer Latin or Greek—I've been studying it by myself for six years—but as it's a prerequisite for medicine at university …"

"So, Ian writes that you're taking a year to study up and then sit the entrance exam again at a later date?"

"If I can't get into the army, sir, yes. That's the plan."

The Boy Who ...

Dr. Sylvester clicked his tongue and shook his head at me. "You've no idea of the number of young men who come through here hell-bent on throwing their lives down the toilet. No; hear me out! I know you think you're doing the right thing. But, Donald, we'll need doctors and qualified engineers and architects for when this ghastly nonsense is over. Ian says in his letter that you've good clinical experience?" I nodded. "Well, you'd best tell me what you know."

I outlined my duties and experience in our outpatients' triage.

"Well, that's a pretty impressive set of skills you have already, young man," he said, with a soft whistle, when I'd finished.

"I started when I was just ten, Dr. Sylvester."

"You started off by mopping floors?"

"Yes, sir, and helping the nurse, Mr. Barry, with the sterilisation of instruments, rolling bandages, changing bedding—"

"And you graduated to helping with minor operations?"

"Yes, sir, and if the doctor is busy, Mr. Barry and I perform basic triage, dress wounds, give injections, stitches, set bones."

"Extraordinary ... well, as you know I'm not a military doctor, I'm a civilian employed by the government to perform medical examinations on those who intend to sign up. The army has allowed me four assistants, and two of those places have already been filled by military personnel from the base. However, as it's a government job, I can't make the decision without some sort of assessment to keep the paper-pushers in the Ministry happy. If you are interested, then I'll give you some reading material to study, and in about six weeks from now there'll be a written test followed by a short practical test in the clinic."

"So, you think I might be all right? I mean ..."

Dr. Sylvester laughed. "You'd be more than all right, Donald. Now, tell me why you're so darned desperate to get into the army."

"It's Spider, sir," I said. "No one calls me Donald."

"Why do they call you Spider?"

"Well, just look at me—I'm all legs and arms and a skinny body, and—"

"All I see is a charming young man, with intelligent, soft brown eyes, and enthusiasm in buckets."

105

I blushed. I couldn't help it. I'd always been the straggler at school. Not educationally, as I was always the brightest in everything I studied. The principal called me "the boy who ... " the boy who could become a doctor, or a physicist, or a linguist, or a mathematician, or a whatever I applied myself to. But, because I'd been sickly as a kid, and was smart, I was always one of those boys the others regarded as a "swot"—despite that, they were fond of me. I was the local gang's mascot, the gawky underdeveloped lad who was always calling out "wait for me!" as the other boys ran off about their business.

I'd grown in their esteem when puberty hit me—like a truck. One day I was skinny and hairless, and the next day a gorilla with a huge phallus and a pair of tennis balls swinging between my legs. I still remained short while the rest of me grew to adult proportion—everything looked bigger, because my body was so scrawny. Anyway, it earned me no end of prestige among my peers, until they themselves began to sprout, to grow, and to lengthen.

"The army, Donald ...?" Dr. Sylvester prompted me.

"My dad was a sapper in France, and Mr. Taylor, out at Mulwidgee Station, well ... everyone knows about him. He and his sister have looked out for me and Gwyneth since Mum died and ... well, Dr. Sylvester; I just think a bloke has to do what a bloke has to do."

I became aware that I'd adopted my "Spider" pose, as my friends called it—my palms pressed together, held between my knees, my legs jiggling nervously. I had confidence in abundance when it came to study, but in day-to-day negotiations with human beings? Well, that was another matter. Dr. Sylvester touched my knee gently, smiling at me. I stopped jiggling.

"Foreskins, scrota, and haemorrhoids—discharges, pruritus, scabies, and parasites."

"Men's genital health?" I said. "Not urology as such, or reproductive health, but afflictions that might affect the enlisting man's clean bill of health?"

I was rewarded with a bright smile. "Not all of those afflictions could substantially jeopardise a man's suitability, Donald, but we do need to know what we're taking on. Have you any experience in any of those areas?"

I was aware that I was nodding enthusiastically. "We get a lot of problems with basic hygiene, adult circumcisions due to phimosis and acute balanitis... I mean, if it's acute then it's more likely to be balanoposthitis—heaps of what Dr. Fletcher calls 'trench crotch'—and then the regular inguinal hernias, straddle injuries, and pubic lice and discharges after weekends in the city... um, have I said something wrong? Dr. Sylvester? I promise you I'm not trying to show off or anything."

The doctor had been staring at me as I spoke, his head cocked at an angle, watching my face—rather like the way the science teacher at school used to do when I solved something awkward in physics classes. I was aware that I could rattle on overmuch when I was talking about something I was interested in.

"Have you conducted any anogenital examinations yourself, or under supervision?"

I shook my head. "No. Dr. Fletcher sometimes asks the patient if they mind if I sit in on the consultation—if I know them personally, they usually do mind—but I don't ever touch, I just observe."

His next question took me completely by surprise. "Are you intact or circumcised, Donald?"

"Circumcised, Dr. Sylvester."

He scribbled on his notepad, and then showed me what he'd written. At the top of the page was my name, and then dozens of ticks. On the last line was written "look for someone uncut".

My face fell. "Oh," I said, quietly.

The doctor laughed. "You misunderstand, Donald. If you're not intact, then the other fellow will have to be—for demonstrations. We'll need one of each."

"Demonstrations?" Even I heard the squeakiness of my voice.

*****

"Nine-penny single, one way, second class to Bullaroo, please," I said to the train conductor. There'd been no one at the ticket office in

Bathurst and I'd lost the return half of my ticket. It had probably fallen from my wallet when I took my last ten-shilling note out to pay for a cup of tea and a ham sandwich at the station tearoom.

I was lost in thought for most of the trip, even though it took a little over half an hour. But, every so often I'd check the brown paper package on my lap, stroke it, and fiddle with the string that held it all together. I couldn't help thinking that my future sat on my knees—two military-issue health manuals and a list of chapters from medical books to read.

I stopped at the Connaught and had a small plate of battered fish and chips. Not being a big man, I didn't have an accompanying big appetite—but I always cleared my plate, even if I'd eaten my fill halfway through my meal, if only to avoid the "eat up your food, Donald; you'll never grow up if you don't eat what's in front of you".

After my early dinner, I stood on the footpath outside the café and watched the world go by, waiting for five o'clock when it would be time for me to make an appearance at Bullaroo hospital. It was a small, country affair, with ten beds—enough to keep Dr. Fletcher, Mr. Barry, and myself busy if there were minor procedures or a few inpatients staying overnight or for a day or two. Anything really serious was sent by road ambulance to Bathurst or to Sydney if it was a really big matter.

It had been harder on us since Dr. Fletcher's eldest son, Lawrence had joined the A.I.F.—he used to do all of the heavy lifting and back-breaking work in the surgery. The doctor's other son, Patrick, was another doctor, but had given up his new practice in the capital city, and was now on his way to England, where, we believed, he would be training to give the Jerries hell from a Wellington bomber four miles up in the sky.

I liked Bullaroo. My dad had always said there were worse places one could live. There was a big library, an Olympic-length swimming pool at the leisure centre, and now they'd put in a new rail bypass this side of Lithgow, it was just over four hours by train from Sydney. I smiled as I went through my list in my mind—it was my order of preferred activities: study, swimming, and travelling to the "big smoke".

Bullaroo was a medium-sized country town of nearly forty-thousand people, if one counted the catchment area of farms, sheep stations, and smallholdings. Small enough to know a lot of people, yet big enough to constantly meet new faces. This was "new faces" time of year—shearing season. The town was packed with itinerant shearers from all over. Good for business at the chemist, where I worked, and at Dr. Fletcher's surgery, and of course, at the outpatients at the hospital.

I checked my watch—four thirty-five. Tucking my parcel under my arm, I lit a smoke and then started to wander down Harris Street—there'd be enough time to finish my cigarette, wash my hands, put on my white lab coat and be ready for five o'clock, when I'd open the hospital doors for outpatients to arrive.

*****

"Short arms inspection," Mr. Barry said.

"I beg your pardon, sir?" I'd never heard the term before.

"That's what you'll be doing, Donald—going by what you've told us of the position description. Once every two weeks, regular as clockwork."

"Men's health," Dr. Fletcher said. "It's a very interesting and complex field, Donald. How long do you have?"

"Six weeks, sir," I replied.

"Well, then, son, your next month and a half will be a world of smelly penises, undescended testicles, and unwashed anuses," the doctor said, patting me on the back. Mr. Barry smirked—Dr. Fletcher's sense of humour was one that took some getting used to.

We'd finished surgery in outpatients for the day, and were in the triage room, cleaning up. There'd been a shearer with a severed finger and a five-year-old with a fever. A quiet evening in all.

"Let's have a look at your list then," he said to me. I gave him Dr. Sylvester's note and he ran through it, humming as he nodded, and stroked his carefully manicured goatee. "Pop into the house after you've cleaned up; I've most of the texts in my consulting room, although you'll probably have to order the *Military Reference Manual to Venereal Diseases and Prophylaxis* from the Mitchell Library in Sydney. Mrs. Pollinger will have a field day with that one." Our head librarian was a wowser of the worst order. "No doubt she'll get her husband to write

109

the request in case she stains her fingers with impure words."

We all laughed.

"Would you like to examine me?" Mr. Barry said, quite out of the blue.

"What an excellent idea, Musgrave," Dr. Fletcher said, and then turned to me. "You've never done a hands-on inspection, have you, Donald?"

I shook my head, feeling at once nervous about the prospect, but yet excited that I might be allowed to actually do some clinical work myself.

"Although the army's bound to have its own ways, a bit of old-fashioned country doctoring will never put you wrong."

"Are you all right with this, Mr. Barry? We've known each other since I was a nipper. I wouldn't want you to be embarrassed."

"Phht," he said. "How do you think I learned? On my brothers. After I came back from the war, I spent an age at the Prince Henry hospital learning the 'latest' techniques in all sorts of nursing. Men's health was just becoming an issue—so many men had lost fighting hours because of gonorrhoea, or syphilis, or infections of the genitals. It wasn't all I did, but it took a lot of my ward time. I'd go home and practice tying circumcision bandages on my brothers, much to their amusement."

*****

Sitting in the examination room, I felt distinctly nervous. As Dr. Fletcher had promised, the previous six weeks of my life had been filled with the study of the things that can go wrong with men "down under". As a result, I'd self-diagnosed with every possible ailment or deformity. Mr. Barry thought it hilarious, and invariably brought me down to earth with quips like "keep a jar handy, Spider, just in case your knob falls off".

Despite my nerves, I felt quietly confident at this, the first of the two assessments I was to perform: the written examination. As I'd had to travel and many of the other men lived locally or on base, my practical test would take place about an hour after finishing my paper. It would give me time to go through my preparatory notes, have a quick sandwich and a cup of tea, before I had to "get my hands dirty".

… The Boy Who …

Of course, while studying, my enquiring mind had to be slapped down every so often. I became fascinated with questions that arose as asides from my main studies, and had to remind myself of the purpose of the piles of volumes I'd started to devour. I'd never admit it, but had even made slides from my own ejaculate and checked it under the hospital microscope, and, after reading one chapter on prostatitis, which was actually not within my specific field of study, had squatted and manipulated myself with my finger, collecting the resultant fluid onto a slide, staining it and inspecting it too. On that particular evening, I'd walked home with a smile on my face, thinking how farcical it would have been had anyone walked in to find me on my haunches, my trousers and underwear around my ankles, one finger up my bum, and a glass slide clenched in the other hand. It was times like that when I wished I had a close mate in my life, one who didn't make judgements, with whom I could share the silliness.

I'd pored over the texts, pestered Mr. Pettis at the chemist for remedies from his youth—even though most of them were of the snake-oil type, I still respected that there could have been something in them. His best revelations were accidental—the bush medicine of the local aboriginal tribes. His father had "gone native" when they'd first settled in the area, and had passed on all sorts of local treatments to old Mr. Pettis, who, for a schooner at the pub, had shared some of the native remedies with me. He was quite glad of the company, as his grown-up son, Kendrick, had just joined up too and had recently left home. None of the preparations were, of course, for venereal diseases, as those had been introductions of the white men, but I'd learned a lot about local plants and their uses for *sprains, pains, and "gains"*—as Mr. Pettis called tonics or pick-me-ups.

If I needed a break away from the books, and had time, I spent every spare moment I could at the leisure centre on men's days, surreptitiously taking note of the forms, shapes, and constructions of the genitals of the blokes who swam there. I wanted to be prepared, and there were, in reality, few examinations at the hospital that I could observe.

I looked around the room. There were ten of us in all, far more than I'd anticipated—it was the main reason for my nervousness. I knew I was prepared in terms of my study, but equally unprepared for the competition—something I was terrible at.

Dr. Sylvester walked around the room, placing the written tests face-down on the table in front of each of us, one spare chair separating each candidate so we could not observe what the others were writing. I found it odd that I was the only one he spoke to. "And this is yours, Donald," he said, as he laid the questionnaire before me.

When the time came for us to start, I turned the paper over and put my head in my hands. Each question was very, very technical—far harder than I could possibly have imagined. Still, I took a deep breath, and then once I started, the answers and the words came to me.

The practical examination, later in the day, was far easier; as far as I was concerned, anyway.

I was too anxious to eat, so went straight to the clinic, an hour before my examination time, and sat under the watchful eye of Sergeant Mitchum until my name was called by a young soldier who was carrying a clipboard. I spent the hour going through my notes one last time, memorising the conditions to be looked for when performing the anogenital triage for the enlistment process.

- Hernia
- Varicose veins (varicocele)
- Haemorrhoids
- Skin disease
- Phimosis
- Balanitis
- Discharges

On the bottom of the page, in Dr. Fletcher's neat hand, and in pale-blue ink, was written: "Keep within the boundaries". It was a reminder to curb my enthusiasm, not to go looking for things that were not on the list of referrable conditions, and to double-check my findings before I spoke.

Dr. Sylvester shook my hand as I was shown into the consulting room where my test was to take place. There was a washbasin, a stainless-steel trolley with the usual triage bits and pieces on it, and a screen in the corner of the room. A corporal with another clipboard waited just inside the door.

"The test is basically a screening test—it's about identifying symptoms, and sorting out those that you feel should be referred to a physician, or those that do not require medical intervention. Do you understand, Donald?"

I nodded.

"You assume that their general medical history, blood pressure, etcetera, have all been dealt with. It's a quick assessment of their anogenital areas. Do you understand how a normal intake is processed?"

"Yes, sir. I've read through the manual and I do understand that initial examinations by medical orderlies and nurses are a basic, quick, precursory look to sort out which conditions, if there are any, should go onto someone with medical training to examine more thoroughly."

"Good. Sometimes we might have over a hundred men to examine in a very limited amount of time and there are few doctors—that's why we need technicians to sort out the wheat from the chaff. Are you ready?" I nodded. "Very good. Then let's start. There are three men whom I've selected; they're all from this morning's intake. Would you like them all at once, or one by one?"

"One at a time, please," I said.

The doctor signalled the corporal, who left the room and then returned a few minutes later with the first of the three young men. He was probably in his early twenties, dressed in a suit, but with an open shirt—it told me a bit about his background.

I waited.

"Go ahead, Donald. Proceed as you would do in Bullaroo."

"Really, sir?"

"You have my permission—just do what you'd do in your hospital."

"Good morning," I said, to the young man. "Please take off your clothes. You may go behind the screen if you wish." He shrugged and proceeded to undress in front of me.

While he was doing that, I took off my jacket, rolled my shirtsleeves up to the elbow, and then washed my hands. When the man was ready, I drew up one of the chairs and started my examination. I examined the man's testicles, took his penis in my hand and gave it a good look over. I carefully retracted his foreskin, and then milked his penis a few times. Dr. Sylvester initially looked concerned when I started my manual examination, but then seemed to watch what I was doing with interest—it made me nervous, but I went ahead and followed the procedure that we normally did in our surgery.

"Turn around, please. Stand with your feet apart and bend over as far as you can."

The man did as I asked; not even flinching as I gently placed my hands on his buttocks and spread his cheeks. "Thank you," I said. "You can get dressed now."

I washed my hands while the man dressed and then wrote up some notes. The second examination proceeded more or less the same as the first. I was dying to ask questions, but tried to stay on track, as Dr. Fletcher had reminded me with his note.

However, with the third man, something didn't seem quite right.

"May I ask him a question?" I said, to Dr. Sylvester.

"Of course. If you think it necessary."

"Do you scratch during the night?" I asked the man.

"Where?"

"Between the legs—around your ... browneye?" I hesitated on using the word "anus" and decided to use a non-medical term. I was used to the sort of bloke he was, talking at his level would not make him as shy.

"I do scratch my bum a bit—but that's heat rash, I reckon."

"Please turn around again, if you wouldn't mind? I'd like to take a closer look. Stand on one leg, place your knee on the back of this chair and lean forward? Thank you." I said to the man. "You can support your weight with one hand on the chair seat."

I washed my hands again and then performed a closer examination of his anus and perineum. Satisfied with what I'd done, I thanked him and told him he could get dressed again. I wrote up my notes after he'd left the room, intensely aware that Dr. Sylvester was staring at me.

"Well, then, Donald," he said, once we were alone. "That was very interesting. Follow me."

I was surprised when he led me first to a small room with an urn, where he made us a cup of tea, and then led me out onto the porch at the back of the medical building and offered me a cigarette. We stood smoking and sipping our tea in silence for what seemed an age while he stared off into the distance, and I became more and more nervous by the minute. I was about to speak when he turned to me.

"We don't normally touch the patients here, Donald, there are simply too many of them to continually wash our hands between each one."

"I'm sorry, doctor. There was no mention of not touching in the notes you sent me. But, you did tell me to do what we did at Bullaroo?"

"So I did—and I have to say I found it most instructive."

"Instructive?" Now I was feeling really nervous. What had I done wrong? What had I revealed about myself that I should not have?

"Instructive in a good way, Donald. The chair business for the anal examination. I've never seen that before."

"Well, there wasn't an examination table, and the light wasn't good in that room—normally we'd have a torch or a lamp to have a better look. I was just thinking on my feet, sir."

He smiled at me. "What were you looking for?"

"That last bloke? Well, I was puzzled. He was very well groomed—did you see his manicured fingernails? He was the only one circumcised, and obviously looked after everything "up front"—it was all well maintained and clean. It worried me that he hadn't wiped properly. His bum wasn't as clean as I would have expected. That's why I asked him about the scratching."

"And?"

"Well, when I first had a look, I noticed that he had what looked like a pimple near his crack—"

Dr. Sylvester laughed. "Another technical term? Like browneye?"

"Sorry," I mumbled, but he looked amused and told me to go on.

"That's why I wanted a second squiz."

"And?"

"It's probably tender—that's why he's not been so thorough with his cleaning. I wanted to have a closer look to see if it was the beginning of a boil, or folliculitis, or just a blind pimple—I didn't think to bring a magnifying glass to see whether it was one hair follicle that was infected or—"

"Well, blow me down! I didn't even notice that myself. Where was it?"

"Just below his freckle—right on the perineal raphe—"

Dr. Sylvester threw his head back and guffawed. I waited. I knew why he was laughing—it was another mixture of slang and medical terminology.

"Well, let's go through them all one by one and tell me what you saw," he said, once he'd stopped laughing.

"The first one was a plant," I said. "Nothing wrong with him. I suppose you were testing me to see if I'd find something that wasn't there. I would find no reason to send him on for further examination by a doctor."

"So, the second man …?"

I looked at him over the top of my glasses. He smiled at me.

"Well, apart from the obvious phimosis—his foreskin is incredibly tight, the poor bugger must have a lot of pain if he tries to retract it—there's the problem of the varicocele on the left side of his scrotum, and the tinea in the groin on the same side."

"So?"

"As the varicocele is one of the conditions on the list, and so is the phimosis, I'd refer him to the physician."

"What aren't you saying, Donald?" I can hear a question catching in your throat."

"He's very smelly, doctor. I'm just concerned that he needs to see someone very quickly. I know my position is not to diagnose, but the smell from his foreskin makes me concerned."

"And you would be right to be concerned. Don't worry; he'll be well taken care of."

"Sorry, doctor."

I was rewarded with another smile, and a pat on the shoulder. "Very well, Donald. What about the third man?"

"He presents with nothing that would require any further examination for the purposes of being suitable for enlistment, doctor. But …"

"But?"

"I know this job's not about anything but *'sorting out the wheat from the chaff'*, as you put it, but where do we stop? If that last man turned out to have a boil, that could be serious if left untreated. And the second bloke, with his tinea—would it be all right to mention that they should see their own doctors? I feel a bit torn about the restrictions of this test, and the moral implications of not saying anything if their conditions turned worse and could have been prevented."

Dr. Sylvester's grin could not have been greater.

"Well, if I'd been in your position, I'd certainly have said something to both of them. But, you have to remember, that if you were one of the triage technicians, you'd have perhaps a minute, two at the most, so it would have to be a quick word. Tell me something, Donald?"

"Sir?"

"Are you always so gentle in your examinations?" he asked. "I noticed you rested your hand beside each man's knee and then ran it over the side of his thigh before you actually started your manual examinations—I couldn't help but wonder why?"

"So far, I've only done a few examinations that require touching ... but yes, Dr. Fletcher tells me it is important to make the patient feel calm before you touch them anywhere private. I've always found it very reassuring to be touched somewhere gently before any procedure I've had done to me, so I think it must be the same for anyone else."

He placed his hand on my shoulder and gave it a friendly shake. "Very good, young man. Now, let's have another cup of tea and then you can tell me what you've got planned for the weekend."

I knew it was a diversionary tactic, to avoid talking about how I'd fared in my test. No doubt, in due course, I'd hear, but I was relieved it was all over. Now there was nothing to do but wait.

*****

I'd given up hope; nothing had arrived in the mail and two weeks had passed. I couldn't help it, but although I tried to be cheerful, felt very down in the dumps.

Arriving early on Saturday morning to mop the floors in the hospital, I'd found a note from Dr. Fletcher asking me to pop into the consulting room in his surgery, which was just across the road.

I broke into a sweat when I walked up the drive and saw him on his front veranda, yakking to a visitor. It was Dr. Sylvester. Had I really done that badly? Had I broken some unspoken professional code by offering a diagnosis? Had I inappropriately touched the test subject? I felt the heat rising to my face, and it was all I could do to shake Dr. Sylvester's hand.

"What did I tell you, Peter?" Dr. Fletcher said. "He's been like this for weeks."

I sat in a chair in Dr. Fletcher's consulting room, the two doctors facing me.

"I'd like to tell you that I don't want to offer you the position, Donald." My face fell. "You see this?" He passed me a sheet of paper—on it were five, simple, men's health questions. "This is what everyone else got." And then he showed me the sheet of questions that I'd answered; there were twelve.

"Did I do that badly?" I asked, timidly.

He laughed. "No, you flattened the test, young man, and that's why I don't want to offer you the position. Not only were your written answers exemplary, but I had to go to check some of the facts myself, so excellent were your responses. But for me, the icing on the cake was your physical examination skills. They were worthy of any young, already-qualified physician."

"What Peter is saying, Donald, is that he doesn't want you to waste your time in a backwater military hospital, he wants you to go to university and study medicine—become a doctor yourself."

"What? You're not offering me the job because you think I'm too good?" I said. I couldn't believe what I'd heard. It was as if someone had slapped my face—I almost started to cry with the shock.

"Listen to me, Donald," Dr. Sylvester said. He crouched in front of me and took my hands in his. "I've never met anyone as young as you with such a talent for clinical observation—the little that I've seen you do, and in the area that we set for you to study, that is. Won't you reconsider?"

I lowered my chin and shook my head; there were tears on the lenses of my spectacles—so much for trying to keep myself under control.

The Boy Who ...

"Spider?" he said, softly, rubbing my back, between my shoulder blades. I couldn't help smiling—he'd not used my nickname before and I found it rather comforting.

"I'm sorry, Dr. Sylvester. I'm sorry for not having better control of my emotions. It's just that I've had my heart set on this job. And what with failing Latin for my university entrance, and on top of that, not being old enough, or tall enough to join up ... I just feel like I'm chasing after things that are always out of arm's reach—again." I bit my tongue the moment the words were out of my head; I sounded like a spoiled child and it made me angry that I didn't have better self-control.

"Donald—" Dr. Fletcher started to say, but I cut him off.

"Please, Dr. Fletcher, let me say something. Since Dad died you've been a father to me—you know me better than anyone else. In my heart I want to be like my mates, off training to fight the Japs and the Germans. All I want is to do my bit in some way. I'm sorry, Dr. Sylvester, I really wanted that job—at least I'd be somehow in the army, even if I wasn't eligible for service."

"No, no! It's me who should be sorry. I wanted what I thought would be best for you—I'd no idea it would make you so upset. Just let me think for a minute. Go outside and have a smoke while I have a chat with Ian."

I went out onto Dr. Fletcher's back porch and tried to roll a cigarette, but my hands were shaking so much that all I did was spill the makings all over my shoes. As I bent down to pick up the cigarette paper, I began to sob—now that I was alone, I could allow the disappointment to really sink in. First Mum, and then Dad, and after that, missing out on university, and now this opportunity to do something for my country ... I straightened up quickly and wiped my eyes as I heard the back screen-door open. The hinges had always squeaked noisily.

"Listen to me, Donald—against my better judgement I'll offer you the job," Dr. Sylvester said, after a few minutes. "But on one condition, all right? It's just for twelve months, until the next matriculation exam. You'll spend your spare time studying under me, as if you were already at university doing a medical degree. At the start, there'll be a lot of time spent in the clinic doing what I discussed with you at your exam—

sorting *'the wheat from the chaff'*. You'll give talks on personal hygiene and prophylaxis to new soldiers, but I promise you that I'll make sure there'll also be time to study for your university entrance exams next year. My Latin's not that great, but I still remember enough to help you. If you accept my conditions, we could start your medical studies with urology, as that's where you'll be working for the first few months, and then we'll go from there. Is it a deal?"

I mumbled a "yessir", too ashamed at my lack of control and what I saw as a childish display of emotion to meet his eyes.

But then he put his arm around my shoulder and handed me his pack of tailor-mades. He waited for me to take one and light it. "You're one in a million, Spider Henderson," he said, ruffling my hair, "and don't let anyone tell you otherwise. You've got two weeks to pack up your Latin grammars, your medical text books, and report to base, ready to start."

I grinned, and chuckled, despite myself—feeling foolish and yet terribly pleased.

"There's one thing more," he said. "It would be unfair and selfish of me not to mention this, but you'll get to know anyway, and I don't want you to think that I've tricked you, or deceived you. I've heard that sometime next year the height requirement will be lowered to five foot."

I lifted my head, my eyes wide. "That means?"

"Yes, it means you'll be able to enlist. But it also means that you could be able to work in the army and in medicine at the same time. If you joined up and applied to become a field medical officer, and elected to postpone university study, I'd arrange it so you could have a very promising career as an assistant to a battlefield surgeon—one that you already know, and will have trained alongside."

"You're going to enlist too?"

"The way I see it, I'll have little choice, Donald. So, there you have it. Work alongside me until you're eligible to sign up, and then, after a short amount of training, you'll be an army medical officer, but with a lot of experience already under your belt, so that when the war's over, you can finally go to university, fly through medical school, and set up your own practice. What do you think of that?"

I almost started to cry again. But, this time, the tears would have been for another reason.

"I think you and Pekko will get on just fine, too. He's a perfect foil for you."

"Pekko?"

"Pekko Laine—his family's Finnish. But he goes by the name of Parker Lane. He's the other civvie assistant, and you and he will work as a team. He's a beaut bloke—bit of a larrikin—but it'll be a good balance to you. He's shy too, though …"

Shy? Larrikin? How did those two things go together? Still, I was bound to find out if he and I were to work together.

*****

I could not believe how quickly nine months could pass. In that time, I'd gone from poddy-calf, to chief bull in the "short arms inspection" paddock.

For the first five of those months, I'd lived on base during the week and returned home at the weekends, where I continued to work at the hospital with Dr. Fletcher, passing on information and experience to him about the latest male urological information and procedures I'd learned. Almost simultaneously with the end of my stint as the "sorter of rotten cocks and bungholes" of those wishing to enlist—a name bestowed upon me in the night, written in an unknown hand on the roster sheet, *Donald "Spider" Henderson, S.O.R.C.A.B.*—the directive came down from on high that allowed me to finally undergo my own medical examination and physical tests for enlistment. I sailed through the medical. I was puny, but healthy. I had to perform the physical tests three times, and then it was only with a wink and a nod from Sergeant Mitchum—who'd been promoted from behind a desk—and a gentle nudge from Dr. Sylvester, that I was issued with a uniform and sent off to Holsworthy for basic training.

Straight after that, I returned to the 104th Australian General Hospital in Bathurst for field medic training, most of which I avoided, electing to do the exams during the first week—Dr. Sylvester was now in charge of the surgical wards there. He'd put in a good word for me, so I'd been allowed to skip the basics—things that I'd been doing for almost ten years. I had two weeks of nightmarish stuff after the tests that made me aware of the gruesome side of being a field medical officer: pretend corpse retrieval, disposal of body parts—they used bits from the local abattoir—stretcher practice, and field first aid. We trained out in the bush, our final exam under battlefield conditions, with live ammunition, mud, and volunteers with dreadful injuries, pinned on their blouses as descriptions. I nearly fainted when attending one groaning man, whose blouse, when opened, disgorged a bucketful of concealed bullock's intestines and blood, which went all over me—it fell out of his jacket with a "glerp".

Now, two months after I'd finished training, I found myself busy—my time divided between field manoeuvres, sidearm practice, parade drills, compulsory ward duties, and my favourite—two hours a day either in theatre, watching Dr. Sylvester operate, or helping him in his afternoon clinic. But, I wasn't so busy that I wasn't also able to spend more time with my medical texts and horsing around with my new pal, Pekko, or Parker, as everyone called him, in our little cubby-hole behind operating room number three.

He was a giant—a draft horse to my Shetland pony, the Goliath to my David. He towered over me by over a foot and outweighed me three times over. He had hands the size of dinner plates and feet larger than the boxes my shoes came in. However, I thought he was the best thing since the invention of the electric light bulb. From the first moment we met, and he introduced himself with "I'm shy"—to which I'd craned my neck to look up at him, shading my eyes, and replied, "Compared to what?"—I knew we'd get on. He'd laughed at me then, and since that day, had laughed with me, the best mate I'd ever had. His laugh was unique—his shoulders shook and so did his chin with his guffaws, but no sound came out. A silent moving picture laugh, and it could not have been funnier, or more infectious.

We'd bonded as mates before the end of the first week, which in itself was a godsend, as in those early days we'd shared a small room with a double-bunk. Me up top, him below. He'd wait until I'd fallen asleep and then slowly raise my mattress with his foot until he heard the first, soft snore and then let me fall with a thud. I'd peer over the edge of the bed and see him guffawing silently under his sheet, which he'd drawn up over his face.

We shared a wash area and a four-man shower room with the two army medics who'd been assigned to Dr. Sylvester before Parker and I had joined up. They seemed to be drunk every evening, and from the sounds I sometimes heard from their rooms when I went to have a pee in the middle of the night, suspected they were diddling each other when the lights were out. I didn't care—it was their business and they were nice enough blokes, even if they did keep to themselves.

One of them slipped while walking home from the mess boozer late one night—he'd been trying to walk along the top style of the boundary fence and landed legs akimbo—he'd asked me to have a look. I was the expert on straddle injuries. Parker and I had spoken of it after, when I remarked that the man had a slightly patulous rectum. "Perhaps he and Smithy are up bum chums?" he said, casually, and then rolled onto his stomach, still reading his text. "Or maybe he likes to finger himself while he's having a pull. It's not uncommon …"

"Really?"

"Sure. I do it—don't you?" I shook my head so violently that I thought my glasses would fly off. "Don, you need to get out more."

"Are you telling me that when we're lying in bed at night and I hear you slapping away down there that you've got one finger up your bum?"

"Nope; two, as a rule."

I hit him with my book. Despite his joke, I couldn't get that conversation out of my head.

*****

We became the oddballs of the army base; always up to mischief. Once, we were reprimanded by the C.O., and consigned to kitchen duties for four days after Parker had picked me up underneath his arm while I was studying, and had casually strolled through the mess hall, with me still dangling at his side and calmly continuing to turn pages, and had then deposited me on the bench in the middle of the other guys. "What's he supposed to be?" one of the W.O.1's had asked. "My bookmark. Why?"

Parker had replied and then had gone off to fetch his lunch.

Around most people he spoke in few words; it was only me that he opened up to. I learned about his bookmaker father, a serial philanderer, and his absent mother, who worked as a dance hostess at the Trocadero nightclub. He'd been parked as a kid with various "uncles" while his parents were away at night. I read between the lines—even though it was something that didn't seem to worry him. I'd made assumptions about his sexuality, but as he'd never actually spoken about it, nor had he demonstrated anything that might prove it, I filed it away as part of who he was and never allowed the knowledge to interfere with the closeness of our friendship.

It was not long after we'd graduated from our training courses that our friendship took a different turn. We'd been promoted to corporals—it was so the men would follow our orders, rather than as a rank awarded for merit—and therefore had been moved into new quarters. It was a white weatherboard building behind the main hospital block, with a communal day room at one end and four single rooms, separated in the middle by toilets, and another four-man shower room. Smithy and Williams had rooms at the end of the long corridor that ran along one side of the building, and Parker and I had the other two rooms. I missed his company during the night, but we spent most of our time together anyway. Sometimes, while we were talking or studying, I'd fall asleep on his bed or he on mine, and we'd wake up in the morning with our arms around each other. No one cared.

The change in our relationship came by way of a simple request. I was lying on my bed, late at night, reading about field amputations during the Great War, when Parker called out my name down the corridor.

"What's up?" I yelled back.

"Come here!" I closed my book and sighed, and was about to get off my bed when he added, "Bring your kit."

I grabbed my canvas pack and went to his room. Oddly enough, the door was closed. I'd never seen it closed before, even if he was in bed masturbating, he didn't seem to need privacy. I knocked.

"Close it when you come in," he said, as I opened the door a crack. He was naked, lying on his back, his knees drawn up onto his stomach, and his shaving mirror propped up between his legs with a pillow. "Something here, Don. I can feel it."

I kneeled beside his bed and lifted his penis and testicles with one hand, pushing them out of the way onto his belly while I peered between his legs. He was quite hairy, so it took me a while to find out what he'd been looking for. "It's a tick," I said. "Right in the crease between your perineum and your groin. Here, hold these," I added, glancing at his genitals. My face was burning as I looked in my kit bag for my needle-nosed pliers. He'd thrown a long erection under my hand while I'd been inspecting him.

"Roll onto your tummy, Parker," I said. "Hang over the side of the mattress and spread your knees apart." He did as I asked; pushing his bits down between his legs so everything was dangling over the edge of the mattress.

I'd thought long and hard about my own sexuality after realising Parker was "that way" inclined. I'd never had any sexual feelings when examining the genitals of countless hundreds of men, nor did I admire other men's bodies in the shower. I'd always thought my sexual arousal was on some sort of biological timetable of need, somehow opportunistic—unaroused by external forces. But, I never really thought about it much. I just always knew when it was time to take care of myself, as if an alarm clock had rung inside my head and reminded me that I was due for a tug. My fantasies while I masturbated were fleeting images, more like sounds and colours than shapes or forms. I enjoyed the physical sensations when my hand was on my dick—which was where my attention was always focused.

So, as I gently teased the tick from Parker's groin—his erection pointing backward between his legs and almost touching my chest—I couldn't explain the tightness in my throat, or the lump there that I couldn't dislodge by swallowing the copious amount of saliva that had gathered in my mouth.

"Gotcha!" I said, triumphantly holding the tweezers in the air so he could see. He looked at me over his shoulder and smiled. "It's not swollen, so it's not been there long. I'll just whack some tea tree oil on it for you and you should be okay."

He nodded and then relaxed his head back into the crook of his elbow. I grabbed my precious bottle of oil and uncorked it carefully, tipped it upside down over my thumb and then recorked it, returning it to my bag. "Ready, soldier?" I asked.

"Yes, Don," he said, his shoulders shaking silently. I slapped his arse and laughed with him. The phrase was what we said to soldiers when they were about to get an injection in the bum. I placed my oiled thumb over the small red mark that the tick bite had left, massaging the spot slowly.

"Is this all right?" I asked. "Not hurting?"

"No," he mumbled, into his elbow. "It's nice, Don. You have the gentlest touch."

The tracking motion of my thumb hesitated for the merest fraction of a second. "Parker," I said, "you know I'm not …"

"I know, Don. It's okay."

I couldn't help myself. I made one of those decisions that wasn't really a decision. It was a moment when you do something that seems spontaneous, but which you somehow know is a decision that's already been made for you, without you knowing it, long beforehand.

"Just a moment," I said, and then moved around and kneeled between his knees, spreading them a little further apart. I reached into my kit bag and found my bottle of Faulding's olive oil, and then poured a small quantity into the palm of my hand. I rubbed it over both of my hands and through my fingers, and then began to give my pal a perineal massage, alternating both thumbs with the palms of my hands. It was a therapeutic tool I'd read about, but never used before. The area between his legs, despite the hair, was muscular, but silky smooth.

I couldn't believe the knot in my belly and the shallowness of my breath—even I recognised it as sexual arousal. I tried not to agonise over it—there'd be time for that later—but something drove me on; I felt compelled to continue, intensely aware of his quickening breaths, which, after five minutes or so, started to become ragged. Before I knew what was happening, the thickened muscle between his legs began to spasm and he let out a soft moan—a long, thick rope of ejaculate flew from the end of his penis and splattered across my thigh. It was surprisingly warm and not at all unpleasant. I'd never seen any man let it go before; I'd have thought I might have turned my head, because it was such a private thing. But I'd been transfixed; amazed at how I'd felt when I'd watched and felt his semen splash over me—it was exactly the same feeling I always had when my own spurted through the air and sprayed over my chest and tummy. I smiled for the same reasons—it was an achievement, and I knew how good it must have felt for him, if it was anything like my own orgasms.

After a moment, I moved my hands to his backside and massaged his arse and the small of his back until my palms were no longer oily.

"Thank you, Don," he said, softly, into the crook of his elbow.

"Shower," I muttered, looking around for a towel to wipe myself with. As I stood, he turned on his elbow and ran his hand over my thigh, gathering his semen onto his fingers, which he then licked clean. Strangely enough, I wasn't shocked—I just started to run through in my mind what the composition of semen was. Mostly starch and a few sugars. I accepted it as odd, but apparently not something out of the ordinary for him—he was far too casual about it. Perhaps that's why he never seemed to have a crusty handkerchief or a hand towel under his pillow, like most of us did.

"Do you always do that?" I asked.

"A lot of guys do ... it's only spunk," he said as he licked the mess from the web between his thumb and forefinger.

When I stood up, I felt my own erection pushing painfully against my skivvies, a large wet patch near my hip. For a moment, I couldn't move—he was staring at the unmistakable protrusion in my undies while he licked his fingers clean. I could feel the fluttering in the base of my stomach, but, like a coward, I decided flight was the best course of action. I wasn't ready for what might happen next.

"Right you are," I managed to stammer, and then left the room and headed to our communal washroom. "Night, Parker," I said, over my shoulder, before closing the door. I wanted to bring myself off in the shower the moment the water hit me—the need in my guts was almost unbearable. But, even after a few minutes of frantic manipulation with my soapy hand, I couldn't. I was too preoccupied—I needed to think through what he and I had just done.

Ten minutes later, I was back in my own bed, the light turned off, my hands behind the back of my neck, and deciding that perhaps now was the time I could think about what had just happened, when a voice came from the doorway, in the dark.

"Hello, Don," Parker said, softly. He'd also just come from the shower, his hair still damp and a towel around his waist. He sat on the side of my bed and began to rub my shoulder. "I didn't get to say goodnight to you—you ran off. Did you take care of yourself already?" he asked, glancing down at the obvious log shape between my legs, outlined by the sheets.

"No …" I said, aware that the same tightness in my chest and the lump in my throat had returned. "I tried, but I couldn't."

"Let me," he said. His voice was barely a whisper.

"No. I'm fine, Parker. Thank you—"

"Shh, mate. Just let me, please … I want to."

He let his towel fall open, and then folded down my sheet, precisely along the line of the top hem, and then flattened it with the palm of his hand, smoothing it out perfectly. I was mesmerised, watching him continue the process until the last fold fell onto my upper thighs and my erection sprang free. He hummed low in his throat as my penis slapped hard against the base of my belly, and then placed the palm of his hand on my sternum and ran it over my chest, about an eighth of an inch away from my skin, so that the hair on my chest tickled against his palm.

"Parker—" I began to say, but he shushed me again, this time running his hand down over my body until he circled the base of my penis with his fingers.

"Stone the crows, Don!" he said. "And you're such a skinny boy, too …" He slapped my erection against my belly button a few times, and then swiftly leaned down and took me in his mouth.

I'd never felt anything like it in my life—part of me wanted to protest that he didn't need to, despite how wonderful it felt. What I'd done to him before was merely because I wanted to give him pleasure. He was my friend—I didn't expect anything in return. But then, as I turned my head to one side, I saw that he was hard again. I made another of those "not so instant" decisions, and ran my hand over his thigh and began to tug on his scrotum and to roll his testicles between my fingers. He let out a soft groan, and tipped his pelvis so that I could wrap my hand around his cock. Although I'd seen plenty in the clinic, I'd never touched an erection, other than my own, while I was sexually excited. The electric shudder that it gave me, as I closed my fist around it, and then began to rub his frenulum with my thumb, made my mouth dry and my toes curl.

As I fondled him, I found myself increasingly lost in what I was doing—it was totally unexpected, but I felt my arousal growing as I worked on his penis and, as a result, he became more energetic with his mouth. It was as if the harder I squeezed on his shaft, the more intense the sensations were in my own cock, and the more energetically he worked to make me unload. Before long, the movement of his lips and his tongue began to turn my world into an explosion of sensation—sharp, demanding, and all-encompassing—I felt as if my body was being turned inside out through the length of my penis.

I attempted to pull his head away, but he brushed my hand aside. I tried to warn him. "Careful, I'm going to—" I said, urgently. But he bobbed his head faster and groaned as he did so. I exploded in his mouth and, at the same time, he moaned and swallowed my semen in gulps, his head pushed down hard so that his nose was pressed against my pubic bone. I wasn't small down there—I couldn't help wondering where it had all disappeared to.

He stayed for an age with my dick in his mouth, massaging my shaft with his tongue, and rubbing the hair across my belly with the underside of his forearm. His penis felt soft and fat in my hand—I kneaded it languidly. He'd come again—it was dripping down the inside of my forearm and over my hand. I let my arm fall, curling my hand behind his calf, and began to tease the hair on the back of his leg between my fingers.

I smiled to myself. I'd liked it that he'd shown such obvious enjoyment while sucking me off—there was no mistaking the fact that he'd really enjoyed doing it, it wasn't just about making me feel good. I was curious, but knew him well enough that it wasn't something he'd ever want to talk about. I tried to examine what I felt, but I had nothing more than good feelings: contentment… warmth… pleasure… happiness? It had been my first sexual experience with another human being. We'd done things that I'd never really imagined beforehand, but which had given me intense pleasure. I felt no shame, repugnance, disquiet, or anything other than how natural it had been—as if I'd been following the instructions in an internal, already-written manual.

Eventually, he stood and took my arm, and then licked it clean, while staring into my eyes. I got hard again. He wrapped his hand around my dick and then dragged me by it to the shower room, where he stood me under the spray and slowly and carefully washed my body from my ankles to the crown of my head, letting out small grunts of satisfaction as he ran his huge, soapy hands over my skin. Satisfied, he pulled me into his arms—I rested my head against his sternum, his chin on the top of my head.

"Please, Don?" he said.

I knew he wanted more—my erection, and the ache in my balls, told me that I did too. So, I nodded. He manoeuvred me from under the shower spray and leaned his backside against the bathroom tiles, spreading his knees. I ran my hands over his shoulders, to bring him down so that our hips were touching, and then took the bar of soap from him. I ran my hand between his legs, soaping up his arse and his penis, and then, while one hand was busy between his legs, I grasped both of our cocks in the other and massaged them in my clenched fist. Warm water and soap; as inexperienced as I was, I managed to bring us both off at the same time.

Afterwards, we stood for what seemed an age, pressed up against one another, slowly running our hands over each other's bodies under the warm water and in the semi-dark.

"Thank you, Don," he eventually said, his voice soft and gentle.

"No, thank you, Parker."

He laughed quietly, but my eyes were fixed on his face. I'd never felt worshipped before and it was the oddest yet somehow the most welcomed of sensations.

*****

In December of 1941, we found ourselves stationed in Malaya, with orders to proceed to Singapore to join some of the 8th division, who'd been there since the beginning of the year. With Dr. Sylvester at our head, we'd been attached, as a three-man medical team, to the 1st Independent Company, one of Australia's new commando units, and we'd moved around with them through the islands in the Pacific—New Ireland, the New Hebrides, Bougainville, and then finally in October to northern Malaya.

On the 10th of December, we heard news that *the Repulse* and the *Prince of Wales* had gone down—news that had left everyone disheartened and in a great deal of despair. On the next day, our orders came to fly out at the end of the week.

Around two, early on the following morning, Parker staggered into our bush hut; he'd been out on patrol with one of the smaller reccy squads and one of the men had accidentally shot another in the leg. They'd not been able to get the man back on a stretcher, mainly because of the denseness of the tropical rainforest, so Parker had fixed him up as best he could and then piggybacked him to base—a distance of seven miles of rugged, densely forested terrain. He was exhausted.

I followed him into the shower and scrubbed his back, while he hung his head wearily on his chest. "I know what's best for you," I said, bending him forward in the shower and then squatting behind him. I spread his cheeks with both hands and then rubbed the stubble on the point of my chin from the base of his scrotum up through his buttocks to the base of his neck, and then wrapped my arms around him and squeezed him tight. He laughed, and then reached behind and ran his soapy hand around my cock, kneading it forcefully. I was instantly hard in his hand.

"I want it in me, please, Don," he whispered, over his shoulder.

We hadn't done that often—had penetrative sex, I mean—usually only when I was very drunk. But, I knew that he liked it a lot, and wanted it much more frequently than I did. It's not that it didn't feel good to me—I really liked doing it to him—but I preferred to watch him swallow my penis. I'd learned to love the look of pleasure on his face as he brought me to orgasm, always with the same satisfied moan when he forced my length down into the back of his throat and as I spewed into his mouth. I'd never developed his love for the taste of semen—to me it was starchy and felt glutinous in my mouth—it made me gag a bit if I caught it in the back of my throat. He thought that semen spilled was semen wasted, but I didn't like the texture, or the smell, as inoffensive as it was.

As for him, it was anything to do with his arse. I found it odd at first that his central erogenous zone was not in his dick, as it was with most men, but further back—his perineum and anus. Timid at first, I'd been awkward. But, after a while, wanting to repay his ministrations, and to make him feel good, I'd become more adventurous—and when really drunk would do anything. I'd often teased him that he plied me with liquor so I'd spread his cheeks, dive in head first, and tongue him to orgasm.

That night, in the shower, he lay down on the bathroom floor on his back, and pulled me down on top of him. We'd never done it face-to-face before—it had always been me on top and him face-down with my hand reaching around and underneath to bring him off while I went at it. But he raised his knees and guided me into him, sighing loudly as I entered his body. I'd never realised how much he really liked it until that night, when I saw an unmistakable smile of pleasure spread across his face as his sphincter relaxed and I slipped all the way inside. He pushed my soapy hand down on his cock and, as I pumped away, he pulled my head down towards his.

I was reluctant—I fought him. Kissing was not on my agenda—I wasn't sure if I was up to two "firsts" on the same night. But his smile and his half-closed eyes, and his "come on, Don … it'll be nice," broke my resolve. I lowered my head and my lips touched his.

And then, once he started to do to my tongue what he'd been doing to my dick for the past year, I closed my eyes and wished I could die. I opened my mouth and gave him what he wanted—it was beautiful—all I could think of was all the time wasted when I could have been plundering his mouth and playing with him at the same time.

*****

For the first two months, life in Singapore was challenging, but satisfying.

Dr. Sylvester had his own operating theatre and I spent a lot of my time at his side, observing operations on Commonwealth troops and on Malays who had been brought in from skirmishes with the Japanese on the Thai border. Parker was the head of triage and of the nurses in the twenty-five man ward that was associated with our surgical unit, and life was pretty darned good.

He and I had a small room in a hut, which was about thirty yards from the hospital. We shared the hut with ten other men. It was crowded but we all got on well together. Despite that, there were still opportunities to be intimate, although not so frequently as we'd done during the previous two years. Face-to-face penetration, although we both yearned for it, was infrequent, mainly due to location or the proximity of other men. It often included me shuddering an early orgasm into him, brought on by nervousness and over-excitement. He was usually disappointed on those occasions, but I'd learned to take care of him with my mouth and to swallow the evidence. If we were in a hurry, a few oily fingers got him home and away in a matter of minutes. I'd learned to like the sensation of the warmth of his ejaculate as he exploded in my mouth, although I never got used to or appreciated the taste as much as he did.

It was during our time in Singapore that I'd finally understood my relationship with him. I wasn't interested in other men, nor had I developed "homosexuality" because of what he and I had done. I realised it was because I'd grown to love him not long after we'd first met, and that our physical intimacy had arisen as the result of our close emotional bond. He loved me too, and wasn't as reluctant as I was to tell me so, but the reasons behind his physical desire came from his already-established sexuality. For me, though, as far as I was concerned, there was only ever going to be one physically intimate relationship in my life, and it was with Pekko Laine.

On the 15th of February, Singapore fell—or rather was handed over to the Japs by Percival—and for the next eighteen months, things changed drastically. The Allies' General Hospital, Roberts Barracks, became our "home". We thought it miserable—our lives after Japanese occupation—but in comparison to what came next, after the

The Boys of Bullaroo

August of 1943, it was in retrospect, very good living.

"L Force" we were called—advised we were going to well-equipped hospitals in Thailand. Well-equipped? Yes, in a manner of speaking they were, not for the preservation of life, but for the slow and painful destruction of it.

The next twelve months demonstrated to me that the difference between the races of mankind is nothing to do with their genetics—the colour of their hair or the shape of their eyes—but the way in which they are brought up to value life.

I had never imagined that cruelty could exist, merely for its own sake.

*****

The sun, shining on the sea far beyond us, made me raise my hand to shade my eyes. Between us and the ocean, a vast expanse of rainforest spread out as far as the horizon to both sides. To the north, only the train line cut through the dark-green monotony.

We were sitting on top of a railway carriage: Dr. Sylvester on my left, and Parker on my right. Peter had his arm around my waist, and Pekko his around my shoulder. I leaned with my head on Parker's chest.

However, I knew what I was seeing and experiencing wasn't real; it wasn't happening in the here and now. The journey itself had been an actual one, which had taken place not long after leaving Singapore more than twelve months ago. Then, the roofs of the trains and the freight wagons behind the engine were packed with captured allied servicemen; Japanese officers seated comfortably below us in a French Indochinese, turn of the century, Pullman car.

This train journey was quite different—now, on the roof of the train carriage, were the souls of we three men, alone, clad in our reimagined mortal husks, living a happy memory dragged from the depths of my being, right in the moment that I moved from one state of life to another, perhaps greater, but as-yet unknown.

I was dead—or dying—at that tiny interval of time between when a man takes his last breath and when the light fades in his eyes. It was the moment in which men who'd been resuscitated had said their lives had flashed before their eyes, or that they'd seen a bright light at the end

The Boy Who ...

of a tunnel. I'd seen that leap into eternity countless times since we'd landed in Singapore in mid-December, 1941.

Japanese voices drifted up from the plush carriage below. *"Mite! Mite!'* they shouted. As I looked into the clouds, I saw an imagined flight of four Supermarine Spitfires soaring overhead. I knew they were Aussie planes—the outer circle on the underside of the port wings was gold and that on the starboard side dark blue. As they peeled off into formation, the familiar dark-blue circle with the centre red spot showed clearly on the tops of the wings and on the rear fuselage, and the pilots gave us a smile and a thumbs up. My heart sang, even though I knew that the aircraft were too perfect, and too far away for me to notice such detail.

Peter raised his arm and pointed. I marvelled at the fullness of the flesh on his forearm and the roundness of the bump of his ulna at the base of his wrist. His hands were perfect. So many times I'd stood beside him in theatre, watching his long nimble fingers performing the most delicate surgery. I'd loved his hands—it was what had truly started the descent into my inner destruction—the day the Japanese took them away.

He caught my eye and laughed, turning his wrists in the air. I smiled at the beauty of them, and then glanced around, mumbling something about the magnificence of what I imagined would be our eternal surroundings, but he shook his head, and squeezed my leg gently, in exactly the same way I'd squeezed his when he'd died.

His gesture confirmed that "this" wasn't it. I wasn't dead yet, but I soon would be. Perhaps I'd already taken my last breath, and this imaginary scene was painted with the few remaining cells in my brain that still had enough oxygen to create such images. What would come next, I'd no idea, but I cast my mind back to how we'd got to this place. Three men who loved and cared for each other, two of whom I'd held in my arms as they'd died, and I was about to join them wherever good men went, after the last chemical reaction no longer ignited the spark of life.

"The boy who ..." was curious about where he might go; "the boy who had been" just wanted peace and some sort of resolution to endless humiliation, helplessness, and pain.

The Boys of Bullaroo

*****

For the best part of a year after leaving Singapore, as part of "L Force", we'd struggled from one "medical camp" to another, only moving when enough of us had died that the outpost was no longer sustainable. We'd tramp through the jungle, force-marched, made to sleep in the rain or the heat, while the guards pitched tents and cooked their food. By early 1944, we were surviving on a cup of cooked rice a day and whatever we could forage from the forest around us when we were out clearing trees, or building huts, or aimlessly ordered to dig trenches, just to give us something to do. Getting enough protein was always a worry; sometimes, if we were lucky, we'd find dead animals. More often than not it was small amounts of dried fish or meat, wrapped in banana leaves near where we worked in the jungle and left for us out of kindness by the local natives. I became a connoisseur of edible insects, lizards, and frogs, and could spot wild spinach from twenty yards away.

The Japanese had confiscated all of our medical supplies and equipment. We had nothing to treat anyone with—no way of rehydrating men or of treating the commonest illnesses they suffered from: malaria, dysentery, ulcers, and beriberi. We made bandages from banana leaves, or boiled strips of clothing from those who'd already died. More often than not, men who could have been saved died from simple causes—dehydration and infections of their ulcers. As for cholera and typhus; it was hopeless. Those men were isolated and cared for by either coolies that had come with us, or by Thais, press-ganged from the local villages.

Each camp varied, depending on who was in charge. The most dreaded were those run by N.C.O.s—if we arrived somewhere new and it was a fat Nip with the rank of sergeant, we knew we'd be in for a miserable time.

The absolute worst of all was our last camp, on the Tapi River, not far from the sea. I knew it would be bad when I raised my head from my bow. Sergeant Mitsuharu was about my height, round, and with thick-lensed spectacles. I almost smiled—he was the living embodiment of every cartoon character Japanese I'd ever seen. But the man was a nightmare; cruel beyond belief, taken to lashing out for no reason at the closest prisoner he could find.

He'd laughingly send us to the river, under escort, to fish for our food with our bare hands. It stopped very quickly when one of the guards had reported that we'd help those with the worst leg ulcers down to the riverbank and place them in the water up to their waists, so that the tiny "poddy" fish could nibble away the dead flesh on their sores.

I was beaten senseless for that act of kindness—made to watch as my glasses were broken under his heel while he smacked me around the head with the butt of a pistol—one that, as a non-commissioned officer, he was not entitled to wear. Parker came off worse than me; he had moved to help me. They strapped him onto two crossed bamboo poles, suspended three feet from the ground, and left him there with no water for three days; Sergeant Mitsuharu's orders were that every Japanese soldier that passed by him should crack his shins with their rifle butt. It took him two weeks to be able to walk again, and then it was with a heavy limp.

Dr. Sylvester and I became like the Graeae sisters—the daughters of Phorcys in the story of Perseus—who shared an eye. He and I, despite different prescriptions, shared his spectacles. It was for that, that Mitsuharu punished him. One morning, during the ritual morning greeting, when the entire camp lined up and bowed to the sergeant, he saw Dr. Sylvester slip his glasses to me. He pulled Peter from the line and began to shriek at him, calling for the guards. To my absolute horror, I watched as they stretched his arms out before him on the ground, and the sergeant hacked his hands off at the wrists with the wood axe the soldiers used to cut up firewood for their cooking stove. After he'd finished, Mitsuharu barked orders and one of the soldiers stepped forward, fixed his bayonet to his rifle, and then skewered each hand and threw it over the low bamboo fence, near where we were gathered, into our latrine. And then, in heavily accented and broken English, he said, "you fix him now" and kicked me in the stomach. I blacked out.

We hadn't been able to stop the bleeding and I knew he wouldn't last—if the shock didn't kill him, then he'd no doubt get an infection, and then that would be the end of him. I'd not been able to stop throwing up after the kick, and there'd been blood in my vomitus for a few days. Parker had been beside himself with worry.

"Promise me you'll go to university and study medicine," Peter had said to me, as I'd held him in my arms.

"Yes, I promise, Dr. Sylvester," I whispered. He was so weak and malnourished; it felt like I was holding a bag of bones in my arms.

"I love you, Spider Henderson. Did you know that?"

"Yes, and I love you too," I replied. He started to shake.

"But not in the same way as Parker," he said with a wan smile.

"No, not in the same way, Peter, but just as much," I replied. I leaned forward and kissed his forehead, my heart crushing painfully in my chest. My body was too starved of water to make tears, but in my mind I felt them pouring down my face.

"Give my best to Ian Fletcher when you get home, Donald. Tell him I'm so proud of the boy who ..." He coughed, and then said something indistinct, which I couldn't make out as his voice gave out on him.

As I squeezed his knee, his head fell to one side. I knew what had happened, but sat numbly, until I felt Parker sobbing behind me.

Parker became very ill after Dr. Sylvester died. He spent most of the day under a threadbare cotton sheet that I'd swapped for my copy of Dante's "Inferno"—a book I'd dragged with me over much of Southeast Asia. It was in Italian, but it didn't matter to the man I'd given it to in exchange for Parker's covering. It was simply something to read.

"Nel mezzo camin di nostra vita, mi ritrovai per una selva oscura; che la diritta via era smarrita ..."

It could not have been more pertinent to where Parker and I found ourselves, although only in our mid-twenties, and not even *"halfway through our lives, in a shadowy, dark forest, having lost our way forward ..."*

Despite being almost on the equator, it was nearly always cold in the early hours of the morning, something that, until after Dr. Sylvester's death, I realised I'd never really appreciated, for it had given Parker and me the opportunity to spend our nights curled up with our arms around each other. All the men slept huddled in pairs or in groups—it was an unspoken acknowledgment that it wasn't just to keep warm, but for the touch of another human's skin.

Parker always held me in his arms, and every night, before we went to sleep, he'd kiss the back of my ear, and then whisper, "Night, Don," as he'd always done since that first evening we'd met and I'd chosen the upper bunk in our room at Bathurst.

One morning, about three weeks after we'd buried Peter, when I was sitting at the end of our "hut", my feet dangling over its edge, wondering if there was anything in my stomach that would come up when I vomited, I heard his voice from behind me. "Hello, Don," he said, so softly that it was almost inaudible. He let himself down behind me with a great deal of difficulty, and wrapped me in his arms, resting his head on my shoulder with his legs on either side of mine.

"Are you feeling better?" I was astounded. It had been days since he'd barely moved.

"No," he said, and then mumbled something.

"What did you say, P.?"

And then, his voice the merest thread, he said, "Goodbye, Don," and fell against me.

I know that I lost control, shouting and screaming, what little moisture I had left in my body streaming from my mouth as I howled to the sky. The last thing I remembered was a crowd of guards coming towards me, red-faced, and barking orders at me in Japanese. One of them turned his rifle and I saw the butt descending towards my face.

*****

I guess that was what had killed me, or what I was dying from. Part of me wanted to go back, to see the bundle of sticks I'd become, lying in the mud with a huddle of pale-brown uniforms jabbing their rifle butts into my broken body, but Parker pulled me against him.

"Come on, Don. No time to go back. Don't you want to go up there?" Parker asked, nodding at the tight formation of Spitfires, which had not moved since I last looked at them. They were suspended, their propellers whirling, but frozen in the air.

'No, Parker," I said. "Let's go down to the sea. Do you think we'll become those glints of light on the top of the waves? The reflections of the sun as it hits the ocean?"

"I don't know, Don," he said. "But let's see, shall we?"

He ran his hand around my chin and kissed me. It was as beautiful as I remembered it to be. And then, I felt myself fall into his body, the outside of my skin fitting against the inside of his, like a hand into a glove, and we soared above the train carriage as one. Up and up into the air, the voices of the Japs below us becoming dimmer and dimmer as we rose.

"Ready, soldier?" he said to me, his invisible shoulders shaking with unvoiced laughter.

"I love you," I said, laughing along with him.

"I know, Don … me too. I always have."

I felt it, rather than saw what happened next.

We disintegrated into a cloud of countless, incandescent, tiny sparks of life. And then the breeze caught us, and we flew off into the sky, like a mass of dust-mites, caught in a ray of sunshine that swirls in the gust of air that rushes into a room when a door is opened, and then swiftly closed.

The Stock Route to Starlight

P arcels—that's how he earned his keep.

It'd been because of the war. So many men had marched off in the later months of 1939, waving gaily and promising to be back within six months. "For King and Country!" they'd shouted from tightly packed enlistment trains. He'd even stood on the platform with his mother waving a tiny Union Jack and holding her hand as his father, his Uncle Derrick (after whom he'd been named), and his brother Simon blew kisses from the carriage window and cheered as the train pulled away from the station in clouds of billowing steam.

That was the last he'd seen of them, along with most of the rest of the young men and adults who'd joined up in those early, patriotically fuelled and gung-ho frenzied days of doing one's duty.

The three male members of his family had all been captured during the fall of Singapore.

There was just him and his mum left; and then he woke up one morning and she was gone too, leaving a hastily scribbled note on the kitchen table next to a slightly stale devon and tomato sauce sandwich and a glass of milk, both obviously laid out the night before. He remembered sniffing the milk and prodding its surface with a finger—a thick, tight skin had formed over the top, rather like an overbaked custard.

He'd tipped it down the sink and rinsed the glass, filling it with water, before sitting down at the kitchen table to read his mother's note.

> *"Gone to live with your Auntie Rose in Adelaide. You're a big boy now, Derrick, you can fend for yourself. There's five pounds in a*

jam tin in the top of the broom closet. Don't expect me back, I can't bear it. Life without your father and his brother and Simon is beyond me. Don't judge me please; you're a good boy, but you are who you are. If you weren't so closed off, I could have borne the pain. I understand, but I need loving and looking after. Be good, remember to pay the rent on time, and eat properly."

"I need loving and looking after." The words stung him more than he could have imagined. His mother was cloying, needy, and fretful. He was only withdrawn from her, and not from anyone else, because of her smothering and desperate need for attention.

It was Monday, the 20th of August, 1945. Five days after the Japanese had finally surrendered, and two and a bit months before his eighteenth birthday.

He'd taken the rest of the day off work. Opened all the windows, cleaned out everything that wasn't necessary, packed it into cardboard boxes, and taken the lot to the tip. "I guess I needed her out of my life as much as she needed to get away from me," he'd said to himself as he'd watched a few tip vultures rummaging through his mother's clothes and knick-knacks.

One by one, from the end of 1944 onward, the three telegrams had arrived. He worked in the parcels section of the post office, not in letters and telegrams, but Mr. Mulley, the mailroom supervisor, had come to him each time, tapping the brown envelope thoughtfully, his eyes full of concern, and asking, even before he'd said sorry, whether Derrick wanted to take the bad news home himself.

Each time he'd shaken his head, asked who it was, and then had taken himself off into the men's toilet and howled his eyes out.

Forty-nine men from Bullaroo had enlisted; only seventeen had returned by the end of 1946. That's how he'd got his job; no blokes around to do the heavy jobs—teenagers, especially strong bush boys, were in heavy demand.

A job for the post office delivering parcels while he was waiting to turn eighteen in November of 1945, so that he could join up, seemed to him like he'd been handed life on a plate. He'd been given a car of his own for deliveries, and could run his own timetable, as long as all the packages, parcels, and newspapers were delivered on time. He couldn't have wished for more.

*****

He felt it strange he'd gotten used to a life without men in it.

That was until the beginning of September in 1945, when one by one the seventeen locals who'd survived the war began to limp back into town. After that, over the following two or three years, ex-servicemen from other parts of Australia began to arrive, wanting to relocate to the bush, either to escape memories of their past, or to make new lives for themselves.

He missed men in his life.

He'd grown up with men around him. He'd slept in a huge bed, shuffled between his father, his Uncle Derrick, and Simon. All four of them had been banished (including his father from the matrimonial bed) by his mother, who complained that they all snored. He'd spent eleven years in that bed with the other three men and had never heard anything more than a gentle rattle in the back of his father's throat if he ever turned onto his back while asleep.

It was when he began to realise his mother was not like other mothers.

For the first few months after the men had left, he'd been distraught when it came time to go to sleep. He knew he'd be alone in that wide, empty bed in a large and empty room that had been set up as the "men's bedroom" on the ground floor of the family house. He'd grown up waking with his nose filled with the smell of men's bodies—that warm, nutty smell of sleep, and brilliantine on the pillowcases. He'd become used to thick, strong arms around him, holding him tight as he slept; someone spooned up behind him, with his nose pressed into the back of the man who he himself was curled up against.

The nights he loved the most among those men were those when thunderstorms threatened and the air was hot and close. His father would lie on his back with Derrick curled up under his left arm, his head upon his dad's shoulder, and one arm flung across the broad expanse of his father's furry chest. Simon and his uncle would lie in a tangle, twisted around them both, listening quietly while his father told ghost stories or fairy tales.

Was it any wonder then that, together with the opening of a new "leisure" swimming pool and the emptiness in his heart for the men he had loved and who had gone off to war and never returned, he'd discovered a whole new world of intimacy with other men that went beyond family affection.

*****

The rules were unequivocal at Bullaroo Leisure Centre—conspicuously posted on placards around the walls of the swimming enclosure and in the changing rooms.

Tuesdays and Thursdays were for ladies only. For them, the rules stated that their bathing costumes must be modest, covering all parts of the torso.

> *"Shoulder straps must be at least one and a half inches wide and not be tied behind the neck in a bow. Long hair must be contained by a swimming cap."*

Mondays, Wednesdays, and Fridays were for men only.

> *"As per State regulations for competitive swimming and diving, no bathing costumes are to be worn. No exceptions."*

Weekends were for mixed bathing. Occasionally a naked man might make an appearance, but more often than not it was a family occasion, so men normally covered up.

It wasn't a new thing—nude swimming for men. It had always been so, and not only in Bullaroo either. Derrick had grown up in the heat of summer sleeping with three other men who'd only donned fleecy-cotton pyjamas in the winter; at other times of the year they didn't wear a stitch to bed, so he was no stranger to the unclothed male.

However, coinciding with the advent of Derrick's eighteenth birthday and his first visit to the leisure centre since his mother had left to live with his aunt, something new and wonderful had happened. He'd discovered a previously unknown and locked door—one to which he never knew he'd held the key.

It had been Michael Passdale, the twenty-one-year-old son of one of the local graziers, who'd been the first to come knocking at that door. Derrick had been swimming and was sitting on a bench in the changing room, his towel around his neck, his mind filled with how he could plan a new parcel delivery route that would allow him a daily half hour somewhere out of the way, so he could put his feet up on the back seat of his car, eat his lunch, and then pull his hat over his eyes and snooze for a short while.

It was only when he'd glanced up, he realised while he'd been concentrating on ways to manipulate his schedule he'd been idly inspecting Michael's body. The grazier's son had towelled off his hair and was languidly drying the "family jewels", perhaps with more attention than he might have had he not been aware that Derrick's steady gaze was locked on the parts of his anatomy he was attending to. He'd given Derrick a cheeky, lopsided grin, and then, after glancing at the obvious tumescence between Derrick's legs, had asked, "Need a hand with that, Derrick?"

Derrick wasn't really shocked; that was too strong a word for it. His reaction had been visceral—a cold grip in the guts and his testicles that he couldn't ignore. He knew instantly what that feeling meant; he'd taken care of those sorts of needs with his hand ever since he turned fifteen.

Michael Passdale had pulled him roughly into a change cubicle and had closed the door, wedging it shut with one knee as he leaned against Derrick, pushing him back against the cubicle wall. It was then, with Michael's urgent manipulations and hot breath against his cheek, he'd realised that other men could do with each other what he'd been doing by himself on a daily basis for the past three years. "Jesus, Michael ..." he'd whispered, a few minutes later, as Michael Passdale groaned into his neck and collapsed against him. Derrick was amazed to realise he'd also "banged the billy" at the same time as his lanky friend.

They'd grinned at each other as Derrick had wiped himself off with his towel, and then had whispered a quick "See ya later."

He'd flattened himself against the cubicle wall, feeling oddly nervous, yet elated and pleased, to allow Michael to open the door to leave. "Later," the grazier's son had whispered, winking at him, and gently pinching one of Derrick's nipples as he peered cautiously into the change room and then left, pushing the door behind him.

"Crickey," Derrick had said to himself, rubbing his palm across the flat of his belly, and wondering if the hairs would dry stiff and matted like they usually did if he didn't have a hankie handy and had let it go all over himself. He had no idea if other blokes' spoof was the same as his own. It looked the same, it had felt as warm. The memory of Michael Passdale's clenching and release, and the soft groan against his neck as the man's knees buckled slightly, made Derrick hard again. He knew he wanted more. Just like the cubicle in which he stood, a door had opened he knew would never completely close again.

He'd left the stall door ajar and had sat back, his body hidden, but his legs from his knees down plainly visible to anyone who might have been outside in the changing room. Idly, he'd wondered if anyone else might gently prod the door open to see what was going on. He'd hoped another man with heat in his guts might do so. He ran his hand slowly between his legs, smiling at the heaviness he felt there, secretly wishing for a quiet tap at the cubicle door.

He was hooked.

*****

In the four years that had passed since his first encounter at the leisure centre, things had moved on well, everything panning out to Derrick's satisfaction. Clever planning, combined with his honest good looks, his flashing, toothy, and cheeky grin, had allowed him to have his cake and to eat it too.

At the start, there'd been no end to the succession of encounters at the swimming pool. Initially conducted furtively behind closed cubicle doors, he gradually moved away from the leisure centre to meetings in more private places—in the flat he'd taken after moving out of the rented family home, in the other men's garden sheds, out in the bush, in haysheds, shearing sheds, stock pens, or at watering holes—anywhere that was quiet and where he could get down to brass tacks with whomever he was with at the time. His vocabulary of experience developed quickly and he was happy to engage in any activity that was neither unnatural (in his eyes) nor involved pain. For that, he was immensely popular with the twenty or so locals who liked to play, and with the several men from surrounding small towns who'd heard of the changing room at the Bullaroo Leisure Centre.

Gradually, he whittled down his choices to a few. Those he not only liked the most but who also satisfied his various needs. He made a roster, one which suited all involved.

At the end of each day of the week, he'd designed his parcel delivery route to call past his "regulars", have a chin wag, maybe a beer, then a bit of hanky-panky.

Monday started off with Tobias, the local baker's assistant. Tobias was all chuckles and flour; he loved a beer and always had a cold longneck ready at the back of the bakery. It would be accompanied by a thickly sliced white bread butty or a few sausage rolls, before a pants-around-the-ankles face-to-face frottage that culminated in a mutual sticky mess. Derrick loved the way Tobias would laugh with delight as he ground his hips against Derrick's and slap his floury hands on the postman's arse cheeks, grinning and chortling as he drove himself to completion against Derrick's firm belly. Derrick always left with a dusting of flour in his hair and the promise of a family-sized meat pie for the weekend.

Tuesday was his day for Michael Passdale; the man who'd first shown Derrick what went where. Now twenty-five, Michael's easy grin and lanky walk got Derrick's motor going with very little need for encouragement. It was he who'd introduced Derrick to the nuts and bolts of serious enjoyment; tentative and uncomfortable at first, he'd gradually given in to the grazier's son, and now needed no encouragement to shuck off his clothes and lie, spread-eagled and face-down, over bales of straw in the hayshed while Michael went to work, ploughing him as he would fifty acres of his father's hayfield.

Michael was an excellent root. He was forceful, yet thoughtful, turning Derrick on his back after he was finished and taking care of him in any way that Derrick asked for. With Michael, he preferred to lie on his face, his nose full of the smell of hay, and simply enjoy the sensation.

He knew it gave the grazier's son a huge amount of satisfaction to think that he was taking care of Derrick, and Derrick was happy to provide a ride. He was like that, he reasoned—he liked to give as well as receive.

His Wednesday man was the local pharmacist—Kendrick Pettis, the chemist. Mr. Pettis had been a gunnery sergeant during the war, but had been sent home after his machine gun emplacement had taken a direct hit by a Japanese mortar in Bougainville. Ken was the only man who had stood up and walked away, losing most of his hearing, while everyone else in the foxhole lost their lives. He'd never discussed it with anyone, apart from Derrick, and he'd only opened up to him when Derrick had asked him where he'd learned man-to-man stuff and how come he was so good with his mouth—Ken loved to lie top-to-tail and whisper, "Come on, Derrick, aren't you hungry?" He'd lick his lips and then wait for Derrick's grin and affirmative answer before they laughed and then swallowed each other down to the root. It was a ritual Derrick loved.

Ken was the oldest of Derrick's "stable" by far—nearly forty. But he had eyes the colour of the sea on a bright summer's day and, despite his experiences in the Islands, had a wicked sense of humour and an insatiable appetite for chowing down on what was between Derrick's legs. Eventually the story had come out—Ken had learned the manful art of fellatio when he'd been found, pissed out of his mind, by two toey American soldiers who'd been out on patrol and had decided to take advantage of the tall and muscular Aussie. They'd shown him that with the right sort of attention, even brewer's droop could be rescued by a warm, wet mouth.

*****

Thursdays were sports nights for Derrick. In the summer it was water polo, and in the winter, field hockey. It gave him a night off to rest up for his next delivery day and whatever he had planned for the following weekend.

The only spanner in Derrick's works was his "Mr. Friday". Patrick Fletcher was the local G.P. and he was the only one of his men that he hadn't met at the local pool. It was Thursday nights and hockey that had brought them together.

Patrick had inherited his father's practice after Dr. Fletcher Senior had suffered a stroke and died while his son was away, interred in a prisoner-of-war camp somewhere in Germany. Everyone had thought Patrick was dead, but one morning, out of the blue, he'd stepped out of a first-class carriage of the Western Plains Express, neatly attired in an unmistakeably expensive suit and hat, leaning on a walking stick. He'd come back from four years of captivity with a sombre demeanour and without his left leg. No one had ever been sure why Patrick had abandoned his own new medical practice in Sydney to go to Britain and become a bomber pilot. Despite entreaties to become a medical officer, he'd been adamant that he needed to be on the pointy end of the stick.

Derrick's first meeting with Patrick, who he vaguely remembered from his childhood, came after a mishap during a grudge match with the Bellarang hockey team. He'd been whacked in the knackers by a mistimed attempt to goal by one of his fellow team members. The Fletcher surgery was not more than a hundred yards from the hockey field.

Two weeks after his examination, Derrick returned to see Patrick for a follow-up visit, his stomach in knots. Patrick Fletcher was as handsome as the day was long and when he smiled, Derrick felt a little weak in the knees. He recognised the sensations.

"Turn around so that I can examine you please, Derrick," Dr. Fletcher had said, after Derrick had taken off his pants and stood nervously, facing away from the doctor. "Come on, I've seen it once before, and I don't bite," he'd added, jokingly.

"You haven't seen it like this before," Derrick had replied, swallowing, and then turned shyly to reveal his engorged, aching erection.

There'd been a sudden lock of eye contact and an immediate moment of unvoiced understanding. Derrick noticed that the young doctor's hands were shaking ever so slightly. "Go ahead, Doc," he'd whispered, his voice thick and husky, clouded with desire. "No one will know but us."

Patrick had shaken his head and then muttered that he couldn't; it was unethical. His resolve lasted four uneven footsteps, the four it took him to reach out for Derrick's penis while pulling the young man's lips to his own.

*****

Despite his numerous encounters with men over the past four years, kissing was something he'd avoided. Mainly because the second man he'd met in the changing room, although expert and gentle, was a terrible kisser with rotten breath. It had put him off.

When Derrick was a nipper, the family had gone to visit his Auntie Rose in Adelaide. She had a huge orchard at the back of the house and was famed for her "peach kisses"—poached white-fleshed peaches with the stone deftly removed from the centre, leaving a fruity, sweet ball with a hole through it, rather like a soft, cooked, and cored apple. Derrick had sat for what seemed like half an hour, softly sucking the juice from the inside of that peach, teasing small bits of flesh from the inside of the hole with his tongue. It was luxurious.

So, no one was more surprised than he that when the doctor's lips touched his own, he'd felt the man's mouth open under his and his tongue slide into a living "peach kiss". It had been entirely involuntary. Doctor Patrick Fletcher's mouth was warm, wet, sweet, and inviting, swallowing Derrick's tongue, gently teasing its tip with his own as he moaned in unison with Derrick at the sheer sensuality and lusciousness of the kiss.

Derrick had never felt anything like it. His legs turned to jelly.

He was hooked.

*****

Despite his "crush" on Doctor Fletcher, Derrick continued his regular parcel delivery route, keeping up his regular visits to his stable of men.

Even though times had changed, in 1949 it still didn't do for two men to be seen to be too close. Patrick was "almost everything" in a man that Derrick could ever have wanted. He was sophisticated, cultured, interested in politics, art and music, and was a terrific cook as well—dinner on Friday nights, after mutual, toe-curling explosions, was the treat of Derrick's week. Sometimes he would sleep over, his arms wrapped around the doctor as Patrick moaned and flinched in his sleep. Like Ken, he'd only hinted at what had gone on in the internment camp in Germany. All he'd let on was that before he'd been captured he'd never played around with a man before, and that hunger was a great motivator to learn what needed to be done to stay alive.

It was the conditional "almost everything" that stopped Derrick from telling his other blokes he was moving on, and into a more frequent and serious monogamous relationship with the doctor. The "almost" was because of Patrick's unwillingness and inability to satisfy one of Derrick's basic needs in bed—to give him every so often what Michael Passdale gave him—a sound and thorough pounding when he needed it. Derrick loved all aspects of sex; he didn't care what went on as long as it felt good, but he knew that if Patrick couldn't bring himself to occasionally give him a good hard ride, he'd end up looking for it elsewhere. In good conscience, he couldn't promise that he'd be faithful to Patrick otherwise.

They'd talked of it only once. Patrick had started talking about buying a practice in a town where no one knew them, where they could set up shop together as a doctor/handyman team, pretending to be cousins. A lot of guys who suffered in the war went into business with their mates; a friend to share the horrors with who understood.

They'd fallen out for a while over it; Patrick unwilling to understand Derrick's needs and Derrick equally as unwilling to give up his Tuesday hammerings from Michael Passdale. He'd argued that if Patrick would only—

"It's just not my style, Derrick. Don't you understand?" The doctor had pleaded.

After ten days of staying away from him, the lure of Patrick's pliant lips and soft warm mouth had him banging on Patrick's bedroom window. The memory of the small patch of fur on the small of his doctor's back and the way he obligingly lifted his hips so that Derrick could penetrate him was more than Derrick could bear. Patrick had opened his window and Derrick had so frantically grabbed his face in both hands to kiss him, the doctor had almost fallen out of the window and into the garden.

Maybe he could get used to being "the man" in the relationship, and go without his need to be ridden, Derrick had reasoned, in a vain attempt to fool himself.

… and maybe it might have worked, had it not been for The Gyppo.

★★★★★

The Gyppo's real name was Johnathon Smart. He was an itinerant farrier and tinker from Starlight, a small country town a hundred miles to the north of Bullaroo, famous for its annual muster horse races.

Derrick had noticed the smoke first. He was on his last Thursday parcel delivery of the day, on the week before water polo started up for the summer, not more than two months after he and Patrick had started reshaping the mattress in the doctor's bedroom. It was out along the highway on the road, which eventually leads to Dubbo, he'd seen the thin wisp of smoke coming from the bush down near the river. As it was getting close to bushfire season, he thought he'd better check it out. Right at the end of the track that led to the river, he spied a dirty green Dodge ute parked underneath a gum tree, partially hidden in the bushes. A blue cattle dog was sitting obediently on the tray and observed him as he stepped out of his car. Not far from the rear of the vehicle a billy sat simmering at the edge of a small, almost burned-out campfire. He threw another log on the fire. He was gasping for a cuppa, and meant to ask for one once he'd found the owner of the ute.

"Cooee," he'd yelled out, and then heard a returned hello from the creek. He'd wandered down to the water's edge. Not more than six yards away a man stood in the middle of the stream with his back to Derrick. Derrick ran his gaze over the man's broad, olive-skinned, muscular back. The bloke was busy, squeezing the water from his hair with both hands; the rounded tops of the cheeks of his arse barely showing above the surface of the water.

"You must be The Gyppo," Derrick had said.

"That's me," the man had replied, without turning around. "Actually, my name's Johnathon, but people call me The Gyppo because they think I'm an Arab or something. Mainly because of the colour of my skin and hair," he added.

"You're dark enough," Derrick said.

"Centuries of Spanish Invaders," the man said, with a wink. "How else do you think I got these coal-black eyes and ebony locks?"

"Where you from?"

"Coonabarabran originally, but my family's from Youghal, in County Cork," the man said, falling into a thick Irish brogue. "Those Iberian raiders, if they missed the southern shores of England, loved to leave little presents with our Irish lasses."

Derrick suddenly remembered his manners. "Derrick," he called out. It was the way bushies said hello when first meeting each other. First names only.

The man turned to smile at him and then began to wade out of the water. "What's the matter, mate," he added with a toothy grin as he held out his hand to Derrick's introduction. "Haven't you seen a grown-up man's cock before?"

Derrick remembered swallowing loudly, louder than he had done in Patrick's clinic. He'd recognised the look in the man's eye. Something bold took control of him and the words were out of his mouth before he could stop them. "Plenty of cocks, mate, and close up too. I just didn't know 'grown-up' meant one like mine, only smaller."

The Gyppo had roared with laughter and then beckoned Derrick to sit with him on the back flap of the ute's tray while they had a cup of tea.

"Wanna fuck me?" the man had said, half an hour later and quite out of the blue, running his hand down the front of Derrick's trousers.

The word made Derrick go cold and hot at the same time—it was a word he never used. His father had taught him not to use strong language. But the growl in the Irishman's voice as he'd said it had made an instant tent in Derrick's pants.

"You're going to pop those buttons on your dacks ... Derrick," the man had said, his eyes fixed on his hand, which kneaded the swelling underneath Derrick's flies.

"Then you'd best move your hand so I can undo them and relieve the pressure."

The Gyppo smiled at him and shook his head softly, before pressing his mouth to Derrick's and kissing him deeply. The man's tongue was thick and demanding, filling Derrick's mouth—it was all Derrick could do not to voice a protest when they eventually drew apart.

"You'll do," the man said, after having deftly opened the buttons on Derrick's pants with one hand to retrieve the young man's penis. "Nice kissing—I think I'm gonna enjoy a taste of your *shillelagh*," he added, glancing down at his hand, which was slowly working up and down over the length of Derrick's shaft, " … before you throw it up me."

He then proceeded to rip Derrick's clothes off roughly.

The dark man's hands were strong and calloused, unlike Patrick's soft and gentle fingers. He grabbed handfuls of the flesh at Derrick's waist and twisted it, moaning and groaning obscenities that only goaded Derrick to plunge harder and more forcefully into the man's body. How odd it had felt to see someone so muscular and "blokey" roll onto his back and lift his knees, drawing Derrick into him while fiercely squeezing the postman's buttocks. The Gyppo used dirty words in ways that Derrick had only ever heard before when used in bar brawls—the coarseness of the words, combined with what the dark-haired man was goading him to do to him, made the blood rise in his ears. And then, when The Gyppo reached behind and roughly squeezed Derrick's testicles at the moment of his climax, it temporarily took his breath away—he couldn't get any air in, such was his amazement. It lasted but a second or two, but then he screamed out his orgasm into the bush around them.

For a brief moment, lost in the haze of what had happened, Derrick felt a small twinge of disappointment; that was only until The Gyppo extricated himself from underneath Derrick and pushed the young man flat on his stomach on the back of his ute. "My turn," he said, growling out the words. "I'm gonna fuck you till my spunk flows out your ears." Derrick heard himself muttering some encouragement; the words didn't matter, he was relieved that The Gyppo wasn't like Patrick—one way only in his preferences.

Despite one of the man's hands groping roughly at his genitals and the other hand clutching a fistful of Derrick's hair, pushing his face against the cold, hard metal of the floor of the ute tray, Derrick lifted his hips to meet The Gyppo's urgent and violent thrusting. After it was over, and he lay, pinned down by the weight of the larger man who remained sprawled on top of him, he sighed with pleasure, feeling doubly satisfied, unashamedly admitting to himself that it was due to the man's rough, coarse coupling, and dirty mouth. He wiggled his hips.

"More?" the man had whispered, before pushing his tongue wetly into Derrick's ear.

"Fuck, yes," he'd replied, amazed that he'd used the word and that the word, coming from his own mouth, had made him hard again. He didn't want it to ever end, this feral coupling out in the bush. "But, mate?"

"Yes, Warwick?"

"Derrick."

"Ah, yes, sorry—Derrick. What can I do for you?"

"Chew my arse out first, will ya?"

The Gyppo arched his back and let forth a long, visceral wolf howl, his erection still hard and deep in Derrick's body.

Derrick couldn't give a stuff if he'd got his name wrong. He spread his knees as the dark-haired man withdrew. The Gyppo moaned softly as he bit each of Derrick's buttocks, running his tongue over the lightly furred flesh, one after the other. Even though he tried for a moment, Derrick couldn't recall The Gyppo's real name either; the warm and wet feelings from back there as he lifted his hips and spread his knees wider to open himself for more had caused the world to dim around him.

He was hooked.

★★★★★

The Gyppo was the only man he hadn't told Patrick about. His doctor knew who the others were in his stable and tacitly, if not willingly, accepted they were part of something he could not give Derrick. Derrick knew that it pained Patrick, but he also knew himself well enough that it would all end in disaster if he tried to make a permanent and monogamous connection with the doctor.

He'd continued to meet up with the itinerant farrier once a fortnight, when The Gyppo made his visits to the few farmers who still used workhorses, mainly to check on their shoes. He'd meet up with the Irishman at the same place on the river and they'd go for it like rabbits.

"This visit's going to be the last time," Johnathon had said, after their last coupling. "For the foreseeable future anyway."

"What?"

"No real work here, Derrick. No reason to come down this way anymore ... except for you, that is, and my thinking is that if you want any more of my thick Irish cock and dirty mouth, then you'll just have to make your way north to Starlight and shack up with me."

"I wouldn't know how to find it," he'd replied, trying to make light of it, even though he felt like he'd been punched in the belly.

"It's simple, mate, just turn north at the bridge and follow the drover's trail. It's the Stock Route to Starlight—the gypsy in me can tell your fortune, and your future has years and years of you and me fucking in it. If I close my eyes, I can hear my balls slapping against your scrawny arse."

Derrick had laughed. "What about *my* balls?"

"Whacking against my chin, Derrick, while your cock is down the back of my throat," The Gyppo had replied with a smirk, and then, his voice suddenly serious, added, "Tell you what—I'll come down next Saturday, if you like. Passdale's mare needs some work on her feet. I told him I'd come if I could. I'll make a special trip, look after his nag during the day, and spend the night at his farm. The next morning I'll wait for you in the lane at the back of your place until nine. Your choice, Derrick. Pack up your swag and throw it in the back, then it'll be you and me and the bright green sea, or that's the last you'll see of me, unless you follow the Stock Route north to Starlight ..."

*****

"I've two tickets for the nine-twenty on Sunday morning," Patrick had said on the Friday night after Derrick's last meeting with The Gyppo. "There's a private surgical practice for sale in Condoblin. It's got a small hospital attached so there'd be a job for you as a general handyman. I know we'd have to pretend to be brothers or cousins, but it would be a way we could be together."

Derrick could not believe his ears. This had to be a cruel and ironic coincidence. He finally had his life where he'd wanted it to be—happy

The Stock Route to Starlight

with his stable of lovers, Patrick's all-encompassing kisses and willing, greedy arse, and his fortnightly rough-housing with The Gyppo—and now this?

"I promise I'll try, Derrick," Patrick had added, noticing Derrick's frown. "To give you what you need, I mean. I'm not very good at it, but if some future together means I have to occasionally swap roles in bed, then I'll do my best."

Derrick could have cried at the sincerity and pain in his doctor's voice. If only he could have both Patrick and The Gyppo in his life and in his bed together at the same time and forever more, he said to himself.

"What's wrong, Derrick?" Patrick asked.

"Nothing. Nothing at all."

"Well, you can't say I'm not trying. We'll see. If you turn up at the station, then I'll know whether you want a future with me or not. If you're not there ... I don't know what I'll do, to be perfectly honest. All I know is I can't go on like this."

*****

From the distance, Derrick could see Patrick's lean form, his walking cane in his hand, a small travel case at his feet, as the man stood at the end of the platform where the first-class carriages drew up, waiting for the nine-twenty to Condoblin. As he drew closer, he could see the doctor take his watch from his pocket and check the time. Derrick glanced at his own wristwatch—it was nine-twelve.

"Penny for them."

"Not enough," Derrick replied with a smile.

The Gyppo slowly unbuttoned his flies with one hand, the other still firmly grasping the steering wheel of his car, and pulled out his *shillelagh na hÉireann*, as he'd taught Derrick to call it. It stood up proudly in the slanting morning light. "How about this? This enough for you?"

"You know it's plenty enough for me," Derrick said, as he lowered his head into the man's lap.

"Next stop Starlight," the Irishman said, fondling the back of Derrick's head. "It's just at the other end of the Stock Route, my young friend."

Derrick knew they were driving past the train station; he could hear the bells of the railway crossing ringing. He stopped what he was doing briefly and rested his head on Johnathon's thigh. It was to give himself a silent moment to send a mental wave goodbye to the brave, quiet, and loving man who was still waiting for him on the station platform, and who was unaware that Derrick was in the dirty green Dodge that sped down the road past the station in a cloud of red-dirt dust.

He could always come back, he'd argued with himself nearly all night long; he'd try to mend the doctor's broken heart if it didn't work out with the Irishman. That's what he told himself, anyway. For a second, a stab of pain ran through his own heart, and then the dog barked in the back of the ute, as if saying, "get back to what you were doing".

He lowered his head once more.

The dog's bark, the feel of the man's hand fondling the back of his head, his mouth full of The Gyppo's "Irish walking stick", and the fire in his guts told him what he already knew—he'd never go back.

It was too late.

He was hooked.

The Connaught

"Hey, Robin! Hang on a minute! Slow down, mate!"

Any Aussie kid would tell you they rarely react to their proper Christian names, unless it came from Mum or Dad, in which case they'd know they'd be really in deep trouble for something real or imagined their parents were going to wallop them for.

"Robin! Mate! Oi!"

There was still no indication Robin had heard his name called out, so Fergus cursed under his breath, and then tore off up the street behind his friend, eventually catching up to him and grabbing him by the seat of his pants. "ERROL!" he yelled in his ear from behind him.

Robin spun around. "Hey! Gidday, Spud. Sorry, lost in the clouds. No need to shout, cobber. Where's the fire?"

Anyone who lived in Bullaroo, watching this encounter from the other side of the street, would merely have smiled and raised their eyebrows. The "terrible twins", the boys had been nicknamed. They'd grown up during the war as two of what the locals had dubbed the "absent babies"—children who'd been born in 1939 after their fathers had shipped off to war. They were nice young men; perhaps a bit too rowdy, and a bit too affectionate with each other in public. But they'd been best mates since they'd been sat next to each other on the first day of primary school, back in 1944.

Hard to believe, really, that those two tots, sharing sandwiches, and walking in file to class hand in hand, should have grown up to be as close as boys could be, had they not been born twins.

Fergus "Spud" O'Neill pulled his friend, who'd been hurrying back to work after a quick cuppa and a cream bun at the baker's, into the empty shop entrance next door to Pettis's, the chemist shop.

Robin "Errol" McLaughlin had earned his moniker after a Saturday afternoon kids' matinee of *The Adventures of Robin Hood*; all his peers had started calling him by the leading actor's name the moment they'd left the cinema, and it had stuck—adopted right throughout the community. It had been in 1948, when he was nine years old, and one of those showings where children were encouraged to come in fancy dress. Despite his mother's misgivings he'd pestered her to dress him in green, and he'd arrived carrying a hastily put together bow and arrow, fashioned from a limp length of river willow and butcher's string, which had been confiscated at the door.

"Hey, Errol, guess what?"

"You're mad, and I'm not?"

"Hardy, ha, ha, ha …" Spud rolled his eyes briefly. "Go on, guess!"

"I've no idea, Fergus." Robin was the only person in Spud's life, including his parents, who called him by his real name. He twisted Fergus's nipple through his shirt.

"Ah, fuck off, you loser!" Spud spluttered, laughing loudly while attempting to bat Errol's hand away. They threw mock punches at each other for a moment, Spud eventually grabbing his mate and pulling him back, further into the shop doorway, and out of view of the footpath. They wrestled light-heartedly, Spud pushing Errol up against the closed doorway of the empty shop while he pretend-tickled him.

"Ow, get off, you dick!" Errol said, laughing, as Spud briefly but roughly grabbed his testicles and gave them a lingering squeeze. The two of them snickered like five-year-olds; it was stuff boys did together—rough-housing and groping each other as some strange way of using inappropriate physical contact to reinforce their masculinity.

A loud, imprecise "harrumph" interrupted their horseplay. They offered a half-hearted apology to Mrs. Robinson, who'd just appeared on the footpath in front of them. Most likely she'd come from the chemist's next door. It was well known that she had an unhealthy and unwelcomed infatuation with Mr. Pettis, the chemist, oblivious to the fact that the man enjoyed long "hiking" weekends away with her unmarried, thirty-something-year-old son, in preference to her ceaseless invitations to come to Sunday afternoon teas. She was always more offended than any situation warranted and didn't like young people; especially rowdy boys.

"Want more?" Errol said, once Mrs. R. had disappeared around the corner into Harris Street, his hands outstretched, ready for a renewed squeeze of Fergus's nipples.

"Fair suck of the sav, mate," Spud replied, his cheeky grin returning anew. And then, with a wink, added, "Well, not my tits, anyway ... and not in the main street."

The two man-boys laughed. They were at that age when their fathers would have already been men; nevertheless, in 1959, they had to wait another year until their twenty-first birthdays before they could officially assume that title. They'd been best pals all of their lives. Different as chalk and cheese—Robin McLaughlin, an odd combination of larrikin and intellectual, and Fergus O'Neill, the sports hero, the boy all the girls in town swooned over. Not that Fergus was stupid—that'd be stereotyping the footy front-row forward—he had plenty of smarts, but he had secrets to hide, and being an athlete was the perfect front for the things he wanted to keep to himself.

"Okay, what's your news then, Fergus?" Robin took a pack of Kents from his shirt pocket and expertly whacked it on his forearm. Two cigarettes slid forward out of the torn opening at the corner of the packet. Fergus took them both, lit them, and then handed one to Robin. They walked a few paces and then leaned against the front window of the chemist's shop.

"Morning, boys," Kendrick Pettis said, before Spud could answer Robin's question. The chemist had come out, chasing after Mrs. Robinson, and waving a package in the air. No doubt, she'd left something behind "accidentally".

"Morning, Mr. P.," they both chimed, in unison.

"How're they hanging?" Spud added, with a quick twist of the head and a wink, speaking loudly, as everyone did. Mr. P had returned from the war with almost no hearing.

"Same as always, boys—knocking against my knees," the chemist replied, with a wink, grabbing Spud's cigarette and taking a quick puff, before he waved goodbye and went back into his shop.

"Okay, then, Fergus. What's this news?" Robin was only partially interested, mainly because he needed to get back to work. He glanced at his watch. Five minutes and Ewan, the editor-in-chief, would be standing on the footpath, thwacking his armbands in irritation that the junior copy-editor had taken too long over his morning tea break—again.

"The Connaught's been sold."

"What? Really? Who to?"

"Eye-ties, so I heard. Their name's Barber, or something like that."

The Connaught was going to reopen? The famous milk bar-cum-café, that'd been closed for two years now, was going to reopen, and had been bought by immigrants? Robin could scarcely believe it. It'd been their favourite meeting place and lunchtime eatery for as long as he could remember. When old Mr. Peagren closed it years ago, the inhabitants of Bullaroo had let out a collective sigh of disappointment, and then had moved on to pies, sandwiches, and pasties from Falls's Bakery for their lunches—those of them that worked, that is. But it was in many ways a poor substitute; there was nowhere to sit, have a ciggie, and a milkshake. The pub did lunches; however, that always led to having a beer and everyone apart from the cow-cockies thought it wasn't "the done thing" to drink during the day.

Italians? Over the past eight or ten years, a few post-war migrant families, mostly from the Mediterranean, had settled around the area. They usually made a go of small farms that ex-serviceman had started, with hope in their hearts and with the starry-eyed prospect of a secure future, but then had abandoned. Those men had been, on the whole, city blokes. Farms and them? Well, let's just say there's a big difference between a whole lot of hope and a whole lot of hard yakka. The Greeks and Italians who'd arrived in the early 1950s had snapped up acreages and smallholdings, usually turning their hand to growing exotic-looking and extremely foreign-sounding vegetables, and keeping themselves to themselves.

The Connaught

But, Robin thought, an Italian family running a milk bar? What the hell would they know about milkshakes, spiders, and the best hamburgers that ever there were this side of the Black Stump?

"Who'dathoughtit it? Eye-ties. Fuck me …" Robin's voice trailed off, some other thought yet to be spoken. He didn't get a chance.

"Promises, promises," Fergus said, under his breath with a leer, poking his mate in the ribs with his finger. "When you gonna let me near your pearly white arse cheeks then, Errol?" Even blind Harry could have told that it was only half-joking.

"When you can bring yourself to roll off your stomach, Spud," Robin replied, his grin just as cheeky as his mate's. He playfully kneed Fergus in the groin, and then took off down around the corner before Spud could react.

Again, any passer-by would just think it was crude, bush-boy teasing—behaviour typical of the "terrible twins". However, there was a story behind it. A story that didn't involve Italians, milk bars, or even Bullaroo. It was a story about growing up in a country town in the 1950s and all that it entailed. Secrets, secrets, and even more secrets.

*****

Any relationship, or friendship, unless it's a superficial one, will have its ups and downs, complications, smooth and rough passages.

That between Fergus and Robin was no different—except for one basic, recurring problem: a combination of religion and sex that twisted their lives, affecting them both deeply, and unhappily, for different reasons.

They, like many other boys during adolescence, had discovered sex with each other in the course of juvenile tomfoolery, mock wrestling, and natural inquisitiveness. Unlike most other boys, however, they hadn't outgrown it, but had continued to preserve a regular, if fraught, physical relationship that didn't mirror their naturally playful and public daytime friendship. While the latter was fun, games, and teasing, the more intimate times they spent together were always marred after the event by anxiety, caused by Fergus's Roman Catholicism and his obsessive fear of being "found out".

While Robin was also careful and protective of their privacy, he was an occasional Protestant and had no such pangs of guilt. So, when he'd rather have been luxuriating in the afterglow of release, he usually ended up having a row with Fergus, who invariably would blame him for "leading him to sin" or perverting him. Nothing could be further from the truth, Robin always argued, for it was invariably Fergus who instigated their sexual activity.

It wasn't that Robin had no interest in sex—far from it. He wanted it to be part of their normal friendship; full of fun, teasing, and with the intensity of connection only close friends could share. He wanted there to be affection with the lust. No, that wasn't it, he'd argued with himself, because Fergus wasn't cold or just physical, at times he was very affectionate; but there was another dimension, a line that Fergus couldn't or wouldn't cross. Robin knew the word—he was a copy-editor after all—he was just too shy to admit what he needed was intimacy.

Once or twice a week, Fergus would meet up with Robin with a certain "look in his eye": one that signalled a quiet place somewhere, Fergus's eyes would be glazed with lust, his hands and legs trembling as he pulled Robin into some corner, scrabbling frantically at the buttons of his friend's flies with one hand while trying to undo his own belt at the same time. He was always demanding; kissing Robin as if he was possessed, willing to go the mile, to make sure that Robin panted into his mouth at the same time he did.

Those were the good times, Robin always thought—the "needy and greedy" times, he called them.

But then, there were Saturday nights.

Every Saturday night, after an evening of back-seat fumbling with the girl of the moment, and a belly full of beer, Fergus would park his father's FJ Holden on the small hill behind Robin's family's orchard, and flash its headlights twice.

There was something robotic, almost compulsive, about the way Robin would always, despite misgivings, crawl out of his bedroom window, along the corrugated iron roof of the kitchen below, and then drop into the garden noiselessly to make his way through the rows of

The Connaught

apples and pears to the top of the hill, where Fergus would be ready and waiting for him.

It was always the same: the car parked with the back passenger door open, Fergus stretched out on the rear leather-covered bench seat with his pants around his ankles, waiting for Robin to take care of him. Whether face-up or face-down, eventually Fergus would roll onto his belly, retrieve a towel from under the seat, place it under himself and then, without looking over his shoulder, pass a jar of Vaseline to Robin.

"Take good care of me, mate," he'd always say, and then moan softly into the crook of his elbow as he arched his back and spread his legs, waiting for Robin to "take the dive".

Robin couldn't help himself. No matter how much he resented the fact that Fergus was always pissed out of his mind and that he would just lie there, writhing and moaning while Robin was on top of him, it still filled him with unbearable lust. It was a lust that was overwhelming—ice in his guts, a sickeningly overpowering heat in his ears, and his heart pounding like a sledgehammer in his chest. Sometimes the combination of his own inability to walk away and Fergus's inebriated focus on what Robin was doing, rather than sharing their mutual pleasure, made him so angry he tried to punish his friend by being rough—only the harder and more powerfully he pounded away, the more Fergus groaned and begged for more.

More than once Robin had cried tears of frustration after the act, but never failed to groan and curse like a barbarian. He was a "yeller"—he made an excess of noise and swore in the crudest manner while they went at it—but it was only on Saturday nights when they coupled, not during the week when they never had the time, nor the place, for anything but opportunistic, non-penetrative activities. It was the intensity of his lust on Saturday nights that made him yell. His cursing always grew in power, eventually becoming an incoherent bellow at the moment of his climax. Fergus loved it—Robin's cursing and groaning always tipped him over the edge too, and at the same time. Even at the times Robin was annoyed with Fergus and tried to punish him with brutal manhandling, he still roared like a wild animal. And always, at those times, despite his attempts at self-control, he invariably arched his neck, kicked his feet against the running board of the car, and shouted his head off at the stars in the moment of his release.

And after? Well, it was more like a battlefield than an exchange of "thanks, mate", or "that was fun", or "are you okay?", or "did you enjoy that?". As they cleaned up and got dressed, there was always sullenness in the air—Fergus's unfailing and irrational anger over what he saw as being "taken advantage of"—of being used by Robin. Shouting, recriminations, punches thrown—there was no reasoning with Fergus during his post-coital, drunken self-loathing, and Catholic shame. Robin had often tried to talk it over with him the following day, but it always finished the same way—Fergus mortified with his own behaviour, often in tears, begging for forgiveness, and blaming the booze and the church.

Of late, Robin had become more and more fed up. He gave as good as he got, not averse to returning punches himself, more in frustration than anything else. He couldn't understand the compulsive nature of their Saturday night meetings and loathed how badly the aftermath invariably affected them both.

So he devised a plan.

They went away camping for the weekend; just the two of them. There'd been lots of sex but no penetration—Fergus couldn't do it without being drunk and they were fifty miles from the nearest pub. Robin had offered his body, but Fergus told him not to be stupid and rolled him back on his side before turning around so they were head to tail and they could suck each other off at the same time. The weekend had ended in a dismal silence after Robin had asked Fergus if he could kiss him. No sex, just kissing.

For the briefest of moments it had been beautiful—just how Robin had always imagined it could have been between them. Soft pliant lips, gentle, nipping teeth, and supple, luxuriant, exploring tongues. But Fergus had abruptly pulled away. "No, sorry, Errol. I just can't do this. This is something else. I'm happy for us to smooch while we're having sex—but I don't want this."

For half an hour, the drive back home was thick with both Robin's unspoken anger and Fergus's annoyance that Robin just didn't understand. And then, raising his knees to control the steering wheel, Fergus undid the belt on his trousers, unbuttoned his flies, and lifted his hips, pulling his pants down to his knees. He reached into the glovebox of the car and pulled out his jar of Vaseline.

"Stick your finger in here," he said to Robin, handing him the small, round jar, his normal cheekiness restored.

"Then what?" Robin was still annoyed.

"Then stick it in here," Fergus replied, as he spread his knees, and rolled his hips forward on the car seat. "If you finger-fuck me for the next twenty miles, I'll pull the car off the road and gobble you off. Okay?"

Robin clucked his tongue and shook his head, but he was already as hard as an iron bar in his pants. He did what he was told.

*****

Of course, Spud got to know the "Eye-talians", as he called them, long before Robin. It was because they all attended the Holy Spirit for Mass at the same time on Sunday mornings, and the Catholic community had welcomed them into their fold, excluding them possessively from the rest of the population of Bullaroo for as long as humanly possible. Afraid they might get "led astray" by the heathens, Robin couldn't help thinking, ungenerously.

"And this is Silvia," Spud said, on the day of their first visit, almost two months after he'd revealed the news about the Connaught and its new owners.

Robin had already been introduced to the husband and wife team who'd bought the milk bar, Vittorio and Grazia Barbano (Bar-*ba*'-no to the same rhythm as "potato", with an accent on the second syllable, Robin noted, trying to make sure he'd get it close to right when he used their name). They were pleasant, well-mannered people, who spoke English fluently, but haltingly, with charming accents and smiles to match. To him, they looked as if they were most probably in their late fifties—impeccably dressed and their neat clothing partially hidden under long white aprons that reached to mid-calf.

With the new paintwork and a few minimal, but noticeable, changes to the inside of the café, the Connaught and its new owners looked, to Robin's eyes at least, very European, and for that, very exotic and enticing—a place and people that he wanted to get to know better.

Silvia, Spud had explained, was their Australian-born cousin, whose family ran a milk bar in Melbourne, and who had come to help them for a few months to set up their business, or for as long as it took for them to get themselves on their feet. Silvia told Robin that she'd advised the Barbano family to continue with the Connaught's Australian-type menu, with the addition of a few Italian dishes that had gone down well with the locals in Melbourne and therefore might also go down well in Bullaroo too.

Robin was entranced. He'd noticed the smells coming from the back room of the café the moment he'd walked in the door with Spud. It was nothing like he'd ever smelled before and it made his tummy rumble, quite loudly. Mrs. Barbano had noticed it and smiled, turning aside briefly to say something to Silvia in Italian. A few minutes later, he found himself seated in one of the café's booths, looking at something rich, red, and totally unfamiliar, with a smell that made his mouth water.

"*Dai,*" Mrs. Barbano said, "Go on; it won't get eaten by looking at it."

"What is it?"

She handed him a red and white checked cloth napkin and mimed that he should tuck it into his shirtfront, behind the collar. His mother would have died had she seen him do that; napkins were for placing folded and across the knee, not under the chin.

"*Un attimo!*" she said, leaping to her feet, and then crossing to the counter. She returned with a glass dish covered by a silver lid, which she opened and then sprinkled what looked like breadcrumbs over his food.

"What's that?" he asked, his eyes wide.

"Smell," she replied, holding up the round glass container. *"Parmigiano ..."* and then added "cheese", to his querulous look.

Robin had never even heard of *ravioli al sugo di pomodoro*; however, after one mouthful he knew he'd never forget it, nor the accompanying look of absolute satisfaction on Mrs. Barbano's face as she watched him eat her food. He'd seen it often enough to think it must be common to women in all parts of the world: watching someone tuck into and really relish the food they'd cooked.

The Connaught

"How do you say 'that was wonderful' in Italian?" he asked, after pushing back his empty plate with the look of "please, sir, can I have some more?" lingering, unspoken, in his eyes.

She smiled and softly patted the side of his face. "No need, *tesoro*, I can see it in your eyes. I make *i ravioli* for the family on Tuesday, Wednesday, and Friday for our lunch. So, if you are here around noon on those days, perhaps I can put a little aside …"

What a saleswoman, Robin thought. Touting for business without advertising. He'd be there, come hell or high water—he'd never tasted anything like it in his life and couldn't wait to try some of the other "non-Australian" dishes.

"May I ask how you speak such excellent English, Mrs. Barbano?"

"Please, call me Grazia," she replied. "*Firenze* was full of English milords and ladies when I was a girl. They lived there before and between the wars, and of necessity we were taught English at school. Mine is not as good as it once was, but since the Americans left, we've only been speaking it again for three months now in Australia."

"Americans?"

"Yes, during the war. We three worked for the Americans when they came, and before that we fought against the Germans as *partigiani* …"

He'd worked out that *Firenze* was Florence and *partigiani* meant partisans, but Robin was confused.

"Three? I thought Silvia was born in Australia."

"Oh, no," she said. "My son, Ettore. You'll meet him soon. He's in Melbourne right now and will be leaving there to come back here. He's driving, so he'll be here in a few days." She gestured at an empty space on the counter of the Connaught café where Mr. Peagren used to have a cake display case. "He's gone to collect *la macchina*. It arrived a few days ago from *Roma*."

"*La macchina?*"

"Yes … I think you call it an espresso machine?"

"Oh," Robin said, softly, and nodded. He had no idea what an espresso machine might be, but he felt a quick trip to the reference room at work when he got back after lunch would be in order. The *Bullaroo*

Bulletin had the only two sets of *Encyclopaedia Britannicas* and *Encyclopaedia Americanas* this side of the Great Dividing Range.

*****

Ten days later, Robin called in for lunch at the Connaught, this time by himself, as Spud had picked up a day's labouring out at Mulwidgee Station.

It was a Wednesday, and he'd been thinking about Mrs. Barbano's *ravioli* ever since the weekend. However, the first thing to catch his eye as he walked in the door was a large, gleaming, silver contraption, sitting on the counter where the old cake display case used to be. It was the espresso machine—*la macchina*; he'd been fascinated to read all about it when he'd got back to work earlier the week before.

He'd also done a bit of homework and had sent a postal order to Angus and Robertson in George Street, in Sydney, ordering a mint copy of the pre-war Baedeker guide to Italy and a simple Italian grammar and phrase book. It was because he was inquisitive; he liked to learn new things. The whole "foreigner" thing was nonsense, he thought—if he ever went to their country, it'd be him who'd be the foreigner.

He ran his hand slowly over the side of the machine, listening carefully to the soft hiss of steam from the pressure valve—he loved contraptions that made things or manufactured things; especially if they seemed alive. Cautiously, after checking it wasn't too hot to touch, he laid his cheek against the outer casing and listened to the soft and gentle thrumming of the water in the internal boiler. It was alive; as alive as the steam train that he'd loved when he was a kid, and which he and Spud would wait for, standing on Bullaroo station at four thirty every afternoon when the Western Plains Express made its stop on its way down to Sydney.

"Is it telling you that it loves you?"

Robin swung around, startled.

A tall young man, perhaps five to ten years his senior, had been standing watching him, a tea towel over his shoulder, and a broad, toothy grin plastered across his face.

"You must be Errol," the man said, holding out his hand. He

pronounced it "Er-roll-ah", the last syllable a soft *schwa* rather than a clear "ah". Even in those four words, Robin could hear the odd combination of Italian cadence with American-shaped vowels.

"And you must be Ettore?"

"*Sì, certo; sono Ettore,*" the man replied. He'd smiled at Robin's correct pronunciation of his name. The rhythm like "factory", accented on the first syllable—Robin had practised getting it right.

They shook hands, both murmuring "*piacere*" at the same time, and then grinning at the coincidence.

Robin was lost in the moment—at the same time both surprised and transfixed. Ettore was nothing like he'd imagined. Instead of a short, round, and swarthy man like his father, he'd taken after his mother, who described herself as a "Venetian Blonde". He was tall, slim-waisted, and very broad-shouldered—a swimmer's build. He had dark, curly, well-cut hair, and long, thick black eyelashes, surrounding eyes of a colour Robin had never seen before. They were so pale blue they were the colour of the outback sky on a hot, cloudless summer day.

"Have I got something on my face?" Ettore asked, raising an eyebrow as he ran his hand across his chin, as if checking for stubble.

"No, sorry, I was being rude. Sorry for staring. I've just never seen anyone with your eyes before."

"Well, if you had done, that would mean I'd be blind? No?"

*****

A few months later, on a steamy Sunday October afternoon, Robin was lying on his bed, reading his Baedeker, and daydreaming about Ettore and Italian coffee.

He knew it was a stupid crush; nevertheless, he couldn't help himself.

Spud had become keen on a girl who'd come to work as the bookkeeper at the local garage, and often on Saturday nights Robin had fallen asleep waiting for the flashes on his bedroom wall that never came. Fergus was always there the next day with some lame excuse as to why he'd missed their regular rendezvous, and would arrange a what he not-so-subtly called "catch up root" somewhere, to make up for the night before. Robin was fairly sure Fergus didn't go "all the way" with the new arrival, it wasn't his style with girls—he was too muzzled and whip-tied by his church. More than likely, he'd been so aroused by his smooching that he'd simply shot in his pants, and therefore had crossed Robin off his list of "things to do".

Robin didn't really mind, especially since their deferred sexual encounters weren't powered by alcohol and therefore didn't involve the usual, tiresome fights afterwards.

So, on this particular October afternoon, while Robin daydreamed about Ettore—beating himself around the head and self-explaining that with everything he'd read about Italian men being natural flirts, Ettore's friendliness was only the natural expression of his cultural heritage and nothing more—he wasn't particularly surprised to hear the "toot-toot" of Spud's father's car.

"Errol …" his mother called out from downstairs. "Spud's here!"

He'd been lying on his back and sighed as he placed the opened book over his eyes. Even his mother couldn't call him by his real name.

He threw himself off his bed and stuck his head out of his bedroom window; the same window that he'd sneaked out of for years to have his midnight trysts with Spud, who was leaning against the bonnet of the FJ, lighting a smoke.

"Swim?" he called out to Robin.

"Sure thing."

It was a scorcher, and had not the leisure centre been closed since June for renovations, he would have already been there, lying in the shade of the poolside trees and ogling the strong, furry legs of the local men. He knew of the reputation of the changing room, but avoided it—apart from his relationship with Fergus, he didn't think of himself as someone who could engage in opportunistic fumbling in a public place. So, he knew that today they'd head to the river; to a spot about half-a-mile south of the new caravan park, along the highway on the road to Dubbo. No one ever went there these days, even with the sun hot enough to melt the tar on the road. All the locals went to an "enclosure" on the river, near the main road right in town, built as a temporary swimming place while the pool was being tarted up.

The Connaught

Not him and Spud though. The place they liked had a narrow track leading from the highway, down through the bush, ending in a small opening, big enough for the car and a small fire for a billy and a cuppa. It was very secluded, and they had often used it for daytime meetings when they had nowhere else to go. Today, Robin was feeling frisky. On the drive to the river, he couldn't stop visions of Spud's muscular, hairy backside flooding into his mind and what he was going to do to it.

"Sorry about last night," Spud began to say, sliding his hand over Robin's knee.

"It's fine, mate. Truly, it is," Robin replied, taking Spud's hand and guiding it to the aching erection in his pants. "Just put your foot down if you want some of this anytime soon."

Spud turned in the driver's seat and grinned at him.

"Too right, Errol. Just make sure you've got two rounds in the chamber, mate. It's been a while."

The car engine roared as Fergus O'Neill put his foot on the accelerator.

*****

They'd already had one session on the banks of the river, and now they both floated on their backs, Robin cradling Spud in his arms, the two of them drifting around in circles in the gentle eddies at the edge of the river.

Robin had been slowly twisting the hair on Fergus's belly, feeling contented and on the point of asking him if he was ready for another round, when Fergus did something unexpected. He rolled over in Robin's arms, so their bellies were pressed together, and then languidly slid his arms behind Robin's neck. For a brief moment, Fergus stared into his eyes, as if he was going to say something, and then changed his mind and did something that took Robin completely by surprise—he kissed him. It was a soft, warm, luscious kiss. It lasted for barely more than a heartbeat, and was quickly followed by a mumbled sorry and a soft chuckle. It shocked Robin; not the sorry, but the kiss and the simultaneous sighting, on the opposite bank of the river, of a tousled, black curly head—one which sported fashionable tortoiseshell sunglasses and a familiar, Italian grin.

Jesus! he thought. What the hell was Ettore doing there? It was all he could do not to jump four foot in the air with the surprise. But Fergus had another agenda; one that included his tongue and Robin's mouth. Robin didn't know which was the more surprising of the two: Ettore standing behind a tree on the other side of the river watching them with amusement, or Fergus's sudden and completely out-of-character, but intensely aroused, smooching.

To his own astonishment, Robin wasn't actually alarmed that he and Spud had been spied romping in the water by Ettore; in fact, he was strangely unconcerned about "being caught out". However, he did realise he had a snap decision to make. He could either distract Spud and get him out of the water and back to the car or he could go with the flow to see how the young Italian man reacted. As it turned out, the choice was not his to make, as Spud was well and truly on fire.

"Take as long as you like this time, eh?" he mumbled, kissing Robin again. Fergus manoeuvred Robin through the water, his arms still around his neck, steering him to where they'd left their towels on the riverbank. As soon as they bumped against the sandy bottom at the edge of the water, Spud jumped onto his feet, pulling Robin after him, and then turned, throwing himself onto his towel and sliding onto his back with his head towards the river, so that he was facing away from the opposite riverbank.

Robin could see Ettore over Spud's head, on the other side of the river. "Come on, Errol, time for round two," Fergus said, his voice barely a whisper. He lifted his knees and drew them apart, pulling Robin down to his mouth and onto his body. The jar of Vaseline was just within arm's reach, and Robin, feeling as if he was being controlled by a larger, external force, allowed Spud to take him in his hand, grease him up, and guide him in. He was so excited by the situation—Spud beneath him and the object of his daydreams not twenty yards away watching what they were doing—that he began to drool involuntarily and to tremble violently; his thighs and calf muscles shaking. He became aware that he was having his first "knee trembler". He couldn't remember ever feeling so sexually and emotionally aroused.

As he began to thrust, he could see the movement of Ettore's arm. The realisation that the Italian's hand, although out of sight, was doing what all men did, and was matching the rhythm of his own lunges, added another dimension to his lust. And then, when Fergus began to whine softly and pulled his head down to devour his mouth once more with his own, Robin felt something monumental fire up in his belly. It was a blazing fire; one which was so ferocious that it threatened to burn him to the bone.

Fleeting thoughts of "what the heck?" at the unexpected, but demanding kissing, evaporated as the heat grew in intensity in his groin. Knowing he couldn't last much longer, he lifted his head, to see what was happening on the other side of the river. Ettore had moved his sunglasses to the top of his head and, when he saw that Robin was looking at him, lifted the hand that had been playing with a nipple inside his shirt and gave Robin a broad, cheeky, white-toothed smile, accompanied by a thumbs up.

It pushed him over the edge, and, unable to tear his eyes away from Ettore, let forth with a string of obscenities, followed by several loud, guttural shouts.

Taken by surprise, Fergus called out, "No! No! Errol! Wait for me!"

Robin could feel Spud's hand working frantically; it was the first time in his recollection that they'd mistimed so badly. But seeing that the Italian's hand was working just as energetically as Spud's, he grabbed Fergus's buttocks and pulled his friend's hips upwards, taking Fergus into his mouth. His head bobbing frantically, he watched Ettore over the top of Spud's hairy belly, and exactly at the same time as the Italian's body stiffened and jerked with his ejaculation, Fergus cried out loudly and unloaded down the back of his throat.

For a few seconds, exhausted, and panting, Fergus's knees still over his shoulders, he nuzzled what he called the "y-joint"—the area between his friend's scrotum and his thigh—he loved the warm, fuzzy angle of flesh, with its gentle, musky odour.

When he glanced up again, Ettore had disappeared.

Robin smiled, more to himself than anything. He knew exactly what he'd been doing while he took care of Fergus so publicly and in such a wanton manner—he'd been putting on a show to help Ettore bring himself off.

"C'mere," Fergus growled, lowering his backside onto the ground and pulling Robin's head down to his own. This time the kiss was not lust-driven and more than a quick "how's your father"; it was lingering, voluptuous, and devouring. Had Robin not known better, he might have even called it loving.

"What's going on, Spud?" he asked, so quietly that the words barely came out.

Fergus raised himself onto one elbow and twisted his body, craning over his shoulder. "Did he watch?" he asked.

Robin was gobsmacked. "You knew?"

Spud nodded. "Didn't you wonder for a second how the hell he'd even know about this place, Errol?"

"I don't understand …"

"Call it an early Christmas present. You're so fucking timid that you'd be waiting until the 'next of whenever' to make a move. I just moved things along for you."

"How did you even know that he—" Robin stopped, mid-sentence. All of a sudden, some of the Saturday nights when Spud hadn't shown up seemed to make sense.

Fergus chortled at his distraught expression. "Don't worry, Errol. It's you he's into; not me."

"Oh God, Fergus." Robin threw himself onto his back and covered his eyes with his forearm. He didn't know whether to thank his friend or throw him a right hook.

"I enjoyed that," Fergus said, after what seemed an age of silence.

"What?" Robin mumbled.

"The kissing."

"Jesus, Spud! Don't do this to me! Not now! Don't tell me it's taken Ettore for you to open up to me like that?"

"Don't blaspheme, Errol. You can say fuck as much as you want, but don't take the Lord's name in vain. You know I don't like it."

There was no rejoinder for that. It was true. Although they both swore like troopers, Fergus got very upset when Robin blasphemed.

Robin sat up quickly, leaned over, and kissed Spud again. Although he laughed against his mouth, Fergus opened his lips and began to spar with gentle, languid swipes of his tongue.

"Why now?" Robin asked. The kissing was truly beautiful.

"Because I know you've always wanted it, and I'm pretty sure you're going to move on. I wanted it to be special today."

"What? You think me and Ettore …?" Even Robin could hear the longing in his own voice.

"Yeah, you're made for each other. You're the only one who can't see the way you look at each other. He only rooted me to find out more about you."

Robin didn't know whether to be jealous or furious. He punched Spud in the ribs. Not hard, just enough to show he was peeved. "You rotten—"

"Ow!" Spud said, with mock-hurt, and then coughed, sat up, and put one arm around Robin, tousling his hair with the other hand.

Robin groaned and put his head in his hands.

"Besides, there was another reason for the smooching."

"Go on."

"You know I don't mind it when we're … you know. But I needed to be sure."

"Sure about what?"

"Sure that it was just sex and nothing … you know."

"You know you're saying 'you know' too often for my liking."

Spud sighed, and then, for the first time since he'd known him, Robin saw the start of something really painful in his mate's eyes.

"You'd better tell me why, Fergus. I don't know why it's so hard …"

There was a very good reason Spud was unable to speak; it was something that had a relentless grip on his mortal soul, and something he knew he'd never be able to be truly honest about—aloud that was. He'd rather hoped Robin would have picked up on it without him having to man up—after all, they'd been best pals all of their lives.

Fergus "Spud" O'Neill really loved Robin; he *really* loved him. He'd convinced himself that he wasn't in love with him, and most likely never would be. Robin deserved someone who could go the full mile, and Spud had long ago told himself he was not going to be the person who could supply Robin's needs—he could scarcely admit the real truth to himself. So, instead of using the perfect opportunity to confess what had been going on in his heart, he did what all Aussie blokes would do under the circumstances—he talked about the *other* thing on his mind.

With a quick movement of the back of his hand, he wiped his eyes—not that he'd ever admit there was something to wipe away.

"Hey, Fergus," Robin whispered, much moved. "I'm your mate; you can talk to me. I don't understand why you're so upset."

"Because, Errol, as much as I love what we do and I'm going to miss it, it's time for me to settle down."

"What the hell are you saying, Fergus?"

"Me and Jeannie. I'll be as happy with her as I would be with anyone. And, if I'm going to get married, now's a good a time as any."

On the drive back home, Robin was so overwhelmed that all he could do was nod, dumbly. Fergus explained that he'd hooked up with Ettore in the pub one night. In fact, it had been the Italian who'd sought him out, pumping him for information about Robin. The flirting had turned into something else after Spud had asked what it was worth to answer Ettore's questions about his mate, Errol. In fact, there'd been no actual fucking, or kissing; it had only been a face-to-face, yard-apart, masturbation session, each man taking care of himself, looking at what the other one held in his hand. Ettore really only had eyes for Robin; but he was an Italian, and the opportunity had presented itself, and Spud was muscled and handsome …

As for Jeannie and the marriage, Fergus was under unbearable pressure from his family and his religious community to settle down with some girl. He wasn't strong enough to put up with the eternal visits from the local priest and the constant badgering from his parents, so had decided to ask the new accountant at the garage whether she'd tie the knot with him. She seemed keen enough.

To Robin's misgivings, he shrugged. "I'll miss my regular dose of this," he'd said, running the flat of his hand down over Robin's belly to cup his private parts through his jeans. "I dunno … I suppose I'll get used to it."

It was all Robin could do to not grab his friend by the shoulders and shake him, to tell him that getting married would be the biggest mistake of his life.

*****

Fergus dropped Robin off and then parked his car on the ridge of the hill behind the McLaughlin farm, where he so often had waited on Saturday nights.

It was all he could do not to cry. It had taken a monumental effort to appear calm and decisive during their trip back from the river, to hold back tears, and to make himself wait until he got home so that he could take ownership of the pain in his heart. It was a terrible sacrifice to let go of a mate, even if it was to give that mate a chance to be happier with someone else than he could make him.

He sat silently, his hands gripped the steering wheel of his dad's beloved FJ Holden, his knuckles white, and his forehead pressed hard against the topmost arch of the wheel.

"Fucking church!" he shouted, banging his head against the steering wheel, time and time again, cursing his inability to escape what he saw was his inevitable fate—pressed into a marriage he really didn't want, and with the thought of finding himself at fifty, fat, with a family, and nothing for himself.

Finally, he'd banged his head so much that it began to hurt like buggery, so he stopped and began to sob into his hands, only stopping when his heart felt numb and empty. He turned the key in the ignition and drove home, although the road ahead seemed unconscionably blurry.

"It's not fucking fair!" he shouted.

Despite his ferocious and determined attempt to hold them at bay, tears streamed down his cheeks, and dripped onto his shirtfront.

*****

On the following Friday, Robin was a little taken aback when Eileen, the receptionist at the *Bulletin*, came to fetch him. A lady was at the counter asking after him.

His pace slowed as he opened the office door and walked into reception. It was Grazia, from the Connaught. For a moment, his heart leaped into his throat, but then Mrs. Barbano's gentle smile made him settle. He'd thought for a moment that somehow she'd heard about last Sunday.

However, she'd come to place an advertisement in the newspaper and at the same time told Robin that she and her husband had had a doctor's appointment that morning, so she hadn't been able to make *i ravioli*. But, she told him that Ettore was expecting him for lunch and had prepared something special; something he'd never had before. She and her husband were taking the afternoon off, leaving Ettore and Silvia to man the café.

Just after midday, Robin ducked into the Connaught, waving hello to Spud and Jeannie, who were sitting halfway down the café in a booth. Spud looked uncomfortable and waved forlornly at him; Robin grinned and gave him a thumbs up and a wink. Silvia was behind the counter, but Ettore was nowhere to be seen.

"Hey, Silvia, how goes it?"

"Not too bad, Errol. How about you?"

"Yeah, I'm okay. Where's the big fella?"

"He's gone out the back to get stuff out of the fridge for your friends' lunch," she replied, nodding in Spud and Jeannie's direction. A moment later, Ettore appeared, carrying a covered enamel tray.

"I'll put these on, Silvia," he said. "Could you pop out and see that the other stuff doesn't burn?"

"Sure," she said, and then disappeared into the back of the café.

"What's out there?" Robin asked.

"Our lunch," Ettore replied.

Robin finally looked up. He'd avoided Ettore's eyes, mainly because he didn't know what to feel or to expect. The last time he'd seen him, they'd shared a climax; their eyes had locked, separated by twenty yards of gently flowing river water.

"*Ciao, bello,*" Ettore whispered, his cheeks a soft shade of crimson.

"Hello, handsome," Robin replied, echoing the Italian, but in English. He couldn't believe how daring he'd been—saying those two words. Still, he covered it with a wink, so it could be interpreted as a joke, just in case things really weren't as they seemed.

Ettore smiled and then removed the lid from the enamel pan. Robin leaned over the counter to see what he was doing.

"Battered sav and chips, and sausages and chips," Ettore explained. It was obviously Spud and Jeannie's lunch order. "Disgusting," he added, holding the end of the saveloy between his finger and thumb. It drooped onto his fist; he flicked the end with the forefinger of his other hand, bouncing it back and forth. "The saveloy's for her," he said, throwing a quick glance in Jeannie's direction. He winked at Robin, who coloured ferociously. There was no mistaking the innuendo. Fergus did have a long, thin penis.

Ettore threw the bright-orange, slender sausage into a container of batter, and then said, "However, this is more what *he's* used to." He picked out three, fat, Australian beef sausages, and held them bunched in his hand, still grinning as he held Robin's gaze. "Your pal really likes Australian sausage, so I noticed?"

"There's three of them," Robin said, unable to maintain a straight face for a moment longer.

"Well, I was a fair distance away …" Ettore said, with a wink. "But it looks about the right thickness."

They both chuckled; one more than the other.

It was another reason Robin had been saddled with his nickname; Errol Flynn was rumoured to be in possession of an unnaturally mighty member. Nature had been generous with Robin; it was something all the young people in Bullaroo seemed to know. Shower room gossip had worked its way through the community.

Their laughter dissolved into something else. The ice had been broken, the subject of last week's opportunistic encounter done and dusted … for the moment.

Robin felt slightly embarrassed; aware that their eyes were locked and they were smiling at each other in a very public place. It was true. Now that Spud had told him, there was no mistaking Ettore's interest. He just hadn't accepted it before. Something leaped in his chest and he became aware that he'd stopped breathing.

"What are you thinking … Robin?" Ettore's voice was very soft.

Robin's heart caught in his chest. He wasn't used to such intimacy. He was unable to say what he really wanted to say—something from the heart. He had to break the moment, and being coarse and vaguely inappropriate was the Aussie country boy way. "I was wondering what Italian sausages were like. I've never had any before."

To his relief, Ettore covered his mouth with a tea towel and roared his approval into it with loud, unrestrained laughter.

Robin drummed his fingers on the countertop; pleased as punch with himself and with the Italian's reaction. It had been the right thing to say. He knew, at that moment, that there would be plenty of time for "sweet nothings". Now it was about finding the way to get from here, right now, to that place, sometime in the future, which he hoped would not be too far away.

"Silvia!" Ettore called out, to the back of the shop, and then threw two portions of chips into a frying basket, lowered it into the hot fat of the fryer, and then gently placed Spud's three sausages onto the griddle. "Everything's ready to go," he said to Silvia, once she'd joined him behind the counter. "Sav's in the batter."

Robin followed him to the back of the café, where Ettore opened a pass hatch to allow Robin to move into the private quarters at the back of the milk bar. The smells were delicious.

"What can I smell?"

"Italian sausage," Ettore replied. "No, really! *Non ti prendo in giro!* I made them myself this morning. Mama said I should give you something special. I thought that I'd like to give you my Italian sausage."

Robin leaned against a kitchen chair, watching Ettore prod half a dozen large, dark-brown shapes in a frying pan. "I suppose you've been thinking that one up all morning," Robin said, trying not to look too cheeky, despite what was going on in his mind.

"*Ecco,*" Ettore said. He speared one sausage in the pan with a fork, and then, after moving closer to Robin, so they were nearly touching, blew on one end, and held it up to Robin.

"*Dai … assaggiare un pochino!* Taste …"

Robin lifted his hand to take the sausage from the fork, but Ettore stopped his hand, and mimed that he should open his mouth and allow the Italian to feed it to him.

It was one of those moments that he instinctively knew he would never forget. Robin flicked his gaze between Ettore's slightly trembling hand and the end of the sausage as it neared his lips. He could feel Ettore's breath flow into his open mouth, along and over the gleaming, luscious-looking sausage as Ettore blew on it gently, to cool it. As it hovered, perhaps half an inch from his lips, Robin instinctively licked them, and then reached out and ran his hand over Ettore's arm, from wrist to elbow, drawing them closer to each other.

The movement of Robin's hand caused them to look away from the sausage and into each other's eyes. Dark brown staring into pale, crystal blue. It was a questioning and tentative gaze, one that threatened to break on the merest of external disruptions. Robin could almost hear his heart beating, echoing around the room.

"Well?" Ettore murmured. His voice rumbled in his chest. "Ready?"

"I don't think I've ever felt less ready for anything in my life," Robin answered, his voice mere breath.

All at once, the sausage fell between them and the fork clattered onto the floor as he pulled Ettore to him and kissed him deeply.

It was at once the hardest and easiest thing he had ever done.

★★★★★

Almost three years to the day later, Robin stood on the station platform in Sydney, waiting for Ettore to arrive on the evening train from Bullaroo.

Robin had landed a job as a junior political reporter for the *Sydney Morning Herald*, an opportunity too good to refuse. Fortunately, the train trip from home to the capital city took just over three hours, so it was easy for them to spend weekends together. For the two years before he'd left to go to Sydney, they were joined at the hip, Robin happier than he thought it ever possible to be, and Ettore desperately in love with his Australian—attentive, gentle, and romantic on a scale that Robin had never even imagined.

A special job prospect had precipitated Ettore's arrival. With the opening of a new stretch of highway, the eastern coastal road now stretched unbroken as far as Cairns in northern Queensland. No one had wanted the job as a "travel writer", however with the promise of six weeks' paid time away from the office, Robin had jumped at the chance, especially after Ettore had arranged time off too, to travel with Robin, and ostensibly to visit relatives who'd settled as cane farmers in the far north.

"A hired, open-top Caravelle convertible, accommodation in the best available, a food and petrol allowance, and six weeks of Ettore, day and night," Robin heard himself thinking, almost aloud, as the diesel locomotive sounded its horn on its approach, halfway between Redfern and Central stations.

He couldn't help remembering how much he'd missed the arrival of a steam engine on a railway station platform. It was a real occasion—theatrical in its grandeur. Thick black smoke belching from the chimney, the squeal of brakes, and the laboured chuffing of the engine as it shuddered to a halt, shrouded in a cloud of steam. It wasn't the same to see the yellow-decaled, brown locomotive slip, almost silently, to the buffers at the terminus of the rail lines.

"The six forty-five service from Cobar, via Nyngan, Dubbo, Bullaroo, and thence Orange, has just arrived on platform six. Passengers are advised that the service terminates here. Welcome to Sydney Central."

He was nervous—the sort of nervous that combined excited and happy. He was looking forward to a road trip with Ettore to the tropics; the first extended time they'd had together alone in three years. And in the wind, there was also the prospect of something very special—a plan he'd been hatching for some time now, and this holiday seemed the best time to share his idea with the man he loved.

He didn't enjoy political reporting very much. However, the idea of writing about travel excited him. He'd made a proposal to his editor-in-chief, who'd seemed very—no, more than very—interested. The Flotta Lauro Lines' *TN Sydney* was due to be replaced by the *TN Surriento* in six months from now, and her final voyage back to Italy was due to be a special cruise, via Asia, India, around the Cape (rather than her usual Suez route), and arriving in the Mediterranean through the

The Connaught

Strait of Gibraltar. Robin had proposed that he pay for half of the ticket, wiring regular travel articles along the way about life aboard ship, and the exotic ports that the *Sydney* visited. He'd also suggested that once he arrived, he'd spend two months in Italy, sending back a weekly travelogue for the Saturday edition of the newspaper.

The editor-in-chief had not said no, despite his obvious excitement at the idea, and the look of avarice in his eyes when Robin had mentioned paying for half of the trip himself made Robin think it was almost in the bag—although he knew in the back of his mind that with negotiation, he'd wangle something that would end up with getting the newspaper to fund the entire journey.

Of course, Robin had thought, the whole shebang would be so much nicer with a travel companion. A travel companion who not only spoke the language but also knew the country. Said companion's dark, tousled hair, and bright, loving smile had just appeared at the back of the stream of passengers alighting from the Western Plains Express, and was making his way through the crowd towards Robin.

"*Ciao, bello,*" Ettore said, throwing his arms around Robin, despite the flow of people around them.

They hugged, slapping each other's backs, as any close pals might do after not seeing each other for a while. It was 1962 after all, and times had changed a little. People cared less about what went on, as long as it wasn't too overt, that was.

"*Quanto mi ami?*" Robin whispered into Ettore's ear as they embraced.

"How much do I love you?" Ettore whispered back, and then added, "*Ti amo fino alla fine del mondo.*"

"I don't need to the end of the world, Ettore," Robin replied. "Just to Naples will do."

"*Napoli?* Why Naples? I don't understand."

"It has to do with sausages."

"What kind of sausages?"

"Oh, Australian and Italian sausages. The best combination there is. The mixture is a recipe made in heaven."

"You are *pazzo*, Robin. Have I ever told you that?"

"No, but you will do when I tell you about a cross-culture sausage story set in Italy …"

"*Non ho capito. Ma, va bene. Andiamo.*"

Non ho capito—I don't understand. Maybe Ettore didn't understand, but when Robin had seen the love in his man's eyes as he'd spied Robin after getting off the train, he knew that after a bit of perseverance and some tender cajoling, he'd be able to send the telegram he'd been writing in his head to his boss at the *Herald*.

"THE AGE IN MELBOURNE HAS MADE A COUNTEROFFER. THEY MAY BE PREPARED TO FUND THE ENTIRE TRIP. I CAN BOOK MY ITALIAN TRIP FROM THE LAURO OFFICE IN BRISBANE. PLEASE ADVISE YES OR NO. REGARDS MCLAUGHLIN"

He knew it would be a cert. The rivalry between the newspapers was legendary; who knew, perhaps the *Age* might already be thinking about the proposal he'd posted to them last week. It wasn't often that a reporter offered to pay half of his own expenses on a world trip.

Maybe he and Ettore would never come back from Italy?

Maybe that was his plan.

Charlie and Me

I knew he was an American before he even opened his mouth.

It wasn't the blond crewcut, or the aviator glasses. It was his togs that gave him away. Canary-yellow, short shorts splattered with palm trees, leis, hula dancers, and pineapples. He sported a large-linked silver chain on his right wrist and a watch on the other—remarkable for its leather face-cover. I hadn't seen one of those for years.

He'd been lying on the beach on his stomach, reading. Every so often he'd glanced up from his book and given me the briefest of smiles before turning his head to look at the surf. I'd guessed he was staying at one of the large nearby hotels—the Oceanic, or the Coogee Bay—his towel was a giveaway, dark blue with white initials at the corner that I couldn't quite make out due to the angle at which I was lying.

It was the last week in January of 1966, not quite a month since my eighteenth birthday, and I'd come to Sydney for a treat. A concert with my uncle, with whom I was sharing a suite at the Australia Hotel in the city, a few days on the beach by myself, and time away from the bush while I waited until the March intake. I'd sat my exams, done my physicals, and in just over two months, I'd be packing my bag and heading off to Canberra, to the Royal Military College, Duntroon, to start my training at officer's school.

I'd not been disappointed when my number hadn't come up in the national service lottery—I'd already decided on a career in the army. I'd been relieved in fact; happy I'd been allowed a choice on how I would serve and in what capacity. It was in my bones to lead—captain in the army cadets at school and high marks in a choice of subjects that almost guaranteed acceptance for officer training. I'd no real idea why I was so desperate to enlist—perhaps it was because my dad had been a soldier, and my Uncle Patrick had also fought in the last big war. Whatever was driving me also made me not want to become one of the rank and file—hence my relief when I hadn't been called up. I'd long ago come to the conclusion there may have been an element of hubris involved, but I'd also argued I had the sort of mind that loved taking charge, solving problems, and doing it quickly and nearly always successfully too.

I'd only had one misgiving, and I supposed my time by myself on a popular Sydney beach was a litmus test for me.

It was really hot now, so I thought it was time to throw myself in the waves. I stood, brushed the sand off my thighs, and raised both arms above my head, clasping my hands together, and stretched back. The man was staring at me; he caught my eye briefly before I saw his gaze flick down to my speedos, and then he buried his head in his book again. I smiled and walked down to the water.

"You a local?" he asked, perhaps two minutes later. I smiled at his movie-star accent.

"Who's asking?" I said, cheekily.

"Charlie," he replied, holding out his hand. "Charlie Howson."

"Tony." I shook his.

"Tony who?" His smile was broad, toothy, and amazingly white.

"Actually, it's Anthony, but no one calls me that. My name's Anthony Fletcher." I explained. "And no, to answer your question, I'm not local. I'm from the country."

"What brings you to Coogee?"

I smiled at his pronunciation, with a long "oo"; we said the word with a short "u" the same sound as in "put".

He'd joined me, as I'd rather hoped he would, standing ankle-deep at the edge of the water. I'd waited, arms crossed, staring over the water at Wedding Cake Island, watching the breakers, and wondering idly exactly how far away it was and whether I could swim there. I tried to be as nonchalant as I could when I felt him arrive at my side.

"R & R?" I replied to his question with one of my own. As he wasn't wearing dog tags, I supposed, like other Americans, he wanted a bit of incognito time and had left them in the hotel safe.

"Coogee?"

I laughed—he wasn't to be distracted. "It's my coming of age present to myself," I said. "A week away from home before I head off to military school."

He whistled softly. "You look older."

"R & R?"

"How'd you guess?"

"You're the only bastard on the beach who looks like Pat Boone," I said, with a grin. "Coming?" I added, and then, without waiting for a reply, ran into the waves and threw myself under and through the first big breaker.

He surfaced next to me, running both hands through his hair as his head appeared above the water. He struck out, swimming powerfully through the waves—I followed, knowing it was his way of mimicking what I'd just done by waiting for him to join me at the shoreline. A hundred yards out, we turned on our backs and faced the beach, floating, waving our arms slowly through the water.

"Yes, 'Rest and Recuperation'—two weeks of it." I knew better than to pry. I'd been brought up surrounded by men who never talked about their service. However, he was the first I'd met as a grown-up who was actually on active service. I was dying to ask him questions, but knew it was probably the last thing he'd ever want to talk about. "Four more days and then it's back to …" He made a gesture with one hand in the air.

"Air force then?"

He nodded. "When I said older, I thought you were my age."

"How old are you?" I asked.

"Twenty-three; and you?"

"Eighteen and three weeks," I replied. "Does it matter?"

He looked at me oddly, but didn't reply. "Can you drink at eighteen in this country?"

"Yes."

"Do you?"

"Like a fish," I replied. "Why?"

"Fancy a bite to eat and a beer?"

"Sure."

"I've been here for over a week and I've done the Harbour Bridge, the zoo, the art gallery, the museum, as much as there is to see, but I'll be danged if I've actually sat down and talked to an Aussie."

"Aussie," I said, pronouncing it with a "z" and not as he did, with an "s". "Well, I'd love to shout you a beer. As you're a guest in the country, let me buy you lunch too. Where you staying?"

"Coogee Bay Hotel," he replied.

"It's got a reputation."

"For?"

"It's well known as a pick-up place."

He snorted. "I'm not into that sort of thing."

"What sort of thing?"

"Picking up random women."

I tried to read his eyes, but had no vocabulary for what I saw there. My litmus paper was dry—maybe I was barking up the wrong tree—I honestly had never been this far before. But then, he placed a hand on my shoulder. "Last one to shore is a rotten egg."

I hadn't heard such an old-fashioned phrase since I was about six years old. However, it somehow sat well on his short-cropped blond hair, and white, toothy smile. I followed him towards the beach, doing my best to let him get there first, so I could get an eyeful of his broad shoulders and the way his muscles rippled across his back and arse as he swam.

*****

An hour later, I was sitting on the edge of his bed in his hotel room, a towel around my waist, and jiggling my knee nervously.

Here I was, my heart in my throat, with perhaps an unexpected opportunity and I didn't know what to do. When I'd told him I would meet him in the bar of his hotel after I'd changed, he'd invited me back to his room rather than using the public facilities. He'd argued that he needed to rinse off and change before lunch too. We'd shyly stripped off in front of each other—he'd turned his back as he'd let his cossies fall onto his feet—and then he'd headed off into the bathroom, leaving the door half-open. I didn't know what to do, I said to myself for the second time in about as many seconds—it was like a mantra of indecision—even more agitated after seeing a naked man for the first time in my life at such a close distance.

It was all I could do not to reach out and touch him, but he'd gone before the thought had crossed my mind.

Through the partially opened bathroom door, I could hear the shower running, and splashes that interrupted it. I closed my eyes and imagined him turning his lightly tanned body under the running water, rubbing his hands over his skin. I could barely swallow, my mouth was so dry, and my chest heaved with shallow, rapid breaths.

I knew what I wanted; I had done since I was about fifteen, but too terrified to do anything about it. I'd told myself I'd wait until I was eighteen, and then to give it a go, in case it was a phase I'd been going through.

Now, as I sat, my heart in my mouth and my guts gripped into a spasm of anxiety, I was bolted to the bed.

He'd left the door open; it had to be some sort of signal. He started to hum softly. It was clear enough even over the sound of the running water and it broke through my indecision—"The Touch of Your Lips", a Pat Boone song from '64. I wasn't so stupid I couldn't put two and two together, and guessed he remembered I'd said I thought he looked like the singer. I put on my "in charge" brain and tried to imagine how I'd be feeling if it had been me in his situation. An older army guy, on R & R, naked, in a foreign country, in a hotel room with an eighteen-year-old who he'd picked up on the beach? Maybe he was worried I was a trap? A honeytrap they called it spy novels. Perhaps he was as nervous as I was—he had more to lose than I did, that was for sure. However, as he'd left the bathroom door open, I decided he'd been waiting for me to make the first move. So, I stood, dropped my towel, and with my half-erect dick swinging, walked into the bathroom.

He'd a soapy washcloth in one hand and was washing an armpit, his arm bent over his head, and his eyes closed while he hummed. The showerhead was over an old-fashioned white enamel bathtub, with a pale-blue shower curtain that had partially stuck to his leg while he was washing himself.

As I stepped into the bath, I started to hum along with him. It gave him a bit of a start—he opened his eyes wide, and gasped a little, perhaps surprised I'd turned up right next to him without actually having heard me come into the bathroom.

"Give me that," I said.

"What, this?" he asked, holding up the washcloth.

"No this," I said. I reached down and ran my hand over his hip, and then around his penis, which was, like mine, standing up hard against his belly.

"I …"

"No, stop," I said. "I've never done this before, and if you say something, Charlie, I might just chicken out. And, in case you're worried, mate … this is no set up. I can't tell you how much I want this."

There's a look between people; one I'd seen in the movies. I called it the "questioning, waiting for permission" look: gazes locked, eyes flicking from side to side, trying to examine what the other person is thinking and whether it's safe to kiss. It's a combination of confusion, apprehension, and desire. I recognised it, just never imagined I'd get a chance to feel it myself—except for now, when it felt as real as anything could be. He looked so frightened—I wondered if I did too.

"Please be gentle," he said.

I couldn't believe it. Surely I was the inexperienced one here?

"I will, if you will," was all I could come up with. He leaned forward and kissed me, and as my mouth opened under his, my knees went weak, and I leaned against his body. It wasn't a romantic blast—it was just the wetness and warmth of his kiss was so intensely stimulating. I wound my arms around him and pulled him tight against me.

It was over before it started to be honest. Ten minutes later we were sitting on the edge of the bath, side by side, the shower still running behind us, both smoking a cigarette. We were both still hard—I found myself torn in the anxiety of managing the rotation of quick glances. Eyes, mouth, penis …

"Wow!" It was the first thing he'd said since he'd ground his body against mine and then collapsed against me as he came. The warmth of his ejaculation had brought me off too, and I'd continued to kiss him while idly running my soapy hands over his back and arse, until he'd decided to go get his smokes.

I smiled at him, barely turning my head, and hoping my smile told him I'd liked it too.

"First time, Tony?"

"Indeed ... Charlie. You?"

"Uh-huh."

We sat silently for a while, and then he ran his hand over my knee. "There's got to be more to it than that?"

"Yeah," I heard myself saying. "I know what I'd like to try; just warn me if you don't like it."

"Holy Mother of God," he whispered, as I slipped off the edge of the bath, moved his knees apart with both hands, and took him in my mouth.

"Teeth!" he said, almost immediately.

"Sorry," I mumbled, and then somehow and inexplicably, I knew how it should go.

*****

"You got home late last night. You could have woken me."

"I left a message with the concierge, didn't you get it?"

My Uncle Patrick had been staring at me oddly since I joined him for breakfast. He kept glancing at my chin, which was still red with beard rash. My inexpert "blow job", as Charlie had called it, had got better over the evening with practice—I was amazed at how much I really loved doing it. He'd also been keen, and had gone crazy on me down there when we'd returned to his room after dinner, and I'd suggested he swivel on the bed and we try what my mate Harry called the "double gobble". I'd always taken the descriptions of Harry's sexual adventures with his girlfriend Charlene with a grain of salt. She seemed way too straight-laced to get up to the things he'd described them as doing.

I'd felt something akin to power as I'd brought Charlie to orgasm—he'd not allowed me to withdraw at the point of mine, which arrived a split second after he'd ejaculated into my mouth, instead he'd grabbed my arse cheeks with both hands and urged me to do the same. We'd lain together for an age afterwards, panting, and then when we'd settled, we'd both chuckled softly—as it if was something remarkable that we'd done. It was all I could do to drag myself away, get dressed, and leave. My uncle would never have understood a phone call from me telling him I'd be home in the morning.

"So you had a good time at the beach?"

I couldn't help myself; my face went red. I felt the heat growing up my neck and flooding over my cheeks.

"Yes, Patrick, I did—thank you."

"And ..."

"And what?"

He leaned back in his seat and folded his arms, waiting for me to speak.

"Can we talk about this when we get home, please?" I wasn't ready for this conversation; not now, when I'd planned to meet Charlie again tomorrow night.

"Very well. I've never pushed you, Tony. But I hope that as well as being like a father to you, I've been a friend. You can talk about anything you wish ... as I would with you."

I stopped, my fork mid-air, a half-rasher of bacon and a whallop of fried egg impaled on its tines.

"I'll tell you everything, Patrick," I said. "However, tit for tat? Seeing you've just offered to be as open with me, I'll expect to hear all about that photo of you and Derrick Finsome on your dressing table, and Michael Passdale's regular Tuesday and Thursday late, hour-long appointments in your office after your receptionist has gone home."

"Oh ..." he said.

"Yes, Patrick. I may only be eighteen, but I'm not stupid."

He sat quietly for a moment, and then began to eat again, this time slowly. I knew he was measuring his words.

"I've nothing to hide, Tony. Nothing at all. I come from a different age; there are some things we don't offer up without some reluctance— I know it's fusty and old-fashioned, but it's the way I was brought up.

However, as you say, you're eighteen and you're not stupid; my 'oh', was more about what's behind you wanting to 'wait until we get home to talk'. A tit for tat around our private lives makes me feel you're going to tell me less about 'tit' and more about 'tat'."

He'd a way with words that I loved.

"When we get home to Bullaroo, please? I need to sort things out in my head first."

"Understood, Tony. I suppose it's a man-to-man that's been a while in the coming."

"It's not the only thing that's been a while in the coming, Patrick—and at the moment, I'm still basking in the afterglow. Now, can we talk about the concert tonight?"

His jaw dropped at my less-than-subtle play on words, covering his mouth and laughing into his napkin. Although he may have been worried, his eyes only radiated love and acceptance. Perhaps I had grown up more than I thought I had.

*****

My Uncle Patrick had brought me up after my parents had died.

First my mother—something had given way in her brain while she was cooking dinner. One moment she was speaking, the next she lay dead on the kitchen floor. I only had vague memories of it, as I was only three at the time. Then, two years later, my dad took his own life. He'd come back from the war, having survived the horror of Kokoda, to find his father had died, and his brother, my Uncle Patrick, missing—his plane having gone down over Germany in '42, at around the same time Dad had been fighting the Japs "up to his armpits in mud". He'd always said he'd no longer been the man he was when he went away—Mum's sudden and inexplicable death had pushed him over the edge.

My parents had moved to Condoblin in '46, the year before I was born, and my uncle had joined them three years later, closing down the Bullaroo surgery and putting a locum in the hospital. He'd bought into a practice to be near his brother, sister-in-law, and me, his young nephew, the only family he had left. It was a good living; a busy surgery with a small medical facility attached, not unlike the one he'd left behind. Mum and Dad came to work with him, and we all lived together.

My mum's parents lived in the big house, "Mulwidgee", just outside of Bullaroo, but they were overseas with my Great-Uncle Arthur when Dad shot himself. It took them nearly two months to get back home—unable to get passage for two weeks and then six weeks at sea. They'd offered to take me back with them and look after me, but Dad had left a letter saying he wanted his brother to bring me up.

Still, Uncle Patrick had sold up the Condoblin practice and moved back to Bullaroo, reopened his father's surgery, and settled down where he'd grown up, with his sister-in-law's parents close at hand to help with my raising.

I'd grown up with four "fathers". The first was my own dad, Lawrence; the second, his brother, my Uncle Patrick. Then there was Grandpa Emerson, my mother's father; and finally my Great-Uncle Arthur, my grandmother's brother, all of whom seemed to constantly be wagging their fingers at my grandma and saying, "Hold on, Edith; don't spoil the boy!"

Having said that, and in spite of their own admonitions, they all had, and I loved my grandma and every one of those men for it.

*****

I felt proud to be at my uncle's side.

The concert was a vice-regal affair, the culmination of an Australia-wide tour by one of our "boys made good". Uncle Patrick wore tails, as did many other of the male members of the audience— on his chest, his rows of ribbons and bars with their miniature medals attached. I wore the first tuxedo of my life—a snazzy, modern suit, with narrow, silk-ribbon edged lapels, and a waistcoat. We'd hired it from George's, the men's shop underneath the Australia Hotel, where we'd been staying.

The evening contained a double bonus, as Uncle Patrick had promised to take me backstage after the performance. I had no idea how he knew him; however, it seemed that he and Sir Thomas Haupner were pals from the war.

When the famous violinist strode onto the stage and shook hands with the conductor, before bowing to the audience, I was already in a world of awe. In my eyes, both men seemed as handsome as gods—Sir Thomas tall and blond, and Dean Dixon, the conductor, dark-skinned and elegant. I was entranced before the first note. The concert had been billed as an evening of "Love and War", based on one that Sir Thomas had performed in Carnegie Hall during the last war, and then had repeated countless times around the world thereafter. I knew there had to be a story behind why this particular combination of concerti had been performed so often by him, and wondered if I'd ever get the chance to find out.

I'd never even heard of the composer of the first concerto—Wieniawski. It was his first violin concerto in F sharp minor, and the programme notes stated it was one of the few concerti that was considered perilous, except to a few extremely gifted players, the preserve of the very few brave enough to attempt it. The second half of the concert was more familiar territory to me, Tchaikovsky—I knew the violin concerto back to front from one of Uncle Patrick's recordings with Sir Thomas as the soloist and Bruno Walter conducting.

After two encores, I was worn out, both physically by clapping, and emotionally from the world that we'd just left—two hours of the best evening I'd had in my life. Music had always moved me, and tonight, my emotions running high, I felt paralysed with a combination of pleasure and bewilderment—a confusion born from being so emotionally ravaged by something that was so intangible and yet so profoundly affecting. More than once during the concert, I'd had to either wipe the tears from my eyes, or grasp my uncle's hand.

And yet, later, in the dressing room, Sir Thomas was all blokey and very Australian—almost ocker—quite unlike what I'd expected. He'd grabbed my uncle in a huge bear hug, both of them slapping each other's backs and in tears—however, that was not the first of the surprises, for when they spoke it was in rapidly delivered, fluent-sounding German. I'd known my uncle for all of my life and never suspected that he had more than a passing knowledge of the language. It was astounding how incredibly familiar they were with each other—Sir Thomas' "better half", as he'd introduced Heinrich Reiter, a tall ginger-blond with a striking American accent, had even played "Paddy Whack" on my uncle's wooden leg, before lifting him into his arms and twirling him around.

I must have looked a sight, as all three seemed to simultaneously notice that I was still in the room gawking at them.

I was about to congratulate the famous violinist, when his friend stepped forward and took my hand. "My God!" he said, and then ran his other hand behind my head and squeezed the back of my neck, while smiling brightly at me. "Where does time go? Just look at him, Tommy! Can you believe it?"

"How do you do, sir," I said, rather more shyly than I'd anticipated.

"You don't remember me?"

"No, sir. I'm sorry … have we met before?"

"You were a toddler, Tony," my Uncle Patrick said, interrupting. "You sat on Henry's knee and played with him in the garden for hours when he and Tommy visited us, a few weeks after your mother passed away."

"How darned stupid of me, I'm terribly sorry, Anthony," the tall American said. "That was remiss of me—of course you don't remember. It was such a sad time. It was Tommy's first big tour back here after the war and we were so pressed for time—neither of us wanted to go back home without seeing Patrick."

"I'm overwhelmed that you should even remember who I am," I said.

"How could we not, Anthony? Patrick writes about you in every letter," he said.

"He does?" I said, more to my uncle than to him.

"We've known him a very long time, Anthony," Sir Thomas said, holding out his hand to me. "And I'm delighted that you were both able to come to the concert."

"Congratulations, Sir Thomas," I said, shaking his hand. "I feel so incredibly rude; I haven't even thanked you yet. That was extraordinary playing—I've never been so moved in my life. I went through two handkerchiefs—I had to even borrow my uncle's."

He smiled softly and then patted my shoulder. "Thank you, Anthony—I really mean that … and it's Tommy to friends. Please?"

"Wasn't he terrific?" Heinrich said, and then, to my utter disbelief, kissed him full on the lips. "But, he always is. Ain't it so, Patrick?"

My uncle smiled, his face a little red, and then conversed again rapidly, in German, to which the tall man replied in the same language, prefaced by a word I did recognise—"oops!".

"I owe these two everything, Tony," my uncle explained. "I know I've never told you, but it was Tommy and Henry who pulled me out of the rubble of the war and more or less saved my life after it." I'd never heard this story before. I knew I was gaping. "Anyway, please excuse us speaking in German in front of you. I know it's terribly bad manners—I've just promised Henry that I'll tell you *everything* before we all get together on the 12th of February."

The 12th of February? I was feeling very embarrassed at this point. Had I forgotten something I'd already been told?

"Both my twin brother Michael and I went to Duntroon, Anthony," Sir Thomas explained. "When Patrick sent us a telegram in Brisbane and told us you'd been accepted, and we knew we were going to still be here in Australia for another month, we thought we'd have a small party to celebrate—to wish you well!"

I was too flabbergasted to express my thanks. "You were at Duntroon?" I said. I couldn't help staring at his violin case—an officer from military college during the war and now a famous, international, concert artist? I couldn't wait to hear this story!

"Didn't you tell him anything, Patrick?"

"No," my uncle said, quieter than I'd ever heard him in my life.

"That's how Shorty, I mean Heinrich, and I met, young man. Both in uniform at the time and in a stairwell in the middle of an air raid in London, in 1941."

"And we've been together ever since."

"Achilles and Patroclus," Sir Thomas said.

"Alexander and Hephaistos," Heinrich added.

"You're not shocked, I hope," my uncle said after a few moments. I was aware that I was still gaping.

"Only over the 'Shorty' thing," I mumbled, smiling at the very, very tall, reddish-blond haired man.

*****

I thought I was dreaming when I heard a soft American voice say my name.

"Tony?"

I opened my eyes, and there he was, sitting on the edge of my bed—in his uniform.

"Charlie?" It felt like I'd only just crawled into bed after the concert last night. "What are you doing here … what time is it?"

He leaned down and kissed me gently on the lips. "It's eight thirty," he said.

"Where's Uncle Patrick?" I was not the best at waking up in the morning; it always took me ages to surface.

"He's gone down to breakfast. I'm sorry, Tony; there's been a change of plan. I found out myself at six. I hope you don't mind, but I couldn't go without saying goodbye."

"Goodbye?"

"Boy, you have a way with words first thing in the morning, don't you?"

I grinned, and then pulled him down to me and kissed him again. "Sorry for morning breath."

"I could get used to it."

And then, as it usually did for me, the world suddenly snapped into focus. "Goodbye? Wait, I thought we had a date tonight?"

"I'm sorry; duty calls. I've been pulled back early. I have to catch a bus at eleven."

"Where from?"

"Martin Place."

"That's just outside the hotel."

"Uh huh," he said. "Your uncle is one hell of a guy, Tony. You know, he flew 'proper planes'—Wellingtons and Lancasters? Boy, what a hero!"

"I love him," I said.

"And he loves you, too; probably more than you think."

"Why do you say that?"

"He said he'll be gone for two hours and that I shouldn't wear you out."

"What?"

Charlie began to loosen his tie. "He'll be back at ten thirty … until then, Aussie …" He threw back the bed covers and ran his eyes over my body—I didn't sleep in pyjamas. "Don't move, please. I want a snapshot of this in my mind to keep me going until the next time we meet."

I was as hard as a rock, even before he lowered his head.

*****

Two days later, I was in the kitchen early, fixing breakfast for us both, to take on a tray to Uncle Patrick, who was still asleep.

We'd arrived back from Sydney the day before, Charlie's early-morning appearance still not discussed, even during our four-hour-long train journey. We'd chatted about everything else under the sun, other than the things I was desperate to talk through with my uncle.

Uncle Patrick had returned from breakfast precisely at ten thirty on the morning Charlie had left, by which time we were dressed and drinking coffee—I'd ordered breakfast from room service. We'd exchanged addresses, on the understanding that although we'd write, we'd have to be circumspect. Who knows, he'd said—perhaps we'd coincide our own R & Rs, or even manage to catch up "over there". There was no doubt where I'd be going, with our country committed to the Vietnam conflict. And, he'd added, no war lasts forever—there was always "after the war". He and I had grown up with that phrase used on a daily basis in our households.

My uncle had taken several photographs of us together outside on the street in front of the flower cart, near the corner of George Street, and a few more posing in front of the Cenotaph.

"It's been a great honour to meet you, Mr. Fletcher. Thank you for your service, sir," Charlie had said to my Uncle Patrick, before throwing his arms around me and hugging me. "Take care, Tony," he'd whispered into my ear. "Please write."

"I will," I'd said, as he'd stepped back, replaced his cover, and saluted us both, before moving off to join the crowd of his pals who had already started filing onto the army bus.

"Move over, lazy head," I said to my uncle, who'd woken when I'd knocked at his bedroom door.

"Breakfast in bed, eh?"

"Mm."

"Does that mean what I think it means?"

"We need to speak, Patrick," I said. "I'll understand if you find it difficult—but, can you just forget for a while you're my uncle, and you've looked out for me all of my life? I need a friend right now, not someone who's going to come over 'all protective' on me."

He rubbed the back of my neck. "I'll try; however, until you've brought someone up yourself, you'll never know how impossible that is. Shall I go first?"

I spread some marmalade on his toast and handed it to him. "Can you speak with your mouth full?"

"Are we going to start off at that level right off the bat?"

I laughed. "Derrick Finsome," I said.

"There was I, waiting at the church, waiting at the church ..." he sang.

"No!"

"Yes, Tony. I loved that man more than anyone I've ever done in my life, and he left me standing on Bullaroo station waiting for him—he never turned up and I never saw him again."

"Why?"

"He ran off with someone else. It was my fault, really. I couldn't bring myself to give him what he wanted, and I also gave him an ultimatum—never a wise thing to do to any man. 'Come with me to start a new life in Condoblin,' I'd said, 'or ...'."

"What was the 'or'?"

"He ran off with a gypsy."

Damn! That wasn't what I was expecting to hear. "I'm sorry, Patrick, truly I am. He can't have known what he was missing."

"Oh, he knew all right. Handsome bastard that gypsy—rough as guts both in and out of bed ... no, wait! I didn't know from personal experience, but I'd heard of his reputation from others who knew."

"Whatever happened to them? Did you ever see Derrick again?"

He shook his head. "Last I heard they'd moved up north to Queensland. The Gyppo had family up that way somewhere."

"God, that must have been dreadful—didn't you get lonely?"

"Well, after he ran off, I moved to Condoblin to be with your mum and dad, and you, and then came back here after … well, you know what after. I wasn't lonely for long—I picked up Derrick's stable."

"What?"

"I wasn't the only one Derrick was sleeping with, Tony. Don't look so shocked."

"I'm not shocked—more surprised about your use of the word 'stable'."

"It's the best word to describe it," he replied, with a small chuckle. "There were four—no, five—of us, if you include the gypsy. All timetabled out over the week. I got Derrick on Fridays and weekends. The rest of them—well, they were really nice blokes, and once I got back home from Condoblin, we got together, played cards, and then we'd—"

I rolled my eyes. "You dirty old bugger, you!"

"Enough of the old. It did help heal wounds. It wasn't the same of course."

"Do you still see any of them?"

He nodded. "Michael Passdale's one."

"If you don't mind me saying it, he seems a bit rough around the edges."

My uncle smiled at me, and patted my knee. "Sometimes that's just what a man needs."

"If you say so, but I can't see what he has that—"

"A penis you can barely get your hand around, and he fucks like a pile driver."

I howled with laughter, having to put my coffee cup down on the bedside table so I didn't spill it. I rolled onto my stomach and pushed my head into the pillow, shaking with mirth.

"I hope I haven't traumatised you with my honesty," he said, slapping my back. "You're the one who wanted frank speech, after all."

I sat up, red-faced, with tears in my eyes. "No, not at all! In fact, I think I like this new Uncle Patrick much better than the old one."

"Anyway, he's as kind as the day is long, and looks after me."

"Who?"

"Michael Passdale."

"Ah, the pile driver with the dick of death—"

He snorted softly and playfully punched my shoulder. "Who kisses like an angel and makes my eyes roll back in my head when he—"

"Okay! I think that's enough frankness for the first attempt."

He grinned. I was pretty sure there was a lot of truth in what he'd told me, but I was also aware that a lot of what had been said was to cover up the sadness he felt when speaking of Derrick.

"I wish you'd been this open with me years ago, when I was wondering about myself," I said.

"I was really aware of the fact that I didn't want to influence your choices. I was quite scared you might go down paths you may not have, had you been aware of my …"

"Homosexuality?"

"Yes, being 'camp', I think they call it these days."

"The Yanks call it 'gay'," I replied. "Anyway, those are just words; you taught me never to be afraid of words. Do you remember the first time you heard me swear?"

"When you called Peachy Kinster a cunt?"

"Yes; you brought me into the surgery and taught me all the anatomical terms, and why some words were more offensive than others."

"Depending on the context."

"Yes, of course. Depending on the context."

"So then, young man … Charlie."

I sighed—a long sigh, one that combined loss, lust, and longing. "Charlie," I said. "Ironic, isn't it, that I should dream of someone like him since I was fifteen and then only get to be with him for three days."

"There'll be other Charlies," my uncle said. His voice was kind—and I knew what he said was the truth.

"There will be. I'm not silly enough not to realise that. Nonetheless, he'll be the first Charlie in my life, and nothing will ever change that."

"Who taught you to be that wise?"

"Some old cunt," I said, and then was rewarded with another punch to my shoulder.

I took his breakfast tray and placed it on the dressing table, next to the silver-framed photo of Derrick and my uncle, taken down by the river. I picked it up and stared at it for a moment, and then ran a finger over the image of my uncle's face. He looked so happy.

"Was Derrick your first?"

"No," my uncle said, shaking his head. "My first was a German guard in the *Konzentrationslager*—his name was Helmut."

"Did you love him?"

"No, I didn't love him; but, in some ways, I owe him my life."

"I'll understand if you don't want to talk about it."

"I've never told anyone about it … it's not easy, so forgive me if go carefully, Tony."

"Do you want more coffee? I can make some?"

"No, thank you. So, Helmut. I'd never thought of sex with another man until I ended up in the camp. It's amazing what you'll do for food. Hunger and thirst, and then self-preservation—I discovered pretty quickly they're the most important drives in human nature. I gave him what he wanted in exchange for food—it's as simple as that. He was mostly very, very kind to me, but even when I heard years later that the rest of the prisoners had torn him to pieces after the main camp had been bombed, I felt nothing but a small amount of sadness. He didn't deserve to die, as an individual, that is, but as a member of the S.S.? Well, nothing was too bad for them."

"Is that how you lost your leg? In the bombing? I always thought you'd lost it when your plane crashed."

He shook his head and then turned so I couldn't see his face. "Well, it's a long story—the one about my leg."

"Your first appointment is Mrs. Greenle at midday," I said. "But, I do understand. Of course, I do. Let's talk about something else."

"No, no. Really, the story about my leg isn't simple, that's all—and now I've started, it feels right to finally talk about it. Eventually, I did lose it because of the bombing, but I'd suffered with it for a few years before that. Yes, I'd suffered what I suspected was a hairline fracture of the fibula when my plane came down. I wasn't able to treat it properly and it didn't set right, so I walked with a limp as a result. However, it was compounded by a crush injury, some six months later."

"A crush injury?" I tried to make my voice sound hesitant, to give him the opportunity to avoid talking about it, as I sensed that involved something gruesome—he'd winced on the word "crush".

"I suppose you'd call it the result of torture."

My heart almost stopped in my chest.

"I was beaten half to death by one of the sadists in the camp—Germund was his name. He knew I'd rather die than treat any of the *Schutzstaffeln*, but he'd caught the back of his heel on something sharp and the camp doctor was too busy to see him, so he came to me. I refused to look at it, point blank, so he had Leo, one of the other guards, hold me down while he kicked my leg. I still had a rough-made splint on it at the time, but he stood back and gave it his boot until the splint broke, and then kept kicking until I passed out with the pain. Later that night, he came back with Leo and Helmut, all three as drunk as skunks. Germund and Leo knew that I'd been doing 'favours' for Helmut, so they dragged me out into the yard behind the hut, Leo pushed my face into the mud and held me down while the other two took turns."

"Turns?" I didn't want to believe what I thought he meant.

"Yes, Anthony—turns. I'm sure I don't have to spell it out."

He said it with a tone approaching resignation—not in the sense of having given up in despair to something inevitable, nor with horror, but with quiet acceptance, as if it was something that had "just happened" to him.

"I thought you said Helmut was kind? What sort of—"

"He did it to save face and to save me. If he hadn't played along, it would have made his life unbearable among the other guards—most likely he'd have had an 'accident' that would have either crippled him or put him in the ground, and they'd have shot me. Despite his more or less consistent kindness, there was something in him, like every German bastard I ever knew from those days in the camp, who liked to humiliate those of us who were unlucky enough to be captured. I always thought it was something to do with what was expected of being a member of the S.S. So, several times a week after that, all three of them shared me for the best part of eighteen months."

I had no idea what to say. He didn't sound ashamed, as I'd have imagined he might. But then again, I had no point of reference, so I merely remarked, "It's a wonder you allowed anyone to ever touch you again."

"You know, I came to realise I could either give in, to become a victim, or learn to use it as a weapon and turn the tables on them in my mind—I trained myself to close my eyes and make myself ignore the fact that it was Leo and Germund who were doing what they did to me. With Helmut, it was different—once I got used to it, it felt good with him, and that's the truth of it. As I said, he was kind and gentle. If I didn't have to look at the others, or even 'see' them with my eyes open, then I could just concentrate on the feelings in my body. You think that's impossible; I can see it in your face. I was the only allied serviceman to survive that camp out of ninety-six, and it was mainly because I cooperated, gave them what they wanted, and they repaid me with survival. Helmut came to care for me; he told me often enough, even at those times when he'd had too much to drink and would beat me up and throw me around the place first—he'd always apologise after and tell me how much he hated himself. As for Germund and Leo, well, I just got 'used to' whatever they wanted—I always got something in return: camp booze or vegetable scraps. Leo always had access to meat, and invariably gave me a small parcel afterwards—I shared everything I got with the other blokes in my barracks, who pretended I got it some other way. But they all knew what I was forced to go through."

"Didn't they hate you for not resisting?"

"No. I think they were just happy it was me and not them. Food was impossible by early '45—I kept the last six of us alive on the tiny portions of meat I got from Leo—he was easy enough to ignore; he was a three-second wonder. It was Germund who was the hardest to cope with. Although he was a pig, somehow it was easier to use sex as a weapon against him than with Leo, because he made no attempt to pretend he even liked me. Believe it or not, because I hated him so much, it was pretty easy for me to turn it around in my mind, so that it was me who was abusing him, instead of him me. I'd swear at him in English and call him every cursed thing I could think of while urging him on to unload in my guts as quickly as possible—I fought him with my body and with words he didn't understand. Perhaps he thought my filthy talk was some perverse sort of endearment, or that I was telling him 'what a man he was'? Crude and disgusting isn't it, when you hear it said like that? Despite it, I lived, and thousands of others died. I wasn't proud of what I did to stay alive. Pride is an indulgence to impress those around you, not for yourself when you're alone, and not for when you're struggling to survive an impossible situation."

I returned to the bed, sat down on its edge and started to rub the toes of his foot, which was peeping out from under the coverlet. The only experience I'd had of sex was tender—one might even say loving—and gentle and reciprocal, despite the urgency and need. "I think you're amazing, Uncle Patrick," I said, softly.

He turned his head. I could see that he'd been crying while he spoke. "I did what I had to do, Anthony."

"And Sir Thomas and Heinrich?"

"Well, I was 'lucky' enough to be moved to one of the satellite camps of Hinzert, the *Lager* where I'd first been incarcerated. We weren't far from the Luxembourg border, and when Helmut, Leo, and Germund had learned that the Allies had landed in Normandy, the year before, they realised I could be of double benefit to them—as a warm, seemingly willing body for them to sink their dicks into, and someone who might protect them from retribution after the war. Germund and Leo had become distinctly nicer to me by January of '45. And, oh yes, sometimes the sex became reciprocal for a while after that—Leo had hidden talents that only came into light when the others weren't around. However, on the 22nd of February, the camp took hits from allied bombers, as part of the softening-up of areas in Germany near the front, getting ready for the advancing occupation. We thought we'd escaped where we were, a few miles away from the main camp, but then a straggler flew over and dropped his load right on top of us—hundreds of forced labourers were killed, including the last of us allied servicemen in that part of the camp."

"But you survived—obviously. But how?"

"Our hut was half-buried, the back of it built into a hill—there were no shelters for the prisoners, so we had to make do during a raid. That's what saved me—I was hiding at the back of the shed, under one of the big wooden bunks, built out of railway sleepers, when the bombs hit. When I came to, after the explosion, I found that I couldn't move. I was pinned down by one of the timbers of the bunks, which—according to the principle that if anything can go wrong, it will do—had fallen right where I'd first fractured my leg. Then, when I tried to extricate myself, the pain was so terrible that I blacked out, and when I next opened my eyes, I heard voices—English-speaking voices, so I yelled out at the top of my lungs. It was a squad of American soldiers, who'd just moved into the camp from Osburg, further to the west, to round up Germans and to 'liberate' us—more like see if anyone was alive, if you ask me. Two days I'd been trapped, can you believe it? It took six of them to pull the timber off me, and then when the medic got a look at me, he threw me into the back of a jeep and the next thing I remembered was waking up in a hospital, surrounded by more American voices, and without my leg."

"You said that Sir Thomas and Heinrich 'pulled you out of the rubble of war'?"

"Yes. It's a figure of speech, of course. A few days later, I was lying in bed waiting for a transfer to a British hospital, when a tall Yank introduced himself, and asked if it was me who'd been in Hinzert—he'd been looking for some German officer who knew about some secret Nazi treasure that needed retrieving, and this Kraut was the only one who knew where it was—the last they'd heard he was holed up in the same camp as me. I told him I'd never heard of him, but I'd barely said a sentence or two when he asked me if I was an Aussie—he knew that accent, he'd said. When I replied that I was, he called out over his shoulder, 'Hey, Tommy! One of yours over here'."

"No!" I said. "You can't be serious. It was Sir Thomas?" I knew the war was one long sequence of coincidences; it's just that this story must have been right up there with the best of them.

"I'd known Tommy and his brother Michael since we were kids at cattle shows," he said, his face lit up, with a slight smile. "We're the same age. And that's why I thought I'd died when I saw him. He didn't recognise me—I was too beat up; black, bruised. But I said, 'Well fuck me dead, look who it is! Tommy-fucking-Haupner!' He nearly passed out with the shock too. The long and the short of it was that after they sent me back to London, Tommy's great-aunt came to visit me in hospital and looked after me until the war was over, and then I spent a year in their house at Garbala, in the south of France, before I came home."

"Why did you wait so long?"

"I'd sent a telegram as soon as I arrived in England, but your father was still serving in the Pacific War, in Dutch New Guinea, I think, and my father was dead, so I had no reply—I had no idea what was going on at home. And then, in late '45, when he finally did get home, I heard from your dad that our father had died here in Bullaroo in 1942. I needed some time to get used to the idea of losing a leg, what had happened to me during the war, and my own father's death. I thought that, as I was in Europe, there was no real hurry to get home—I hadn't even tossed around the idea of opening my own practice again. It's amazing how numb years of violence and death can make you."

"Holy cow!" I said, almost inaudibly, and then, more for myself than for him, added, "I don't know how you managed to go on, Patrick. I'll be damned if I do!"

"Well, when I heard that my brother had met your mum and had decided to get married, I reckoned it was time to come back, so I sent them a telegram and asked them to hang on so I could be there for the wedding. That was towards the end of '46."

There was something in his voice that made me think there may have been another reason for coming home late. "You and Sir Thomas and Henry never …"

"Oh, no!" he said. "I'd be lying if I didn't say there may have been another man, or men, that delayed my homecoming. Recuperation is as much about the spirit as about the body. Two friends of Tommy's and Henry's in Bayonne—a Frenchie and a Yank. Boy, oh, boy!" he said. Somehow those three words said everything.

I went to make more coffee and toast, as mine had gone cold. I'd been too intrigued at my uncle's story to concentrate on food. While I waited for the percolator to do its thing, I found myself crying. Not sobbing, just profoundly moved over what I'd just been told. The man who'd really been my father—the kindest, most gentle, and loving man in the world—hiding such terrible secrets inside. I didn't want to make judgements about whether I could have done or put up with what he had done. Obviously it wasn't all rape and starvation—there must have been moments of peace and the appreciation of just being alive. I knew him too well to know that he observed life, and then lived it, rather than the other way around.

When I returned to the bedroom, he'd retrieved his photo album, and was sitting up in bed writing a heading to a new page—white ink on the dark-grey paper. I stood beside him.

"Anthony and Charlie" it said, with two neat underlines.

"This will be for when the snaps come back from the chemist's," he said. That's when I broke down and really sobbed out loud. His story had affected me far more than I'd let on, even to myself. "Hey, hey! Come on, Tony," he whispered, as he held me in his arms. "Where's my big lad, eh?"

There were no words for what I wanted to say—anything would have been patronising in the extreme, and sympathy would have been even more unwelcome.

"Oh, Patrick—" I started to say, but then the words stuck in my throat.

"Listen to me, mate," he said, and then pinched the flesh of my forearm and twisted it.

"Ouch!" I said, and then laughed. It was like him to do something like that. I knew a bit of wisdom was heading my way.

"Does it still hurt?"

"A little."

He gave it a rub for a while. "What about now?"

I shook my head.

"What those three men did to me feels about as real as what my pinch feels to you right now. It's faded—gone—it all happened over twenty years ago now. They didn't hurt me inside, Tony. They may have thought they were using me, but ultimately, as I'm still alive and they're not, it's me who won—not them."

I couldn't bear to hear any more. I wanted to know about the good things that happened to him in the camp—the glimpses of a bright spring morning, or the sound of a bird, the intense green of a leaf on a tree, or even the bright flower on a weed in a tangle of barbed wire. Just so that I could colour the thought palette I'd created in my mind of his time in a concentration camp—I couldn't live with myself if I thought it was all shades of black and grey.

"Who's this?" I asked, pointing at one of the photographs in the album, and knowing the subject of his incarceration had been dealt with for the moment.

"Who's this? In this photo?" It was a picture of my grandfather, standing next to him a man of an age similar to his own at the time the photo was taken, and with them a boy, probably about fourteen or fifteen. A scrawny lad, with glasses.

"I know that's your father, my grandfather … who are the other two?"

"That's Musgrave Barry—he used to be the hospital nurse. And the young bloke is Spider Henderson—Donald was his name. Musgrave moved away, back to the city, just before I came home. Donald was my dad's assistant; died in a Japanese P.O.W. camp in '44. His sister, Gwyneth, works for your nan. That's why she's so quiet—she never got over it."

I fiddled with the edge of the blanket for a few minutes while he waited for me to speak. I was used to his waiting silences, and he knew I was trying to find words. "What will become of me?" I asked, very quietly.

"I've no idea, Tony, and that's the truth of it. You're resourceful, brave, and you've got a brain between your ears. You've never asked me what I think you should do. I just accepted the fact you wanted to be in the army. You used to get dressed up in your dad's uniform, do you remember? You'd pull it out of his service trunk and put it on, even when you were four or five."

"No, I don't remember, Patrick. But it doesn't surprise me."

"Now why don't you tell me what's really on your mind—I know it's not about Charlie."

I sighed, and then threw myself on my back on the bed next to him. "I wondered if it was a phase at first—I've sort of known for years that it wasn't. It wasn't until Charlie I realised that it was for keeps. It wasn't some sort of game, something I could 'get over' or 'deal with'. It's a part of me; an important part of who I am."

"And …?"

"And, I've been wondering if there's a place in the army for a man like me—that's all."

"What? A clever, courageous, kind, and intelligent man?"

"You know what I mean, Uncle Patrick."

"Yes, and I just answered your question. You wouldn't be the first and you won't be the last. The army will value you for what you are and how you do the job, rather than who you think of when your blood's hot in your ears. They'll see you as I do—clever, courageous, kind, and intelligent."

I smiled. "You're biased."

"Yes, I am," he replied. "But have I ever lied to you?"

I shook my head.

*****

Later that week, I cooked dinner for the three of us.

I'd asked Patrick to phone Michael Passdale and to invite him for "tea", as the grazier called it. Half past seven for an evening meal was later than Michael was used to, but surprisingly enough, he turned up with a half-decent bottle of plonk, a bunch of flowers under his arm, wearing a tie that matched the colour of his eyes, and a modern, well-fitting jacket.

Patrick had told him I knew what they'd been up to, and that as he'd been Patrick's partner for nearly fifteen years, I wanted him in my life too. My uncle had reported that he'd seemed stunned at first, but then had sounded very grateful for the invitation.

When he arrived, he handed the bottle to me and the flowers to my uncle, blushing as he did so. I felt my grin widen as I watched them.

"What's so funny?" my uncle asked.

"You two! You've apparently been at it like rabbits for years and now you're acting like a pair of timid teenagers."

Michael Passdale had something about him; I hadn't really noticed it before, as it was hidden underneath his grazier's hat and surly countenance. But when he laughed, I saw what it was that my uncle found so attractive.

"Righto, then, nipper," he said to me. "Teenager, huh?" He put his arm around my uncle's waist and kissed him deeply in front of me for a few seconds, before turning back and wiping his mouth with the back of his hand. "Yummo!" he said.

I laughed. Loudly. And for a long time. I had to sit down.

"We'll speak later, Anthony," my uncle said, his face brick-red, with a pretend scowl.

I really warmed to Michael Passdale over dinner. He was almost the archetypal outback squatter—seemingly taciturn, which was indeed just being spare with words; sardonic, another word for our habit of "taking the piss"; but, underneath the veneer of bushie, a man with a good intellect, and a great sense of humour.

"That was truly delicious," he said, placing his knife and fork side by side onto his plate, and then wiping his mouth with a napkin—I'd broken out the white linen and the silverware for the evening. It was my uncle who'd taught me to cook. He was a wonder in the kitchen, having told me that he'd learned about food while convalescing in the *Pays basque*, in the south of France.

"I owe everything I know to the man sitting on your right-hand side," I said, nodding at Patrick.

"So, no troubles in the sack with your Yank, then?"

Patrick nearly choked on his wine.

"Well, some things are instinctual—my uncle didn't have to teach me that."

"I'm pretty curious. Don't get me wrong, it's great to be here—officially that is—for the first time. Is there any reason for this dinner? In the back of my mind I've been wondering if there is to be some huge announcement."

"No, nothing like that, Michael. Far from it. Last week, when we were in Sydney, I fell in love with the look on my uncle's face when he came back to the hotel room after Charlie and I had been … well, you know. I could see in his eyes the look of delight, I suppose you'd call it, for lack of a better word. He knew that I'd had a wonderful time, and he was telling me, without words, that he approved and he was happy for me. I just want that opportunity for myself—to come into the kitchen one morning, knowing you were still in bed, and that Patrick was maybe making you a cuppa or something, but with that same look on his face that I had. I want to be able to acknowledge his happiness, or contentment, or whatever you want to call it. We've spent too much of our lives only knowing part of who we are, and I'll be buggered if I'm going to go off to war without having shared that part of his life with him."

"Well, fuck me …" Michael said, shaking his head at me, with a smile.

"Thank God the walls are thick in this house," I said. "I might want to approve after the act, but I'd rather not live through it with you both, if you don't mind."

Patrick reached over the table and took my hand. He squeezed it—the merest glint of tears in his eyes.

"I'll be gone soon, for God knows how long," I said. "I expect you don't need my permission, Michael, but even while I'm still here, and then after I've gone, I don't want you to pussyfoot around me with late-night appointments. I hope you'll spend many a happy night together without worrying about what I might think."

"I'll drink to that," Michael Passdale said, raising his glass.

"Amen!" I added.

*****

On Saturday, the 5th of February, the week before we were to visit the Haupner farm, I was in the kitchen, boning out a lamb leg for dinner when the phone rang.

"Patrick!" I called out. The phone continued to ring; I guessed he was either out the back watering the garden, or had his head down in a book. If that was the case, the house could burn down and he'd be none the wiser. So, I quickly put the lamb back into the fridge and then wiped my hands on a tea towel before rushing down the hallway to answer the phone. "Coming!" I called out to it, and then shook my head at my silliness. As if the phone could hear me? Ha!

"You took your time."

"Sorry, Nana, I was boning out a leg of lamb for dinner and I thought Patrick would get it. How are you? Is everything all right?"

"Why is it that once you pass sixty and you make a phone call, then everyone assumes it's bad news? Your Uncle Arthur needs a hand down in the grove tomorrow," she said. "Baked dinner at one. Tell Patrick to be here at twelve thirty."

"What time do you need me?" I asked.

She half covered the phone with one hand and called out through the house. "Arthur? What time do you want Anthony here?"

"Tell him to come at eleven, Edith. Ask him if he can collect Viola at the vet and ride her up."

"He says he wants you here at eleven, Anthony—"

"And I'm to pick up Viola at the vet. Yes, I heard him, Nana. What's this all about?"

She chuckled into the receiver. "Why ask me?"

"Because you know everything before it even happens, that's why."

"All I know is that your Uncle Arthur, your grandfather, and Patrick met up for a beer in town yesterday afternoon."

"Uh huh …"

"Anthony, I swear you're just like your mother was. You think I'm omniscient."

"Uh huh …"

"And don't 'uh huh' me, young man."

"Or?"

"Or, you won't get any crackling with your roast pork."

Now those were strong words. My grandmother cooked the best roasts and made the best scones in the shire—she was famous for both. Roast pork without crackling? What was the world coming to?

"Okay, Nana. I'll be good."

"Oh, and Anthony … go steady on your Uncle Arthur tomorrow."

"Why shouldn't I, Nana? I love him."

"I know you do, and I'm counting on you for that. See you tomorrow."

*****

"You know how long coolibah trees live for, Anthony?"

"No, Uncle Arthur, I don't. All I know is that the bastards live forever."

He smiled, his head down, fiddling in his saddlebag, looking for something. "I swear you're Jack come back to keep me honest. I hear his voice every time you open your mouth."

I'd known that Jack Hastings was my Uncle Arthur's best pal during the war. The Great War, as he insisted on calling it. Not like that recent ruckus in the 1940s. There were pictures of them together in Egypt on my uncle's study walls, and a photo of them both sitting on the legs of the Sphinx, in a chased silver frame, on his bedside table. My great-uncle was one of that generation who never talked of personal things, that's why I got a bit of a surprise when he mentioned Jack—he rarely spoke his name.

"Ah, here it is!" he said, and then handed me a sharkskin covered photo wallet, of the type that folded like a book. I opened it.

My Great-Uncle Arthur lay in the arms of another man who was the spitting image of my Grandfather Emerson, under a clump of date palms next to a watering hole. There were two horses tethered to a small bush next to the palm trunk against which they were laying. They were both stark naked, their legs splayed wide open to the camera.

We rode in silence for a few minutes while I got my brain into gear. I wasn't shocked in the least—I'd been dumbstruck by how incredibly handsome my Uncle Arthur was in those days; how the light seemed to shine in his eyes, and his evasive smile—one that we so seldom saw—made him look happier than I'd ever seen him. What was most striking was that it was the first picture I'd seen of him before he lost his arm and when it wasn't covered in a shirtsleeve. His biceps were very muscular, and there was a tattoo that I couldn't make out on the arm that was no longer there.

"Who's that?" I said, eventually.

"That's Kingsman," he replied. "He died under me at Al-Khalasa. He was the most bonzer horse, Anthony. Soft in the mouth, but with the courage of a lion—"

"No, Uncle Arthur. The man."

"That's my Jack," he said. "Who did you think it was?"

"It looks like grandpa," I said.

"That's what I thought when I first met Emerson—almost a spitting image of Jack. Did I ever tell you I fainted? I thought it was my Jack come back from the dead."

"You're naked."

"You noticed."

"Hard not to notice, Uncle Arthur."

We both chortled.

"What's the matter, Anthony? Never seen a naked man before?" I didn't know what to say. In the photograph, they both looked incredibly handsome and seemingly not in the least bashful. It was the most intimate, and therefore, to me, the most beautiful of photographs of my great-uncle.

"Only one, apart from Patrick that is," I said.

"Well, from what your uncle told me about your American and your day at the beach—"

"Uncle Arthur—"

"I don't mean to embarrass you, Anthony. Don't get me wrong. I don't make judgements, and I'm happy for you, if that's what you want. I really mean that. I just want you to be sure. Perhaps I'm going about this the wrong way—you know it's nigh on impossible for me to talk about these sorts of things. I just wanted you to know you're not alone. There are others of us who you can talk to. Surely you've guessed about me and Jack, or at least had a thought that we might have been 'close'."

"No, I hadn't, to be perfectly honest … tell me about him, please, Uncle Arthur. Now that you've taken the first step, please don't clam up on me. I love you, you know that. I want to know about him—if he's as much a part of you as that photo suggests."

"I loved him, Anthony. I loved Jack with all of my heart. I loved him so hard that, apart from your mother and you, I've never loved anyone else in my life …"

As his voice trailed off, I reached across in the space between our horses and took his hand.

"Thank you, Uncle Arthur. I can't tell you how much what you just said means to me."

"I don't understand."

"Well, you must know that you and Patrick and Grandpa have been like fathers to me. You're the men who made me who I am. If I ever learn to love as hard as you've just told me you loved your Jack, then you'll have succeeded in helping me to become the person I hope to be ..."

"You needed little help in becoming a good man, Anthony. You have your mother in you," he said, simply.

"But I have more of you in me than anyone. You're the one who taught me to ride, to handle horses, to see the land around me as a resource and a friend, not something to be exploited for profit. It's you who taught me how to be brave, to be humble, and to thrive in your humility."

He smiled and wiped his eyes with the sleeve of his shirt. "Smartarse kid. When did I teach you all of those things?"

"From the moment I was born, Uncle Jack."

"My name is not Jack, Anthony, it's Arthur."

"I know. But now I know how much you loved him, I think I'm going to find it hard to separate you two out in my mind."

He stopped his horse and stared off down into the clearing below us. I could see the pain and the start of tears in his eyes. "Three hundred years," he said.

"What?"

"I asked you about coolibah trees, young fella. That's how long they live. There were none here when I bought the land. So, when your grandfather returned from Quirindi with a sparkle in his eye and your grandmother on his arm, I asked them to help me plant this lot. Edith brought the seeds from our old family homestead with her. I wrote to her and asked her to gather some up. We put the pods in the ground behind the house, and then, when they were big enough, I planted this circle—that was nearly fifty years ago now, in 1920, the year they got married."

I'd heard the story of my grandmother's abduction. There'd been no further contact with the rest of their family after my Uncle Arthur had sent his station manager and two of his army friends to rescue his sister from the family property. I'd heard there'd been a dreadful row between my great-uncle and one of his brothers before that, but that was all.

"Did I ever tell you how this place got its name?" he said.

"What, 'Mulwidgee'?"

"Yes. Jack wanted it called so."

"No you didn't, Uncle Arthur. Tell me."

So, leaning on the pommel of his saddle, he told me the story of the two aboriginal men who were betrothed to the same woman, but who loved each other and were killed by her father for it, and how she cut out their hearts and buried them underneath a coolibah tree at the place of Mulwidgee.

"This is where mine will go, when I die," he said to me when he'd finished the story, jumping nimbly from his horse, and then squatting down to carefully rearrange the small cairn of granite stones that stood in the middle of the circle of trees.

"Your what?"

"My heart, Anthony. This is where Jack's is buried—mine is to go next to his."

"I thought he was buried in England? You were all away over there visiting his grave when my dad—"

"Yes, we were, son. But only his body is buried in the Mother Country. I brought his heart home with me, as I'd promised him on the night before he died. He wanted to be buried under Australian skies, under a coolibah tree, like the two warriors at Mulwidgee, so I could be close by and tell him about my life."

I was so incredibly moved by what he'd said that my shoulders started to shake. He wrapped his arm around me and pulled me close.

"That's what love's all about, Anthony. Every day for fifty years, I've come here in the morning and told Jack about my dreams and my hopes, my love for my niece, your mother, and my aspirations and my care for you."

"Does he ever answer?" I asked, wiping my eyes.

"Yes, of course. He's talking to me right now."

"What's he saying?" I tried to smile, but in my heart I was mostly serious.

"He says that you're not to tell your grandma about the photo of him and me with our dicks out and our balls blowing in the breeze."

*****

We were mostly quiet on the way back to the house until we reached the stock gate, when I got off Viola and went to open it.

"Uncle Patrick asked you to have this talk with me, didn't he?"

"Yes, he did, Anthony. He's not worried about you—more concerned that you're worried."

"I'm not worried, Uncle Arthur."

"Oh no? Then why did you ask him if there was a place for a man like you in the army?"

"I suppose I didn't know what to expect."

"Did you think you'd be the first man to fight for his country who loved another man? Or that Patrick was, or that I was? Love is love, Anthony. We don't get to choose who we've given our hearts to while we serve—love comes unbidden. We only get to choose why we fight. We might fight for our country, but we die for those we want to protect, be it man, woman, or child. No one gives up their life gladly for an ideal, no matter what they tell you or what you read in the tabloids. In the backs of our minds, we are only fighting for the survival of the person, or the people, we care most about—our comrades and our loved ones. Some of us are lucky enough to have both, in the same person, standing right next to us."

"Wow ..."

"Wow?"

I didn't know what to say. I stood at the gatepost, Viola's reins in my hand, and I began to cry again. This time I cried for my Uncle Patrick's leg, for the loss of his Derrick, and for my Uncle Arthur's arm and the loss of his Jack.

"Don't cry, son," my uncle said. "What I said—those are just words.

Come on, hitch Viola up to Sandy and jump up behind me, there's a lad. Put your arms around me, and let's ride up to the house and show them that true men aren't ashamed to be close and show they care for one another."

So, I did just what he said.

I felt peaceful for the first time in what seemed a very long time. Restless, yet at the same time resigned to the fact that I could love who I liked, yet dedicate my life to my country. Charlie seemed, at that moment, a whole lot closer to me, even though I'd known him for barely a number of days.

I wound my arms around my great-uncle and lay my head on his back, squeezing him as we rode up to the kitchen door.

*****

After lunch, Patrick and I stole the best spot in the house—the hammock on the northern veranda. It had views down over the valley to the river. For as long as I could remember, I'd always loved being in this spot with my uncle. I'd drape one leg over the edge of the hammock and rock us slowly, massaging his foot, while we spoke of "grown-up" things.

"Things go well down at the grove?" he asked. I sighed and nodded. "Sorry if I betrayed your confidence."

"It's fine, Patrick, truly, I don't mind."

"You seemed in such an anguish of thinking you might be 'the only one'."

"Well, I knew that wasn't the case. It was more about wondering if I'd be the only one in the army."

He snorted. "In the armed forces, men will do all sorts of things they wouldn't do at home, let me tell you. It's all about opportunity, or lack thereof. Promise me one thing though, Anthony."

"Sure thing. What?"

"That you'll come back?"

"I promise," I said.

"Afternoon tea in an hour," my grandmother called out from the kitchen.

Charlie and Me

"I tell you, that woman never stops," he said to me.

I couldn't help but agree. "And aren't we glad of it too?"

"Where are you going?" my uncle asked, as I slipped carefully out of the hammock.

"Just going to do something inside," I said. "I'll wake you before tea if you nod off."

"Okay," he said, as I leaned over and kissed his forehead.

I'd taken my shoes off, and padded down through the cool, dark, wood-panelled hallway to my Uncle Arthur's study and knocked softly at the door.

"Come in," he called out, and then after I'd poked my head around the door, "Oh, hello. What's the problem?"

"Nothing, Uncle Arthur. I just wondered if I might use your desk for a bit before afternoon tea."

"Knock yourself out," he replied. "I'm just reading this nonsense. It's bound to knock me out too!"

"What is it?"

He held up the book. James Michener's *The Source*. I'd given it to him for Christmas with the warning that it was historical, but not written chronologically. I knew it would drive him crazy, but that he'd ultimately love it.

I sat down at his desk and took a sheet of notepaper from the stationery stand, and then asked if I might use his fountain pen. He grumbled assent, his eyes still fixed on the book, but then looked over the top of it at me and smiled.

It was time, I thought. I should have done this earlier.

Mulwidgee Station
Via Bullaroo
5th February, 1966.

Dear Charlie,

It's not been two weeks since I waved goodbye to you in Martin Place, with my Uncle Patrick at my side.

I hope this letter finds you well, wherever you may be. I'm sitting in my grandparents' house in the country, having just eaten the most splendid roast for lunch. Perhaps I shouldn't tell you of such things, as I'm not sure myself what you get to eat wherever you may be.

Let me tell you a little of what I've been up to since I last saw you ...

I sucked on the end of my Great-Uncle Arthur's fountain pen, thinking how I could not write what I truly wanted to—that Charlie was on my mind, and had been, ever since the moment I'd stepped over the edge of the bathtub in his room at the Coogee Bay Hotel and had pressed my mouth to his.

That would have been a different letter altogether. One I could only write in my heart, and then perhaps recount to him, somewhere on the other side of the world, at another time, in the steamy heat of a distant jungle.

I slipped my hand into my trousers pocket and fingered the silver, rounded rectangles, threaded on their beaded metal chain, that now went everywhere with me. That night, after we'd said goodbye to Charlie in Martin Place, I'd come back to the hotel to find an envelope on my bed from the chambermaid; on it written:

These were under your pillow, sir.

Charlie's dog tags. If he couldn't leave a piece of himself with me, he'd done the next best thing. I think I was the only soldier in the world who really wanted to go to an overseas conflict, not for the fighting, or for the sake of my country, but for the hope of finding what every man is ultimately looking for—himself.

And, if perchance I managed to catch up with someone with a blond crewcut, sporting a pair of aviator glasses, and a cheeky smile? Well, that'd certainly be the icing on the cake.

Acknowledgements

Archives New Zealand. The Australian War Memorial Collection. Imperial War Museums Archive.

Victoria Milne Professional Editing and Proofreading Services, UK. Tricia Dearborn, Institute of Professional Editors, Australia.

Dr. Catherine Silsbury. Dr. Adam Carroll.

Brendan Smith, Brett O'Neill, Julie Bozza, Christopher Lincoln, JLT.

Oral histories: D. White, J. Pengilley, E & M Dufty, B. Farkas, G. Jones.

Many thanks to the dozens of men who wrote to me, asking to remain anonymous, with their memories of being gay while serving in World War Two, Korea, and in Vietnam.

Christine Wright, who sparked the flame for this collection.

www.ingramcontent.com/pod-product-compliance
Lightning Source LLC
LaVergne TN
LVHW041629060526
838200LV00040B/1500